CLASS ACTION

What You Don't Know CAN Hurt You

Gail Ward Olmsted

Black Rose Writing | Texas

This is a work of fiction. Names, characters, businesses, places, events, and incidents are either the products of the author's imagination or used in a fictitious manner. Any resemblance to actual persons, living or dead, or actual events is purely coincidental.

ISBN: 978-1-68513-684-0
LIBRARY OF CONGRESS CONTROL NUMBER: 2025940426
PUBLISHED BY BLACK ROSE WRITING
www.blackrosewriting.com

Printed in the United States of America
Suggested Retail Price (SRP) $20.95

Class Action is printed in Minion Pro

*As a planet-friendly publisher, Black Rose Writing does its best to eliminate unnecessary waste to reduce paper usage and energy costs, while never compromising the reading experience. As a result, the final word count vs. page count may not meet common expectations.

Advanced Praise for
Class Action

"Gripping and engaging, Class Action explores what it means to choose the harder right over the easier wrong."
–Sublime Book Review

"Class Action is an emotional roller coaster that takes you from the edge of despair to the promise of a new life."
–Gary Gerlacher, best-selling author of the AJ Docker medical thriller series

"Class Action is a multiple-layered legal thriller I couldn't put down once I started reading."
–Diane Hawley Nagatomo, author of *The Butterfly Café, Finding Naomi,* and *The Making of Us*

"This story has it all: intrigue, legal drama, family drama and romance, with a little blackmail tossed in to keep things spicy."
–S.M. Stevens, author of *Beautiful & Terrible Things*

"A smart, emotionally-charged legal drama blending personal stakes with ethical dilemmas. Fans of Megan Miranda's "All the Missing Girls" will find a similar mix of suspense, secrets, and an underestimated protagonist."
–Cam Torrens, bestselling author of the *Tyler Zahn mystery/suspense series*

"Class Action is a smart, fast-paced romp with heart, humor, and just the right doses of suspense and romance."
–Karen E. Osborne, award-winning author of *Tangled Lies, Getting It Right, Reckonings* and *True Grace*

"Once again, Gail Olmsted has created an emotionally charged legal thriller with a strong-willed female protagonist that keeps you on the edge of your seat."
–A.J. McCarthy, author of the *Charlie & Simm mystery series*

CLASS ACTION

Charlene Gallagher
New Year's Eve, 1999

Charlene peered at her reflection in the foggy mirror above the
bathroom sink.

"Damn, you'd think with all of the practice I've had with eyeliner,
I'd be good at it by now." She frowned as she studied the black smudge
pooled in the inner corner of her right eye. Her younger sister, Kelly,
walked by, clad only in a towel, combing out her long tangle of dark
wavy hair. She stopped just long enough to study the problem.

"Yeah," she said. "You look like crap."

"Not helpful," Charlene said. "Now I've got to start over." She
dabbed a cotton ball with makeup remover and swiped it under her eye,
managing to get most of the excess in one try. She wanted to look her
best tonight. It had been nearly three months since she'd smoked meth,
and it had been hell, pure hell. Her skin had finally begun to lose its
sallow color, the zits that went hand in hand with being an addict were
mostly gone, and she had put a few much-needed pounds on her slight
frame. Her black hair had always been short, but she had to admit it
looked kind of nice grown out just a bit. Feeling pretty, she thought she
looked younger than her twenty-six years. Her ten-year high school
reunion would be held next year. Maybe she'd buy a new dress and
score a hot date as well. She smiled, thinking how much she would love

to show up all decked out on some cute guy's arm and prove to those fucktards from her high school she was still a force to be reckoned with. After all, she was Charlene Freakin' Gallagher! Had she fallen down a time or two? Sure, but she had rallied and come back stronger and better than ever. She could just picture the shocked look on her former bestie Randi Quinn's face when she saw how good she was doing. *That stuck-up bitch. False friend. Slut.* Charlene's good mood vanished as she pictured the woman she held responsible for sending her down the rabbit hole of binge-drinking, smoking meth, and sleeping with anyone who could supply her with that meth. Goddamn her. Everything that happened since that summer following graduation was all her fault!

She snapped at her sister, now prancing around their shared bedroom in a thong and push-up bra, acting like she had all the time in the world. "The party's not gonna wait for you, you know," she said. "Get ready, wouldja?"

"What's got your panties in a bunch?" asked Kelly good-naturedly. "Or maybe you're not wearing any," she added, a teasing lilt in her voice.

"Just hurry up. All the free food will be gone by the time we get there."

Kelly cast a critical eye in Charlene's direction. "You might want to skip the chips and guac tonight, Char. Since you quit smoking ice, you've put on a pound or two."

Charlene glared back at her sister. The words stung, but she knew they were true. Probably closer to ten pounds, but what the hell? Wasn't a slightly chubby, relatively sober girl better than a strung-out, scrawny meth head? "Some men like chicks with a bit of meat on their bones, ya know. Now get your coat and let's go." She stood and smoothed down her stone-washed denim skirt, almost short enough to expose her red thong. With a sparkly silver halter top she wore sans bra, fishnet tights, and her unlaced Doc Martens, she was ready to boogie. She grabbed her pleather bomber jacket and tossed her sister's fake fur wrap in her direction. It was time to get themselves down to the Wharf, party like it was 1999, cuz it actually *was* 1999, and get wasted. Hell, the world could end in a few hours if the doomsday Y2Kers had anything to say about it. She sure wasn't gonna face it stone-cold sober.

She sang the lyrics from "It's the End of the World as We Know It" by R.E.M. as they clambered down the stairs. With any luck, the sexy bartender would be on duty tonight. He hadn't been picking up many shifts lately, and she had heard he was in college or trade school . . . *whatever.* He was easy on the eyes, gave a generous pour, and always had girls hanging all over him. Well, tonight was his lucky night. It was Charlene Gallagher's turn at bat.

The bar was packed by the time they arrived. The old guy at the door was collecting a five-dollar cover from the guys, but he waved the Gallagher sisters right on in. Charlene considered smacking him upside his head after catching him leering at her sister's curvy butt and licking his lips. As if he stood a chance! What a perv. But that was ten dollars more for them to spend on drinks, so who had it really hurt?

She scanned the bar. Looked like there were two bartenders working tonight. There he was, the sexy one. He was working the far end of the bar with all the single ladies gathered around him. Mixing drinks and serving up beers on tap and all with an easy smile on those very kissable lips. The last time she'd seen him, she'd been fairly wasted. Well, actually, she had gotten falling down drunk that evening and puked on the sidewalk. Not tonight! She was gonna end the night in that dude's bed. A stool at the packed bar opened up, and she moved along at a fast clip before anyone got to it first. It was go-time, baby.

•   •   •   •   •

The next morning, Charlene let herself into the empty apartment. Against all odds, the world was still turning and the dire predictions everything would go haywire at midnight had been way off. Quite the opposite, she thought with a grin, even though her head ached from the morning-after effects of half a dozen G & T's and the hours spent in a loud, smoke-filled bar. She really had to shower, but first she was in dire need of a few hours of sleep. She flopped onto her unmade bed and burrowed into a cocoon of blankets and a tattered quilt.

Her patience had paid off last night; she'd finally scored with the hot bartender. Several other wannabes had passed out or given up during the wee hours, but Charlene had persisted, staking her claim on the guy and passing up games of pool and offers of weed being passed around out back. She'd commandeered her barstool all night, and it had been worth it.

An hour after last call, he'd beckoned her to him with a single gesture and escorted her to a spare room above the bar. He'd taken her up against the wall before they crash landed on the dingy cot in the corner of the room for round two. Some of the details were a bit fuzzy, but it had been fun, and she was looking forward to spending more time with the sexy bartender. She was fairly certain she'd heard him say he'd call her as she tiptoed out of the room a half hour ago.

The New Year started off with a bang, she thought with a smile before she fell into a deep sleep. The year 2000 would be epic, she just knew it.

Chapter 1

Lennon Gallagher
Present Day

I slammed the heavy textbook closed, the sound reverberating through the library at the University of Connecticut Law School. The other patrons looked up in alarm, and I received a couple glares and several pairs of raised eyebrows for my efforts. I nodded in what I hoped was an apologetic manner, and everyone went back to their reading. Everyone, that is, except me. I had been unable to concentrate since my shift interning at the law firm.

It had been nagging at me for days, and the more I attempted to deny it, the harder it was to put it out of my mind. Now it was impossible to focus my attention on anything else. Like a sore tooth or a hangnail, I couldn't ignore it. Poking and prodding until I thought I would lose my mind. This idea, this thought had appeared out of nowhere, and I could not let it go. If it were true, it could quickly torpedo the life I had been building. Blow it to smithereens, as my grandma used to say.

Talk about a conflict of interest! I wasn't at all certain I could risk it. And to what end? To finally put a name and a face to a ghost? Would it be worth it just to finally know? Besides, I had more than enough going on with finishing up my last semester of law school, putting in the required number of hours at the law firm on the class-action case, interviewing for a job, obsessing about the upcoming bar exam, trying to spend time with my mother, who had just gotten out of prison and was now insisting I call her Charlene for some godforsaken reason, and eking out the bare minimum of a social life to hang with my friends and FaceTime with my boyfriend, Seth, in Brooklyn. I could barely recall the last time we were together. This girl needed her man, *not* these kinds of complications right now.

And it was crazy, right? I mean, c'mon. What were the odds? Out of all the law firms in the world and the never-ending list of class action lawsuits they worked, the one I was assigned to just happened to be the one where the named plaintiff was *him*? There was just no way! But was there a downside to finding out either way? I didn't have to *do* anything with the information. I had no need to act on it. It could be my little secret for now, maybe forever. I needed to run this by Randi. If anyone could help me to sort this out, it was her.

I grabbed my phone and, leaving my belongings behind, hurried out to the lobby. I quickly found her name in my contacts. After a couple rings, *ugh*. Voicemail.

"Hi. You've reached Miranda Quinn, legal-aid attorney. Please leave your name and a number, and I'll call you back."

"Hey, Randi. It's me, Lennon. You know my new client from the class action lawsuit? The lead plaintiff I deposed last week? Um, well, I think he's my father. Call me."

Chapter 2

Not quite two hours later, I pulled into the driveway of the place I had called home for much of the past six years. Summers, college breaks, and many weekends during the school year, Randi and Eric had welcomed me again and again. She and my mom had been besties in high school, and many years later, Randi had been there for me. I watched as the front door opened and she raced down the steps. Her reddish-brown hair with barely a sign of gray was pulled into a messy bun, and her skin was glowing. She looked at least a decade younger than her age, which I knew to be fifty-two. I hopped out of the car and hurried over to meet her.

It was only a couple weeks since I had been here last, but no place in the world ever felt more like home to me in all my twenty-four years, and it was all due to this amazing woman. She hugged me close to her, and the tension smothering me all day literally melted away. Randi pulled back just enough to study me closely. I felt those intelligent green eyes of hers attempting to peer into my brain. It was pointless to try to hide.

"You okay?" she asked.

I shrugged. "Better now."

She nodded. "Eric made dinner," she said, taking my arm and leading me to the door. "We'll eat, then we'll talk."

My stomach growled in anticipation as we stepped inside, and I caught a whiff of what could only be Eric's amazing barbecued ribs. That meant there would be homemade mac n' cheese, cornbread, and coleslaw to accompany those ribs. Despite being only a hair above five feet tall and never quite hitting a hundred pounds, I could pack it away like a much larger person. Eric's teaching schedule at the university provided him with the occasional free afternoon to putter in his garden or prepare amazing dinners. Coming here had made the most sense as there were no two people in the world I trusted like Randi and Eric. A homemade feast with all my favorites was just the icing on the cake. Would there be cake? My sweet tooth was always ready to be taken out for a spin. I followed Randi into the kitchen and quickly confirmed the side dishes I hoped for were on display. *Hmmm*, no cake.

Eric came in from the patio carrying a platter of ribs and wearing a green apron stating, "Grills Just Wanna Have Fun." He was the coolest guy ever, but he could be such a goofball sometimes. He had been a senior partner in a successful architecture firm before joining the faculty at the University of Connecticut in the Architectural Engineering department. He had been granted tenure just last fall. I could easily imagine what a popular professor he must be. His eyes lit up when he saw me standing in the doorway. Just like his wife, he looked much younger than his years, especially with that mischievous grin plastered across his face.

"Of all the kitchens in all the world, you show up in ours," he said. He placed the tray on the huge marble island and crossed the room, sweeping me up in a hug. "How're you doing, kid?" he asked before setting me down to inspect me nearly as closely as his wife had minutes earlier.

"Better now," I repeated. "What can I do to help?"

"Pour yourself something to drink," said Randi, "and we're ready to eat." I turned to grab a glass from the cupboard, nearly tripping over the large gray tiger cat winding himself around my ankles.

"Where did you come from?" I asked Hobie, who looked up at me and began to purr loudly. I scooped him into my arms and carried him over to his cat tree, placing him on the top perch. "I'll be back for you after dinner," I assured him, and taking a glass, I filled it from the water pitcher on the counter. I joined Randi and Eric at the table and gratefully accepted large portions of all the freshly prepared dishes. For the next twenty minutes, we focused on the delicious meal. When I was satisfied I had eaten all I could, I eyed the remaining food suspiciously. The three of us had barely made a dent.

"I know you didn't prepare all of this for my benefit," I said. "There's enough food here to feed the whole neighborhood. What's up?"

Randi got up from the table and stepped into the pantry, returning seconds later with a stack of reusable plastic containers and lids. "Tracey is visiting her parents this week, and Dale is home alone. We invited him over for dinner tonight, but he's still at work, so I'm making him a meal to eat later."

Well, that certainly made sense. Tracey and Randi were best friends, and Dale owned a landscaping firm and worked long hours. Their twin sons had flown the coop a few years ago. Flynn was in Las Vegas pursuing a career in nightlife photography, and Chase was working as a production designer at one of the movie studios in Hollywood.

"That's really nice of you. But there's still a lot left over." Randi was filling containers of mac 'n cheese to the brim and snapping the lids into place.

"True. I'm also making up meals for Pop and Sally. Neither of them is doing much cooking anymore, and I figured they would like a home-cooked meal." When they weren't wintering in Florida, Randi's father and his wife lived in a nearby retirement community and took most of their meals in the dining room with the other residents.

"How're they doing?" I asked. They were like my own grandparents in many ways. Randi had really lucked out with a father like Dez Quinn. Widowed young, he'd had the good fortune to find love again with Sally, a lively divorcée who softened his rough edges. "I've got to get over to see them. I feel bad . . ."

Randi had moved on to the pan of cornbread. She withdrew a knife and pushed the pan toward me. "Four squares of bread in each," she directed, and I got to work. "They're doing fine. I had my doubts early on, but they really love it there. The food is good, there are lectures and clubs and guest speakers several times a week, and they've made new friends. I asked them to come tonight, but Sally was playing mahjong, and you'll never believe it, but Pop was going to his bi-monthly book club."

I looked up in surprise. I never once saw Pop read anything but the sports section of the daily newspaper. "Book club?" I asked in amazement. "How did that come about?"

"They have several different book clubs at Oceanview. Sally is in a historical fiction reading group, and Pop found a bunch of men who meet to discuss military novels. Sally says he's been reading a book a week, sometimes two. Can you imagine?"

"That's great. I'm glad they're enjoying their time up here."

"Snowbirds," agreed Randi. "Living their best life, for sure."

Eric closed the lids on three large containers of spareribs. "I'll put two in the fridge, and I'll drop the other at Dale's. Give you two gals some time to chat." He added containers of cornbread, cole slaw, and mac 'n cheese to a large bag. "Anything you need me to do before I hit the road, babe?" he asked Randi, who smiled at him.

"I'll put on a pot of decaf, and when you get back, we can have dessert." Eric groaned, and I knew it was the idea of decaf setting him off. Both of them were big coffee drinkers but had recently cut back and switched to decaf in the evenings. He gave Randi a kiss and waved in my direction. As he opened the back door, I saw his apron hanging from the doorknob.

"Eric, your apron," I called out, and he looked down at his plaid shirt. "Made you look," I said, and he shook his head good-naturedly at me before closing the door behind him.

"These dishes can wait," Randi said as she glanced around the room. "C'mon." I followed her into the large, but somehow extremely cozy, living room. She pointed the remote control at the gas fireplace, and instantly we were bathed in the amber glow reflected off hundreds of glass beads lining the hearth.

"I feel bad, like I kicked Eric out of his own home," I said, but Randi brushed off my concerns.

"I told him we needed to talk, and this gives him an excuse for enjoying a cigar with Dale. Trust me, he's not feeling put out in the least."

We settled into the cushy confines of the generously upholstered sofa, and for a second I nearly gave in to the idea I could lay back and fall asleep. Randi would cover me with the mohair throw slung over the back of the sofa, and I could—

"So why do you think this guy is your birth father?" she asked, and I sat up straight, all thoughts of a nap forgotten. It was time to talk.

Chapter 3

"Just tell me what you know, Lennon. Stick to the facts," she encouraged me, and I let out a breath. No need to be nervous. I was talking to Randi, the smartest and most compassionate woman I had ever met. Surely she would understand and help me make sense of all this.

"His age," I began slowly. "He's fifty-two." I watched Randi's lack of a visible reaction. Yeah, big whoop. My mom was turning fifty-two, same as Randi. The similarity in ages meant nothing. "His name is Michael Kelliher. He was born in New London, lived there most of his life. Bartended at the Wharf. My mom used to talk about the Wharf. How she and Aunt Kelly used to go there all the time."

Randi's eyes narrowed, and she nodded slowly. "I remember the Wharf," she said. "But hundreds, thousands of people drank there over the years. What are the chances Charlene . . . ?"

I spoke rapidly, desperate to convince her I might be right. That this guy hooked up with my mom, and nine months later she had me. "His hands, for one. They're just like mine." I held up a hand to demonstrate my claim. "See how my index finger is virtually the same size as my middle finger? His are just like mine. And he has a tiny mole on his left cheek, just like mine. Charlene doesn't have one. Neither does Kelly. I had to get it from someone." Randi was looking thoughtful, actually skeptical, and clearly not convinced. I was doing a shit job, my examples were weak, and my evidence was speculative at best. Why did I ever think I could be a lawyer? If I couldn't convince my best friend of something, how would I ever manage with a jury? *My client is innocent because he has a mole. Seriously?*

"Back up a step, okay?" Randi's calm voice brought me back to reality. "Tell me about the case. How did he end up joining the class action lawsuit? And you said he's the lead plaintiff?"

"Yes, he was the first to file and best represents the entire class. The claim is that Data Solutions, a medical billing and coding firm out of Hartford, was negligent in protecting the privacy of their clients' records. Nearly two hundred class representatives are being vetted to join the lawsuit."

"And this Michael Kelliher is a client of Data Solutions?" she asked, and I nodded.

"Yes, he's a licensed therapist, and he contracted with them to handle his billing and insurance claims as well as store his clients' medical records."

"I imagine he's looking for monetary damages to compensate him for financial losses related to the security breach?" she asked.

"Yes, but it's more than that," I said. "He's not just doing it for the money."

Randi smiled. "It's okay if he's in it for the cash, sweetheart. After all, the basis for the claim states due to negligence on the part of the defendants, the claimants suffered losses to varying degrees. Correct?" I nodded, and she went on. "Why did Kelliher file a claim if not to be awarded a financial settlement?"

"One of his clients took his own life after his medical history and issues with gambling went public. I shouldn't reveal his identity, but you probably know who I am referring to." Randi thought for a moment before her eyes grew wide and she stared at me in total surprise.

"You don't mean . . . Sonny Leone, the sportscaster on the Hartford TV station?" she asked, and I nodded slowly.

"Yes, it's him. And the press has been having a field day with it. Well-respected, award-winning sportscaster a degenerate gambler? And Kelliher's own business has suffered irreparable harm as a result. He's lost nearly all his clients and is struggling to maintain his practice."

"Okay, tell me more about meeting him, your first impressions," Randi said.

I spoke slowly as I recalled the first time I saw him about a month ago. He was one of a couple dozen claimants we brought in to review the process. One of the junior partners from the firm walked everyone through the steps of a class action lawsuit, emphasizing there were no guarantees the case would see the light of day, and, even if it did, there might not be much in the way of compensation. I was one of the unnamed law student interns tasked with looking like I was going to be working hard on their behalf. I studied the group of potential claimants from my vantage point near the back of the room, and when I saw him, my heart quite literally skipped a beat. Did I know him, and if I did, would I need to report it to my supervisor at the firm as a possible conflict of interest? He seemed very familiar. Maybe I waited on him while I was working at the Point all those years? I realized he was looking straight at me as well, and, caught in the act, I averted my gaze to the list of attendees. They were wearing numbers on lanyards around their necks, and I glanced up quickly to check. He was claimant number one, the lead named individual claiming damages against Data Solutions.

I studied the names in front of me. Michael J. Kelliher, aged fifty-two, originally from New London, Connecticut. Licensed social worker with a practice in Hartford, claiming damages resulting from a lack of due diligence on the part of the defendant.

Despite my glaringly apparent need for help, I have never consulted a therapist for any of my issues, which include, but are not limited to, a fear of intimacy, a mistrust of authority figures, and challenges with commitment. I'm honestly afraid of starting down that rabbit hole. As long as I could maintain a couple of good relationships, graduate from law school, and pay my bills more or less on time, I was grateful. I never expected to be where I was today, and I didn't complain all that often. And certainly not while lying on some therapist's couch.

I had no good reason why I would know this guy from anywhere, but there was *something*. Had I seen his image in the file I spent hours studying over the past two weeks? As I watched him out of the corner of my eye, I saw him run his left hand through his sandy hair. It felt familiar as I realized I did the exact same gesture multiple times a day. What was it with this guy?

"And then last week, he came in to be deposed. I sat in with my supervisor and we talked, and I had the same feeling, like déjà vu or something, and I swear when we shook hands, he looked at me kind of, I don't know, surprised, maybe? Like he knew me too? And then I noticed his hands, their shape and how fidgety he got the longer we kept him. When he started talking about his client's death, he got kind of choked up. Like, his voice got shaky, and he seemed heartbroken. Then he said it was his fault." Randi drew in a breath as she leaned forward to study me closely.

"Why would he think it was his fault?"

I shrugged my shoulders. "Not sure, but he did say he had been thinking of switching companies lately. Like he was having some concerns about Data Solutions, there had been a few glitches, but he was super busy and kept putting off the process of finding another provider."

"Guilt is a funny thing," Randi said. "It doesn't sound like he's actually culpable to me. But honestly, Len, the idea of him being your father is all somewhat circumstantial. What you've told me isn't much to go on."

I was tired and less than pleased with how this conversation had gone tonight. I was not certain what I hoped would come out of my visit, but it wasn't this. "Ran, you always tell me to go with my gut, to trust my instincts, and that's what I'm doing. The first time I met with him, I felt something. Like I knew him from somewhere or like we met before. It was weird. People say that all the time, but not me. I have never felt that way about anyone before now. You know me. I'm always on the outside looking in. I don't click with people the way you do. Not even family members. Which is fine," I clarified.

I honestly never felt like I was missing out on all that much. Whenever I spent any amount of time with my mother's siblings or cousins, I left feeling like maybe I was adopted. But who would let a single, strung-out drug addict get their hands on a baby? No one, that's who. I was definitely Charlene's daughter, but my father was out there somewhere. He had to be. Maybe it *was* Michael Kelliher.

Randi was shaking her head at me. "Len, I know you're all tied up in this whole lone wolf persona, but you're kidding yourself if you don't recognize the bonds you've forged just since I've known you. The birthday dinner for my niece Clementine that you had to skip because you had the flu? I thought I would need to drag you out of your sickbed to get everyone to calm down."

I smiled, thinking of the cards and flowers I had received. And the food! Homemade chicken soup for days. I was forever grateful to be part of such a wonderful family. Maybe I just needed to leave well enough alone.

"And Tracey and her family love you. And Seth's family too," she added.

"It's true, and I love you all. I know this sounds crazy, and it probably is, but the first time I laid eyes on him, I felt a connection, and every time I've seen him since, the feeling is stronger. The physical similarities, the way he pushes his hair out of his eyes, the freaking mole, the nervous twitch . . . Hell, he just about sits on his hands to keep them still." I stopped and met Randi's gaze. She looked . . . almost convinced.

"And he's married. They just celebrated their fifteenth wedding anniversary. She's a school teacher named Marilyn, but he calls her Lyn, and they have a thirteen-year-old son. His name is John. He named his son after his favorite musician, John Lennon." I swiped at the tears running down my cheeks with the cuff of my sweatshirt. I was more convinced than ever I had finally met my father and I had a half-brother as well. It couldn't just be wishful thinking, could it?

"That's . . . interesting," Randi said, and I nodded, spent. Yeah, it was. "What do you want to do?" Randi asked, and I knew she was almost on board. I thought quickly about my response before answering.

"I could confront Charlene, but I've already asked her a million times, and she either truly doesn't know who knocked her up or she just wants to hold it over me. Keep me guessing. I used to think she didn't want to share me, you know? Like, if I found my dad, I wouldn't love her as much."

Randi was nodding her head. "Unfortunately, that sounds just like the girl I used to know. What's next?"

How much should I share? Everything, of course. This was Randi.

"I, um, may have a sample of his DNA, you know?"

Her eyes widened in surprise. "How on earth did you . . . Wait, do I even want to know?"

"It's a coffee cup. I offered him a cup of coffee last time we met. No biggie. We have a Keurig and plenty of disposable cups in the breakroom. He had a cup of regular black coffee. Just like me, FYI. He went to crumble up the cup when he finished it, and I offered to dispose of it for him. But instead, I took it and sealed it in a plastic bag and tossed it in my backpack. Just in case."

Randi frowned. "You know the chain of evidence is not—"

"I don't want to sue him or arrest him. I just want to find out if he's my, you know, bio-dad. What's wrong with that?"

"Nothing, hon. It's perfectly natural you would want to know. But be careful what you wish for; that's all I'm saying."

"I just don't get it. I hoped you would be proud of me." Tears pooled in my eyes, and I swiped at them, feeling angry and frustrated.

"I'm always proud of you, Len. Always. And I think you're being really brave. I just don't want to see you get hurt. You know very little about this guy, and until his case is resolved, you need to tread carefully. As his attorney, your only responsibility is to help him and all the members of the suit get the highest settlement possible. This kind of information could be damaging to your role in the case. And you're so close to graduation. If you were to be released from the case, it's unlikely you could be reassigned so quickly. Without those hours, you won't be able to graduate."

"I know, I know. I'm not an idiot. I put the cup away for safekeeping. I am not planning on sending it in for testing until all this is behind me. Maybe not even then. I've already got way too much on my plate in addition to the case." I started ticking off on my fingers. "Exams, a paper for Civil Procedures, setting up more job interviews, getting laid," I added with a wicked grin and Randi laughed.

"Well, you do you, or I guess I could say 'you do Seth,' but whatever you do, please don't forget to sign up for a study group," she reminded me. "The right group can make all the difference."

I sighed. I didn't correct her, but they called them *review* groups these days. I had already joined a few groups during my three years in law school, but I hadn't stuck with any of them for more than a couple weeks. I had a basic distrust of people and a hard time relying on others. Safe to say I was a loner, *not* a joiner.

"And if you find the right group to get you through the final exams, you might just be able to stay connected with them while prepping for the bar."

"Three *more* months with a bunch of people I haven't met yet? Kill me now," I said.

"Len, you have to trust me on this," Randi said.

"Okay, I wasn't going to say anything, but a classmate, Erin, told me about a new group forming, and she thinks there's an opening. I'll find out this weekend. Please don't worry about me."

Chastened, Randi nodded. "Groups are good."

"You should know," I reminded her. "You passed the bar on the first try, didn't you?" And was ranked in the top ten percent of her graduating class.

"A million years ago," she conceded. "Or maybe it just feels like that long. While we're on the subject of planning ahead, what are you doing this summer? I know, studying for the bar and interviewing. But are you going to keep your place in Hartford? Your room here is always available. We would love to have you. And we're talking about taking a boatload of vacation time this summer. Eric submitted a paper for a conference in San Diego, which sounds like fun. You can stay here with Hobie and keep him company."

"Thank you. I love being here, and whenever you are planning to get away, just say the word. I'll hang with Hobes anytime. But I'm just not sure about where is the best place for me." I thought about Seth, who had accepted a great job with a tech startup and moved to Brooklyn last summer. It was a terrific opportunity, a once-in-a-lifetime sort of thing, and he'd jumped at it, starting only a day after receiving his degree. I had taken the train in to see him a bunch of times since, and he'd come back to Connecticut for a handful of long weekends and most holidays. Added all together, it was maybe a month's worth of time together in nearly a year. I was worried he and I were drifting apart. He seemed less than interested in just about anything I had to say lately.

I suddenly felt all the stress of the last few months crash-land in my brain. Thinking of the things I needed to accomplish over the next several weeks, wondering where I would be living after graduation and if I'd have a job lined up by then. Seth and I needed to have *the talk* and soon. But there was nothing I could do about that right now. I yawned loudly, not even attempting to cover my mouth. Randi watched me closely.

"Hey, it's late and you're exhausted," she said. "Why don't you stay here tonight instead of driving back to Hartford? You can get a good night's sleep, and Eric will make us breakfast."

She didn't have to ask me twice as returning to my tiny dorm room held no appeal whatsoever. I hugged her gratefully and headed toward my room, Hobie following close behind me. "Tell Eric thanks when he gets back," I called out. "G'night." I peeled off my clothes, pulled on a Ramones *Rocket to Russia* T-shirt from the top drawer in my dresser, and crawled into bed. Within a couple minutes, I fell asleep to the sound of Hobie's slow, rhythmic purring.

Chapter 4

I left Randi and Eric's late Friday morning and spent most of the weekend in the law school library. Sharing my suspicions about my client left me feeling lighter, unburdened, and I got caught up on the assignments I had been putting off. By Sunday afternoon, I had finished two papers and heard from Erin that I was welcome to join the new review group, headed up by some dude named Roger. Must be a bunch of like-minded procrastinators, I assumed. Still Erin was really smart and rumored to be ranked first in the class. We'd had coffee a few times this semester and exchanged contact information, but neither of us had much free time. Still, it would be nice to see a familiar face. I confirmed the details via text; we would be meeting twice weekly until exams were over, then amping up to three times a week all summer to prepare for the bar exam in August. Assuming we made it through final exams intact, it looked like I would be spending most of my summer in Hartford.

I called Seth on Sunday night. We had been missing each other for days, leaving messages on voicemail and relying on texting to communicate. He immediately answered his phone and confirmed it was a good time to talk. Finally!

After a few minutes of catching each other up on the past several days, I told him about my review group. "We're meeting tomorrow night at five to get acquainted and figure out how we might divide up the work. There are six of us, which is good, I think, because we'll be able to get a lot done, but it's not so big anyone can just coast. And for the bar—"

His voice cut in, sounding flat, cold even. "I guess what you're telling me is you're not spending the summer with me after all." He sounded less disappointed and more annoyed, and his reaction surprised me.

"I never promised you I would be able to do that," I explained. "It was always just a possibility. My focus has to be on studying for the bar, Seth. You know that, right?" When he didn't answer right away, I hurried on. "Anyway, we're meeting during the week, so I can still take the train down on weekends. And you'll be coming home for the Fourth of July and your folks thirtieth wedding anniversary party in August. It's on my calendar," I reminded him. Seth's folks threw an epic holiday bash every year, coinciding with his hometown's fireworks display. I imagined us walking on the beach, eating fried clams, and going for ice cream just like we did every summer. "You'll get sick of me," I teased, trying to elicit some form of reaction from him. After an awkward moment of silence lasting a beat too long, he spoke up.

"Yeah, with all my family around and your people, we'll be lucky to have five minutes of alone time. And let's face it, when you come in for a weekend, it's like thirty-six hours from beginning to end, if we're lucky. And you spend half the time catching up on sleep and the other half texting your law school friends about assignments or whatever. Sounds great."

His assessment of our past few weekends together stung. It's like he didn't recognize what kind of effort I had been making all this time. Since we started dating six years ago, I'd earned my bachelor's degree in only three years by taking on additional classes and going to summer school. I had applied and been accepted into law school and would be graduating in a couple months. With Randi's help, I had applied for loans and grants and funded most of my meager living expenses working part-time everywhere I could. I filed papers and answered the phones at the legal aid clinic where Randi worked, handled the reference desk at the law school library, and even filled in for some shifts at the restaurant in New London where I previously worked full-time. The one where I first met Seth.

How did we get here, to this place where we couldn't even have a civil conversation? I wanted to try to understand him better, but in times of stress like this, I reverted to my default. My go-to. The standard Gallagher reaction. *Anger.*

"Are you seriously giving me shit right now? You know I've been working my ass off. What the hell do you expect me to do? Drop everything I've been working for and park my ass in Park Slope for the summer? Wait around till you get off work before we head to a sports bar with all your pals? Oooh, yeah. Sign me up." I let out a breath, shaking with frustration. Where had that come from? Clearly, Seth was wondering the same thing. I could picture him, sitting on the edge of his bed in his Brooklyn apartment, looking at his phone, trying to figure out what had gotten into his girlfriend. "Hey, it's late," I said, willing my voice to sound calm. "Why don't we say good night and plan to catch up later in the week, okay?"

"Sure thing. Catch ya later then," he said, his voice cool and distant.

I was about to tell him I loved him and we would work things out, but he had already disconnected. *Crap.* I sent him a text anyway and he responded immediately, liking what I had written and telling me he loved me too. Crisis averted—or just delayed for the time being? I honestly had no clue.

I tried to recall what I might have said to give Seth the idea I would definitely be moving to New York for the summer and beyond. I had to admit I sometimes shied away from difficult conversations and that commitment was still like a coat I wore but occasionally needed to shrug off and hang in a closet. Not that I was ever unfaithful to Seth. Not even close. We met at the restaurant when I was eighteen. He was my first love, my only one. I could imagine Seth and me spending our lives together someday, I think. But I still needed me-time. To put on an old sweatshirt and a pair of Seth's boxers. To spend a sunny day entirely indoors, eating a pint or two of ice cream and listening to Sabrina Carpenter or Billie Eilish or binge-watching *Grey's Anatomy* reruns.

Oh yeah, and Seth wanted kids and I wanted nothing to do with them. Through Randi's step-brother, I'd had exposure to a few young'uns, and I enjoyed the occasional day at the beach with them, collecting seashells or building sandcastles. Then going home to spend the next twenty-four hours blissfully alone and entirely sand-free. I knew it was a discussion we would need to have at some point in the future. But I had a degree to complete, a bar to pass, and a well-paying job to land. It wasn't my fault Seth was a couple years ahead of me in the adulting process.

I donned my headphones and settled into re-reading my study notes to prepare for my upcoming exams. It felt good to put nearly all my focus on schoolwork. My early education had been chaotic, as I'd shuffled every few months from Aunt Kelly's house, then back in with my mom when she was out of jail, to a variety of foster homes ranging from bad to truly deplorable. When my mom was out, whether it was for a month or two, before she violated her parole and got sent back in, she'd often kept me out of school, claiming we had so much missing time to make up for.

We would hang out at one of the beaches dotting the Connecticut shoreline or wander around the New London Mall, eating free samples in the food court and sneaking into a movie. Needless to say, schoolwork often took a back seat to my role in Charlene's twenty-four-hour-beck-and-call routine. Somehow I'd adapted to the rigors of college, where I flourished academically, and then law school, always making the dean's list, and earning good grades. Amazing what could be accomplished when you didn't have to cater to your narcissistic mother's nonstop whims.

I pulled up the calendar on my phone and studied my schedule for the upcoming week. Crap, I had completely forgotten. I'd promised my mother I would take her to her doctor's appointment tomorrow. It was right there. April 23rd @ 2:00 p.m. I would have to hustle home from

New London and would likely be late for my 5:00 p.m. group meet and greet. Talk about making a poor first impression. What a crap sandwich!

I flipped off my light and bundled into my covers, still surrounded by textbooks and notebooks and my laptop. Ugh. First my possible bio-dad, then a fight with Seth, and now a guilt trip professionally escorted by none other than Charlene Gallagher. Fuck. My. Life. *Why me?*

Chapter 5

I spent the morning sitting in bed enjoying a jumbo cup of takeout coffee from the bodega on the corner and a large, only slightly stale cinnamon roll from the half-price rack. Not a bad way to start the day, all things considered. I had a load of paperwork to get through, and as I would be spending the entire afternoon driving Miss Charlene, the solitude was ideal. I had been assisting with document review and coding for the last few weeks, and since the full-time staff was involved in some sort of off-site training retreat, I had been given the go-ahead to work remotely this morning. As I didn't have actual physical files or reports, I wasn't breaking any of the strict rules regarding confidentiality. I was in the zone, no interruptions and no background chatter to attempt to block out. It was perfect.

I needed to create a timeline of the memoranda, briefs, and other legal documents related to the class action suit. I was making some headway, checking the dates on whatever had already been filed and noting them on a master list. I had scribbled notes and had my go-to index cards spread around me in all their color-coordinated splendor as I worked. Ever since I was assigned to this case back at the start of the semester in January, I felt like this was the work I was meant to do. At first, most of my time had been spent on research—collecting data on relevant laws, regulations, and precedents on cases related to damages incurred following a breach of confidential information. One of the junior partners, a cool guy in his mid-thirties named Calvin, must have seen something he liked in my work. Before long, I'd gotten pulled from the pool of interns and had begun the seemingly monumental task of organizing and analyzing large datasets of information into categories, looking for themes and similarities. I found the work fascinating, all aspects of it. The lectures and legal knowledge I had absorbed for the past three years were finally making sense and being put to good use.

Since I normally concentrated on what others might call scut work, but what I saw as essential data mining and critical pattern identification, last week's time spent on depositions with claimants was new to me. All the impersonal stats and factoids, dates and data suddenly came alive for me. This case truly mattered to those negatively impacted by a corporation's carelessness. They weren't just claimants, they were *S.C.*, a college student working as a nanny who was fired when her employers found out she was being treated for depression, and *T.B.*, who had lost partial custody of his two kids when his vengeful ex-wife discovered he was HIV positive, and of course Michael Kelliher's client, local sportscaster Sonny Leone, who had shot himself in the head after being publicly outed as a gambling addict in treatment.

Data Solutions should pay dearly for their negligence. According to our growing roster of techies who would be paid to testify if the case ever went to court, it was a fairly clear-cut example of trying to save a few bucks by not installing the proper firewalls. When an endodontist from Manchester, Connecticut, logged into his personal email while on the DS network and opened an email which turned out to be a phishing attempt, his dental practice records got hacked along with those of DS's other clients. I was far from an expert in IT, but even I could understand basic security principles.

As my internship ended in only a few weeks, I knew I would not be around for the court proceedings if a settlement was not reached quickly. The rumor currently making its way around the office centered around the firm's plan to bring on additional associates this summer to continue the work of us graduates. I hoped to be included so I could continue with the case. Although I ultimately planned to pursue a career in family law, time spent with a top-rated law firm would be beneficial. Plus, it might take away some of the sting of disappointing Seth.

Lost in my thoughts about the case, I jumped when I heard a knock on my door. I struggled to extricate myself from the tangle of covers without disturbing my files. I looked down to ensure my tank top and baggy gym shorts covered all my private body parts and called out, "Who is it?" I assumed it was Jimmy from next door, bored from studying solo and desperate enough to seek out decidedly un-chatty me.

"It's Sasha Turner," a voice called out. "I need to talk to you, Lennon." Weird, the dorm's resident coordinator needed to talk to me? I could count on one hand the number of times we had exchanged more than a passing greeting in the past three years.

I pulled open the door to find a very irritated woman, a couple years older than me. From her grubby Birkenstocks to her paisley peasant dress paired with a vintage headscarf, everything about her screamed Earth Mother. And let's not forget the cloying scent of patchouli following her everywhere she went. Man, did she look pissed off.

"Hi, Sasha," I began. "Can I help you with something?" I was about to ask if she wanted to come in when she thrust a manila envelope at me. "What's this?"

"We've been trying to get a hold of you for weeks. You're not answering our emails and calls to your number are not going through." My bad. I was never good about checking my personal emails, and I had blocked her number a few months back to avoid the barrage of reminders about proper disposal of trash and recyclables and reported parking violations. I adopted a look of surprised confusion, a mien perfectly suitable for occasions like these.

"Gee, I'll have to check on that. I guess I didn't realize my spam filter was so aggressive. But since you have me, what's up?"

Sasha's face softened a bit as she studied me closely. "Your request to stay for the summer was denied. You need to be out by the middle of June." At my shocked expression, she hurried on. "It's nothing personal, Lennon. We're looking at doing some long overdue renovations, and the budget just got approved." She gestured to the dated wallpaper and dreary carpeting giving the hallway a rather depressing vibe. "You won't recognize this place when we're done," she added gaily.

Are you fucking kidding me right now? I wanted to shout. Back in February, I requested an extension for summer housing here in the law school dorms. At the time, it was more of a backup plan, a place to live while I prepped for the bar or in case I was asked to stay on at the law firm to help with the lawsuit. As the months went by, I never received a written response and had assumed no news was good news. But now I was reeling. I needed to pack up three years' worth of stuff, find a place to live, and, oh yeah, take my final exams, graduate, find a job, study for the bar, figure things out with Seth, determine if it was Michael Kelliher's sperm that fertilized Charlene's egg . . . and crap, Charlene. I checked my watch: 11:33. If I hurried, I might get to her in time to deliver her to her two o'clock appointment.

"Thanks for the heads up," I deadpanned to Sasha, who was clearly waiting for me to argue with her or beg for an extension. "Gotta run."

Her face brightened as she turned to leave. "If you need packing boxes or tape or, well, anything, just holler. We want to help make this transition as painless as possible," she said with uncharacteristic enthusiasm.

Don't shoot the messenger, I told myself, just barely resisting the urge to launch into full Gallagher mode. And I would need boxes and all that stuff to move . . . somewhere. I watched her traipse back down the hallway, presumably to spread tidings of joy and cheer to other poor, unsuspecting souls. Although if they actually read their emails or answered incoming calls, it's likely they already knew. Then why hadn't anyone told me? Oh yeah, probably cuz I was never home and rarely read emails and only occasionally texts. Clearly, I was going to die alone unless Seth and I figured things out. I closed the door with a quite satisfying slam and hurried to get ready to go and pick up Charlene. This day, which had shown such promise only a short while ago, now had me questioning virtually every life choice I'd ever made.

Chapter 6

The last time I'd driven to New London to bring my mother to an appointment, she'd answered the door in her threadbare bathrobe, a cigarette dangling from her lips. I'd had to remind her we needed to be across town in less than twenty minutes for her dental appointment. Somehow, being locked up for the better part of the last decade had caused her to forget the whole concept of being on time, as well as the availability of public transportation. A bus would have been quick and easy, but playing the usual guilt card, she'd talked me into driving the eighty-two miles from Hartford to pick her up. So that morning, I had gotten up at 5:00 a.m., completed the assigned readings for the day, and sat through two lectures. Then I had driven nearly two hours and arrived at her place to find she wasn't even dressed yet. Welcome to Charlene's World, I had thought bitterly.

Today would probably be about the same. I knew this, and yet here I was—rushing to be on time. Bumper-to-bumper traffic made the drive even longer than the hour and a half I had projected. At the rate I was going, I would need to really hurry her along this afternoon. My phone pinged with an incoming text, and I gave it a quick look. I was fairly certain if I didn't actually make physical contact with my phone, they couldn't cite me for distracted driving. It was probably my mom, asking where I was or letting me know her chiropractor visit was canceled or rescheduled. That would be fine with me.

R U in? Need $ ASAP

What the hell? My curiosity won out over the whole "hands-free" mandate. I grabbed the phone, checked the number, and saw it was from a number in the group text my review group had recently created. I was confused, thinking I missed an earlier text. I'd already purchased the required study guide and the other materials I would need. Were we chipping in for pizza tonight? The traffic jam began to break up, and the cars in front of me finally started to move. I focused on the road and less than fifteen minutes later pulled up in front of a run-down rooming house. I could hardly believe my eyes, but there she was, all ninety-five pounds of piss and vinegar, as my grandmother used to say. Charlene Gallagher flicked her cigarette on the sidewalk, sashayed over, and let herself into my car. Before I could say hello, she leaned in for a quick hug.

"I was about to take a bus," she said in her gravelly voice, sounding like she'd already smoked a pack of her long menthol-infused cigarettes today. "What took you so long?"

I pulled away from the curb and U-turned back the way I'd come. Resisting the urge to say, "I wish you had," I just shrugged. I studied her briefly, noting her stained Yankees T-shirt and cut-off shorts leaving little to one's imagination. Fairly typical attire for post-jail Charlene, but something was off. She was staring out the window, pouting.

"You're in a mood," I said. "What's up?" I figured she would have a bug up her butt about something. She always did. Charlene's litany of concerns and injustices ranged from social inequality—*There are too many wheelchairs and bicycles on the sidewalk in front of my place. Where exactly do normal people like me get to walk?*—to the price of just about anything, from a cup of coffee to a pack of smokes—*Twelve dollars! Do you believe that? It's like they want us all to quit or something.*—to being put on hold—*I called my parole officer, and he put me on call-waiting. Do you believe it? He works for me. Why do I have to spend ten minutes of my precious time twiddling my thumbs while he gets someone to bring him a coffee or takes a dump?* But not today. Apparently, I was the problem du jour. She glared at me.

"What're you talking about?" she asked testily. "You're the one who showed up late, no apology for keeping me waiting. What's up with *you*?"

I shrugged again, resigned to be able to count on one hand the number of arguments I would ever win with my mother. She should have been a lawyer. "Just tired, I guess. The chiropractor's in the shopping plaza over on Green Street, right?" Without even looking, I could feel her rolling her eyes at me.

"No, that's the acupuncturist. We need to get over to the high-rise on Park Street. Pronto."

I turned left at the next stop sign. Ever since her release six months earlier, my mother had been on a self-discovery quest. At least that's what she called it. She'd gotten hold of a catalog from the Medicaid office and was like a kid in a candy store. She'd started calling me at all hours, eager to explore her newfound benefits as a free woman. As befitting the true nature of the classic narcissist, time in the spotlight garnering all the attention she felt was her due was the ultimate reward. If it could only be earned by lying spread eagle on an exam table and wearing a johnny gown, that was a price worth paying to Charlene.

Today we were going to a chiropractor despite her total lack of aches and pains. After the past thirty-plus years during which she snorted, smoked, or injected just about every possible substance known to man, smoked two packs of cigarettes a day, and subsisted on beer and barbecue-flavored potato chips, Charlene Gallagher was a healthy woman who, if she could be believed, would outlive us all. But she would gamely schedule appointments with whatever specialists were in her healthcare network, answer their questions, fill out paperwork, and submit to an examination. If she liked the doctor she saw, she would try to finagle a free follow-up visit. But if their breath was anything but minty-fresh or they kept her waiting more than five minutes or called her on her bullshit, she would storm out of the examination room, tell the waiting patients with actual health concerns they were wasting their time on the quacks running this place, and swear she would never see another dermatologist, ophthalmologist, chiropractor . . .

I waited somewhat patiently as she checked in and then sat beside me in the waiting room, filling out forms. At the speed with which she was answering the questions about her medical history, I couldn't help but imagine she was just making it up as she went along. Minutes later, they called her name, and she sailed through the door, chattering away to the nurse who was escorting her. I breathed a sigh of relief. For a tiny woman, she sure sucked up a lot of energy. I pulled out my phone to study the text message I'd received during my drive here. It still made no sense to me. I decided to respond.

In for what?

Seconds later, I got my response.

Crap Yur not...my bad. Wrong #

Well, that told me exactly nothing. Seeing no new texts or messages, not even from Seth, I pressed further.

Who is this?

Three bouncing dots appeared, and I thought I was getting a response, but after a minute or so, nothing.

R U in tonight's group? I asked.

Again dots, then finally:

Yeah, it's Glen No biggie. thought you were someone else. Sorry for confusion.

I remembered a Glen from the list I'd received. Despite my reservations, I really wanted to mesh with the other members. Tonight's meet and greet would provide a sense of the group dynamics, and I hoped I would get there on time. First impressions and all that.

The door to the inner sanctum opened and my mother glided out, still chattering away with the nurse. Must have gone well, I decided, standing as they approached.

Charlene let out a squeal when she saw me. "Oooh, baby girl. Wait till I tell you. What an experience," she drawled, her eyes bright and sparkly. "I feel like a brand-new woman." If I didn't know any better, I would have sworn she was on something. And honestly, knowing her as well as I did, it wouldn't have surprised me if she'd somehow scored back there.

"Hey, Mom." I walked toward them, and she gave a cutesy little wave and pulled me closer.

"Megan is a nurse practitioner." She spoke slowly, drawing out each syllable. "She went to college and everything." The two women beamed at each other, and Charlene leaned closer to the willowy blond. "This little rascal is my baby girl, Lennon. We named her that because her father was a big Beatles fan." I looked at her, trying to disguise my amazement. She had never disclosed that to me, always claiming she just liked the name. Michael Kelliher was a huge Beatles fan and had even named his son after John Lennon. This could *not* be a coincidence.

I decided to have a little fun at her expense. "Hi, Megan. Yeah, my dad sure loved the Beatles all right. There was a jukebox at the place where he bartended, and he would always play his favorites for my mom." I smiled sweetly, delighted to witness the look of surprise on her face that quickly turned to one of barely disguised annoyance.

"All righty, then, see you next time, Megan. I'll call that number you gave me and see if I can get the state to foot the bill. And meanwhile, I'll do those exercises you showed me. Twice a day." She turned to me, grabbing my arm and propelling me toward the exit. "C'mon, you. Places to go and all that." As soon as we were alone in the quiet hallway, she pushed me up against the wall, and I could tell her annoyance had morphed into anger. With an accusing finger in my face, she practically snarled at me. "Just what the fuck was that?" she rasped. "What the hell are you playing at, girl?"

My momentary fear at the change in her behavior quickly subsided, and I turned to face her, my eyes blazing. *Oh, hell no! You don't get to be mad, Char. I do!* "My dad was a Beatles fan, huh? Well, that's interesting. I sure appreciate your sharing that little tidbit with Megan as it represents the sum total of what I know about the man who fathered me."

Her eyes narrowed, and she glared at me. "It's called making conversation, little girl. That's all. I already told you I have no idea who your dad was, so cool your jets, wouldja? Now let's get going. It's one-dollar sliders night at the tavern, and I promised Helen and Joannie I would go with them. I need a change of clothes." She took off at a fast clip down the hall, and there was nothing else I could do besides follow her out to the parking lot. When we got to my car, I spoke up just before she slid inside.

"So, was he a bartender or not?" I asked, receiving a scowl in response. She was silent on the drive, and I noted with some satisfaction I was off the hook for any sort of conversation. I pulled up outside the halfway house. It was no worse than any of the group homes I'd lived in over the years when she was incarcerated and neither my grandma nor my aunt Kelly could take me. I turned to see an all-too-familiar sight. Charlene with one hand on the door handle and the other facing toward me, palm outstretched. I sighed, knowing what was expected. I dug my wallet out of my backpack and pulled out a ten-dollar bill. She raised an eyebrow with an "are you kidding me" look, and I found a second bill and held them out to her. She grabbed the cash and shoved the bills in the back pocket of her ridiculously short shorts. She smiled at me, suddenly in no hurry. Having gotten beer money, a free massage, or whatever, and weaseling her way out of answering my questions, she could afford to be magnanimous.

"You still seeing that Black boyfriend of yours?" she asked, and my heart sank as I pondered her question. Seth and I had argued last night, and I hadn't heard from him all day, so I really wasn't sure how to answer. Well, if I was or if I wasn't, I sure as hell wasn't going to go down that path with her.

"His name is Seth, as you very well know, and yes, I am still seeing him." I knew there was no point in trying to school Charlene on the lack of a need to reference his skin color EVERY SINGLE TIME we talked.

She smiled, an actual smile. "He's good for you." She leaned in to give me a quick peck on the cheek. "Don't fuck it up," she warned as she climbed out of the car.

"Hey, Char, don't forget to do your exercises for Megan," I called out and gave a little wave when she turned to face me. Her look of surprise changed to a smirk.

"You're a riot, girlie. A regular laugh riot." She shook her head and started to walk toward her front door. At the last minute, she turned and called out to me. "I still ain't got my invite to your graduation. You gonna come and get me for it or what?"

I softened, recalling how she had been in prison for most of the milestones in my life. Was it possible she would actually be there for me when I earned my law degree? I started to tear up at the idea.

"Watch your mail, Mom," I told her, wiping at my eyes with the cuff of my UCONN sweatshirt. I made a U-turn and headed toward the highway, shaking my head at the mood shifts she had gone through in the past hour and a half. I recalled an expression from my PSYC 101 class that fit Charlene Gallagher perfectly. My mom clearly had a *dynamic emotional landscape.*

Chapter 7

The traffic gods must have been smiling down at me for a change because I pulled into the parking lot at the law school library with fifteen minutes to spare. I hustled into the lobby, hit the restroom as my bladder was about to burst, and checked the board where they listed all the private rooms, and there it was. The Aetna room was reserved for the evening by Roger Stevens. I could totally murder an iced coffee right now, but I knew there was nothing available in the immediate vicinity. I spied a tired-looking vending machine and patiently fed wrinkled dollar bills into it, receiving a room-temp bottle of water and a package of only slightly crushed orange cheese crackers for my efforts. It would have to do until I made it back to the dorm.

I shoved a couple crackers in my mouth and tried to wash them down with a slug of tepid water when a movement close behind me caused me to jump. What the—I turned to see an extremely tall, extremely hairy man possibly about my age looking down at me curiously. This dude was a giant, like Sasquatch-esque.

"Can I help you with something?" I backed up to the vending machine and glared at him. "Who are you?" A ghost of a smile slightly softened the man's sharp features, hooded dark eyes, and beaky nose. He held out a large hand, a gesture I was unable to return as I was holding my crackers in one hand and my orange-dusted sweaty water bottle in the other.

He saw my dilemma and raised both hands in a kind of "no worries" gesture. "I'm Roger Stevens, and I'm betting you're Lena Gallagher, Erin's friend."

I shook my head slightly and corrected him. "It's Lennon, not Lena, but it's nice to meet you, Roger. I'm looking forward to our meeting." I bent slightly to center my backpack and walked slowly toward our meeting room. A few others were entering the room, and it was exactly 5:00 p.m. "Hate to be late," I quipped when I noticed he was trailing slowly behind me. The forced grin he wore turned downward, and he once again invaded my personal space, moving in closer and speaking softly.

"I understand you got a call earlier today from a wrong number," he murmured. And here I was, about to correct him a second time in as many minutes. I didn't know this guy at all, but I knew his type. Challenging or questioning him was a surefire way to earn a spot on his shitlist. Well, it was too late for that.

"Actually, it was a text, and it was from Glen. But I was not the intended recipient. No worries," I added quickly when I saw his brows knit together and his cheeks flush red. Was this dude seriously pissed at me? "A simple mistake."

"It was a wrong number, and you need to let it go. Put the call and this conversation behind you. They never happened. Please nod to show me you understand." He studied me closely, and I found myself nodding in agreement but was now totally confused. What was he making such a big deal about? He turned away, and I followed him into the room. I saw Erin sitting with her back toward me, reading something on her phone. Her bright red curls were only partially contained by the messenger-style cap she wore. I always marveled at her sense of style. It was quirky, for sure, but she made everything she wore look amazing.

It was a small conference-style room with a large round oak table in the middle. All but two of the six seats were occupied, and it looked like

Erin had saved me a seat. On a sideboard, I saw a bucket with ice-cold water bottles, a small stack of napkins, and a silver bowl heaped with a variety of pre-packaged salty snacks. I dropped my bottle of water and crackers in the trash bin, grabbed a napkin, and wiped my lips and fingers. I snatched a cold bottle and a bag of kettle chips and sat down in the empty chair next to Erin.

"Hey," I greeted her. "So . . . this is weird."

She looked up, immediately breaking into a smile. "Hey, you. Glad you made it. What's weird?"

"Roger is kind of a lot, isn't he?" I asked in a low voice.

She shrugged in response. "Yeah, I guess. But he's wicked smart. And really well connected" she added before looking down at her phone again.

I busied myself assembling my notebook, a pen, and my tablet. I was ready. Roger suddenly looked up and, seeing the rest of us watching him intently, cleared his throat and placed his phone down in front of him. He remained standing but spoke in a voice very different from the whispered frantic tone I'd just heard.

"Good evening. We all know how important this group is to our success in graduating before sitting for the bar in a few months. We'll be working hard toward the ultimate goal of each of us passing on our first try." A small cheer went up, but he continued, needing no acknowledgment or confirmation from us. "My name is Roger Stevens, my focus is criminal law, and I plan to join my father and older brother in the firm founded by my grandfather back in the 1950s." He sat and nodded to the woman to his right. Just as she was about to introduce herself, he held up a hand to stop her. "Sorry, I just realized I haven't gone over the ground rules. Bear with me, won't you?" She nodded, and Roger continued.

"We have agreed to meet on Mondays and Thursdays through the end of classes, after which we will gather Monday, Wednesday, and Thursday through the summer. We are starting early tonight, but going forward we will begin promptly at 6:00 p.m. and conclude no earlier than 9:00. You are expected to arrive on time and attend each session for the duration. If you are sick, you'll need to produce a doctor's note prior to rejoining the group, and two or more unexcused absences will result in your dismissal from the group. It is anticipated any individual or cohort assignments will always be completed and circulated a minimum of twenty-four hours prior to the next group meeting. Is that clear to everyone?"

I looked around and saw the other four members of the group nodding. I thought he was kidding about the doctor's note and just about everything he'd said since then, but it looked like he meant every word. It seemed crazy to me, but maybe this was how all groups operated for graduating seniors with a seriously narrow window in order to get this group thing going. I tried to catch Erin's eye, but she was busy typing notes on her tablet. I tuned back in, realizing he was continuing. His voice was rich, commanding, and I could imagine how a jury might respond to him despite his ungainly size and lumbering gait.

"I should also mention our roster has shifted a bit. For personal reasons, Glen has decided he is unable to join us this session. But I'm pleased to announce Chelsea was happy to step in to take his place." He nodded curtly to a woman sitting across from me who was beaming at Roger like she'd just won first prize at the fair. No one seemed particularly surprised by the announcement. Maybe they didn't know Glen, or maybe they just didn't care. He was the one who had mistakenly texted me earlier today, asking if I was "in" and saying I needed to come up with payment. But for what? Get your head in the game, I told myself. Roger was continuing his opening comments.

"As discussed, the dues are to be paid monthly in advance. If you haven't already paid for May, please take care of that before we end tonight." Clearly, I missed something, lost in my own train of thought. Was this the payment Glen was referring to?

I spoke up. "Excuse me, Roger, can you go over that again, please?" At his blank look, I hurried to explain. "The part about monthly dues, I mean."

He frowned slightly. "Lena, if this is any indication of your ability to concentrate, maybe we should—"

Oh, come on. Seriously? "It's Lennon, Roger. Not Lena. And I apologize. I just missed what you said about payment. Can you please repeat it?" He shook his head at my cluelessness.

"The monthly dues are $150, payable in advance by Venmo, Zelle, or PayPal. I don't take cash, and I don't take credit cards."

I swallowed nervously. The amount was a drop in the bucket compared to what I had invested in my degree, but combined with the registration just to sit for the exam and the study materials I'd already purchased, it was going to be a real blow to my already stretched thin budget this summer. Of course, I would save loads of cash if I took up residence under a bridge after I got kicked out of my dorm room, which, based on the area's tight housing market, was always a possibility.

"But what is it for?" I pressed. "The dues," I added. His look made me want to slide to the floor and slither out of there, but I held firm. I had a right to know where my hard-earned money was going and what it would be used for.

"The room itself," he began. "Refreshments, supplies. Other incidentals. Does that answer your question, Miss Gallagher?" he concluded with barely disguised scorn. Once again, my bullshit sensor went off. I had worked at this library for three years. Students were never charged for reserving meeting rooms like the one we were using. And I was as big a junk food fan as anyone, but not to the tune of $150. What other lies would this guy be telling us?

"Let's please continue going around and introducing ourselves. Chelsea, you were next, I believe." For the next ten minutes, each of the members offered a brief summary of their current status, what type of law they hoped to practice, blah, blah, blah. Chelsea was interested in real estate law, Justin in litigation, Sam in civil law, aka personal injury, and Erin shared what I already knew about her passion for environmental law.

When it was my turn, I spoke quickly, offering the briefest bio ever, delivered in what I'm certain was a robot-like tone, not making eye contact with anyone. I concluded by saying I hoped to practice family law, earning me the briefest of eye-rolls from Roger.

Wow, I am off to a great start. He's warned me, lectured me, and essentially ridiculed me all in the first half hour. If this kept up, it would be a long summer here in Hartford. I wondered if it was too late to find a different group. One with no monthly dues and no Roger.

And what happened to Glen? I wondered, before realizing Roger was once again speaking and my colleagues were all scribbling notes furiously. I joined in and tried to focus in on the logistics and the expectations of the review group. How many different ways could he try to explain the purpose of the group was **not** to study in a group, but to test each other's knowledge? We get it, I wanted to scream. Move on, man!

I was pleased when, at only 6:20, Roger concluded his remarks, and everyone started to pack up. Erin leaned in to say something, and I turned toward her. She was tall and pretty and looked like she spent a lot of time at the beach. Not in a sunburned freckly way, more of an iced cinnamon latte. Yikes, girl crush much?

"What a way to spend a summer, am I right?" she said with a grin.

"Yeah, you're right," I agreed. "We should pay big-time for the privilege. Oh, wait . . ."

Her grin turned even wider. "I knew I liked you," she said with a wink. "Smart *and* funny," she added, and I felt myself blushing. I generally kept to myself, but I really liked Erin and felt like we could be friends.

"That's me," I said feeling tongue-tied and suddenly extremely shy as she studied me closely.

"A few of us are going next door for a beer. If we hurry, we can still get a couple pitchers for half off. What do you say?" I groaned silently, wondering how many times the offer for drinks would be made before my team members would come to the same conclusion reached by so many others over the years. I don't drink, I dislike bars, and I suck at small talk. I am *not* a whole lot of fun.

I smiled at her, appreciating her efforts to draw me out. "Thanks for asking, but not tonight. Raincheck, yeah?"

She smiled back at me. "No worries," she said. "Next time." With a brief wave, she hurried off behind the others. I watched her back disappearing down the hall, and for the briefest of moments I considered calling out to her and joining the group. Then I remembered how my mom had all but cleaned me out of cash earlier. It would be a perfect night to raid the group fridge at the house and turn in early. I checked my phone, finding no recent calls or texts from my boyfriend or anyone else for that matter. There was no doubt in my mind I would spend the balance of the evening firmly ensconced on the overstuffed sofa in the lounge, watching Jeopardy, and eating, well, anything I could find. Answer: Lonely couch-potato with no friends. The question, of course, is: *Who* is Lennon Gallagher?

And that's where I was half an hour later, stuffing myself with someone's leftover lasagna, which probably should have been tossed yesterday, when I got a text. Unknown number. I glanced down at my phone and read:

Don't tell anyone

What the hell?

Who is this? I texted back, but got no response.

Chapter 8

I may have alluded to the fact I was never much of a student all the way through high school. I'm still not certain why I even bothered to get my GED a year after I dropped out at sixteen. It's not like I'd had any parental units pressuring me or anything. I'd worked a string of part-time jobs ever since I was thirteen, so I could see the writing on the wall and wanted to have better options going forward. Maybe that's why I borrowed a GED review guide from the library and studied it for a week straight. Randi had encouraged me to start slowly by taking a few college courses at a time, but honestly, once I got started, it was balls to the wall. I got a taste of what was out there, and I was hooked. Kind of like my mom and meth, only infinitely better, with no health risks other than perpetual exhaustion and high levels of stress.

I was lucky to have snagged one of the bedrooms in the row of Victorian-styled homes circling the perimeter of the grounds surrounding the UCONN law school. I'd enjoyed the three years I spent as an undergrad majoring in psychology on the huge, semi-rural campus in the town of Storrs, but I really loved the urban surroundings and convenience of the west end of Hartford. The times Seth spent here with me had been fun, checking out the nearby cafés and bars when we weren't holed up in my room. I had hoped I could live here until I took the bar exam, but apparently that was not in the cards. Should I go on Craigslist or put up a notice on the boards?

Single nerdy female seeks private room with kitchen privileges and little to no need for chitchat. Non-smoker on a tight budget.

Call me!

Right now, however, I had more important things on my mind. I had looked up Michael Kelliher's home address the other day, and since I had a little time to kill before my 10:00 a.m. class, I decided to take a drive, just to see what I could find out about the man who might be my father. 73 Farmington Avenue was located nearby in the west end of the city, and I found it easily. It was just before eight when I parked across the street from a well-kept colonial with dark gray shutters and a detached garage.

It was a busy time of the morning for school buses and commuters, and I waited patiently for several minutes before deciding I was wasting my time. I started my car and was about to drive away when the front door opened and Michael came out, followed by a petite, dark-haired woman and a tall, gangly teenaged boy. Michael hugged the woman and gave her a quick kiss before turning and walking down the street. He called something over his shoulder, and I watched the boy laugh and say something back. He continued on in the direction of what I assumed was his office. As I watched, the boy walked quickly to the corner as a school bus pulled up. He got on the bus and it pulled away, the dark-haired woman who I knew had to be his mom watched it leave before she walked to the car parked in the driveway and got in. Small in stature with short dark hair. Michael sure has a type, I noted.

I decided to follow him, so I drove slowly, allowing other cars to pass me or cut in front of me. We traveled a couple blocks in this way before Michael entered a small café. I pulled over and left my car running, assuming he was popping in for a quick coffee to go before continuing on his way to the office. I was surprised when he emerged carrying a tray with two coffees and took a seat at one of the small metal tables placed out front. It looked like he was waiting for someone, and a couple minutes after he sat down, a pretty blond woman came around the corner and greeted him warmly. He stood, and they hugged before sitting down to chat excitedly. She was easily twenty years younger than Michael. As I watched, she leaned across the table and grabbed his hand. They stayed that way, drinking coffee and talking for several more minutes. As I watched them, I felt angry but mostly disappointed. A wife at home and a sidepiece young enough to be his daughter. What a cliché!

I shouldn't have been surprised he had a roving eye. Charlene always had the absolute worst taste in men. Figuring I'd seen all I needed, I drove back home wishing I had stayed in bed. Had I thought my father might be a good guy? A man who knew nothing about me but would welcome me into his family with open arms? Yes, I had. When would I ever learn happy endings were not in the cards for people like me? I parked my car in the tiny back lot and climbed the stairs to my room, hoping I wouldn't run into one of my housemates. My luck held, and I entered my messy room and flopped face-first on my unmade bed. I lay that way, half dozing, until I heard music playing in the room next door. Jimmy and his penchant for early Eminem at full volume. I groaned and rolled over and saw it was 9:45. My class!

I was more grateful than ever on this particular morning, that I lived just a few minutes' brisk walk from the large building housing most of the classrooms. As I hurried down the street, my mind drifted back to the weird text messages I had been receiving. If they really were out to get you, that meant you weren't paranoid, right? The line in front of the elevator looked longer than usual, so I took the stairs two at a time and nearly collided with the hulking figure blocking my way into the classroom.

"Excuse me," I said with a huff only partially attributed to the two flights of stairs I had just scaled. When the man mountain turned slightly, I was amazed to see it was . . . "Roger? What're you doing here?"

His smile was more of a pained grimace, but his tone was light as he handed me a large, steaming cup of coffee. What parallel universe had I wandered into?

"I thought you might need this today," he said. "I guessed at black, but if you want cream and sugar . . ." He gestured to a small white bag of what looked like little tubs of creamer and packets of sugar in his left hand.

"What, no almond milk?" I quipped, receiving a frown in response. Realizing I was just kidding, he began to smile that creepy smile again and, after I took the coffee cup, shook an accusing finger at me.

"You with that sense of humor," he said, his grin stretching his brutish face into a cartoonish leer. Cautiously, I sniffed the coffee cup. He wouldn't try to poison me, would he?

"Well, um, thanks, Roger. For the coffee. How did you know . . . ?" Crap, my paranoid brain was working overtime. Had he followed me? Was he stalking me?

He smiled and nodded at my professor before he looked back at me. Was that some sort of a "hold on, Professor Stein" kind of gesture? Did he just suggest to my professor that what he had to say to me was more important than what she had to say to the whole class?

"Not too hard to figure out. I knew you and Erin had coffee a few times and I couldn't recall seeing you in Federal Income Tax last semester, ergo . . ."

"But what do you want with me?" I pressed, before enjoying a long sip of the most delicious coffee I had ever—

"We got off to a rough start," he said, all signs of kidding put to rest. "I just thought we should clear the air, you know? The work in front of our group is downright brutal." He spoke in a low tone, as if he were confiding a little-known fact, some hidden nugget of knowledge recognized by only a select few. "It wouldn't do to have two of the members at each other's throats."

While I would hardly classify our limited contact with each other in that way, it still came as a bit of a surprise to hear him this eager to clear the air with me.

"Sure, no worries," I told him. I was getting death glares from several of my classmates, so I gave him a slight smile. "All right, then, we're good. Thanks for the coffee. See you tonight." He reached for my arm, and just for a second I thought he might try to hug me, and I recoiled. *Ugh.* Again with the creepy smile.

"We need to talk further. Meet me at 5:00 tonight. We could grab a bite to eat before the group session. I know a place I think you'll love. My treat," he added magnanimously. Well, duh, I wanted to add. No way was I going to pay for the dubious honor of breaking bread with the honorable R. Stevens, (soon-to-be) Esquire. But did I want to play Little Orphan Annie to his Daddy Warbucks? Was I that starved for attention *and* food? Yes, yes, I was.

"Five o'clock at the clock tower?" I confirmed, and he nodded before turning on his heel and stomping off down the hallway. I entered the classroom and blushed at the greeting I received from my professor.

"Nice of you to join us, Ms. Gallagher," she said, earning smirks from several of my classmates. I slunk into my seat, convinced the whole world had gone screwy. Just the other night, Roger had acted like I was something that could be wiped away from the bottom of his shoe, and now he wanted to buy me dinner. Why? Yet another question that would nag at me all day. All of this drama left me no doubt whatsoever: My life was indeed a cheesy daytime soap opera. I took a long sip of my coffee and groaned as I heard the professor's announcement. Pop quiz on this past weekend's reading. Terrific, just what I needed.

Chapter 9

My last class of the day ended in time for me to return to my room and relax for a bit before heading out to meet Roger. I had the strangest feeling, like I should leave a note in my room indicating who I was going to meet and where, just in case I disappeared or something. I chided myself for being ridiculous as I blew dry my hair and dabbed a bit of concealer under my eyes. I looked like I felt: exhausted and more than a little freaked out. I sent Randi a quick text:

Meeting up with group shortly. Quick meal with our "leader" first. Wish me luck.

Confident I had covered my bases despite feeling like I was overreacting, I slid my tablet into my backpack, grabbed my keys, and headed out. I wasn't too surprised to find Roger waiting for me out in front, even though our agreement was to meet a couple blocks from here. He grinned when he saw me, that same slightly creepy expression he'd worn earlier.

"Hope you're hungry," he said, opening the passenger door of a flashy-looking yellow sports car and gesturing for me to get in. What was going on here? I would have thought we would grab a bite at a nearby café.

"Where are we going?" I asked. He slammed the door with a satisfying thunk and hurried around to the driver's side. He eased his considerable length in and buckled his seat belt before starting the engine. I repeated my question. As he pulled out into heavy traffic, he glanced over at me briefly.

"I figured you would be sick of all the local spots, and I thought we might go someplace new. Well, new to you, probably. I have been eating at Russo's for years. It's really good." He added almost shyly, "I think you'll like it."

I studied him closely as he wove his way through heavy end-of-the-day commuter traffic. Was it my imagination, or was he nervous? And if he was, why?

"I've never heard of it," I admitted. "Where is it?"

"Franklin Avenue in the North End. Not too far." Not too far? Was he kidding me? At this time of night with the current traffic levels, I could imagine it was close to a half hour each way.

"I don't understand," I admitted. "By the time we get there, we're going to have to turn around right away if we want to make it back for the group."

He appeared to be concentrating on the road as he admitted, "Yeah, about that. I reached out to the rest of the group to cancel tonight's session. It just seemed—"

"What are you talking about?" I asked. "The whole point of this dinner was to clear the air before we all met up. This is feeling off, you know?" I didn't actually feel unsafe, but I sensed there was something else going on at the same time. He had not canceled our group session just to get me alone. Had he?

He concentrated on the road, and after several more minutes of awkward silence, we were driving through the densely populated North End of Hartford with more pizza shops and family restaurants than I had ever seen in one place. We pulled up in front of an impressive-looking brownstone, and a pair of young men hurried out. One went around to greet Roger and give him a claim ticket. The other opened my door and allowed me to grasp his hand to pull me up out of the car's buttery leather depths. I joined Roger on the sidewalk.

"After you," he said graciously and followed me up the wide staircase to where a distinguished-looking gentleman in a dark shirt and tie was waiting. Roger gave his name, and the man grabbed two large menus and beckoned us to follow him. We were led to a quiet table in the far corner of the room

"Nick will be your server this evening," the host announced as he placed the menus in front of us. I looked around the dimly lit space and decided this was the most romantic dining room I had ever seen. The flickering candlelight, the blush-colored napkins and low bouquets of fresh flowers everywhere. This was the perfect spot for a quiet supper. And here I was with Roger. As a busboy poured iced-cold sparkling water into mason jars decorated with burlap ties and sprigs of freshly cut lavender, we glanced over tonight's dinner selections. Lots of pasta dishes and—holy crap, they were charging sixty-eight dollars for a steak, and the scallops were market price, which was code for "if you have to ask, you can't afford it." Roger reached over and placed his oaf-sized hand over mine. "Order whatever you like," he said in a confidential whisper. "It's on me." I pulled my hand away as if it were on fire.

"Thank you. That's nice of you." I studied the menu carefully and decided if I was going to put up with my creepy dinner companion all night, at the very least I would be extremely well fed. *Mmmm. Lots of excellent choices. Let's see . . .*

I flagged down the young waiter hovering nearby and got the ball rolling. "Good evening, Nick, we are ready to order. I'll have the citrus grilled halibut, the fingerling potatoes, and a chopped salad with extra blue cheese dressing on the side, thank you." He nodded, as if my menu choices pleased him. I recalled feeling that way myself at times when I waited tables over the years.

"And to start?" he asked, and I picked the menu back up. Why not?

"How many shrimp do you get with the shrimp cocktail?" I asked.

"Only three, but they're a nice size." Nick spoke as if apologizing for the unfair situation of his customers being forced to put up with the indignity of a measly trio of jumbo shrimp. "What some do—" he began.

"Way ahead of you. I'll have a double order. Please and thank you." I beamed at him, and I detected a ghost of a smile cross his face. He was of medium height with a slight build and light brown hair. But that smile and those eyes! He was seriously good-looking. And *you* have a boyfriend, I reminded myself.

Roger ordered a well-done ribeye and the French onion soup to start, sounding more than a little distracted. When Nick collected the menus and left us, I looked up to find Roger watching me closely. I returned his gaze, and for a short time we sat silently, sizing each other up, both wary, uncertain of the other's next move. At least that's how I felt. Just as things were starting to feel even more uncomfortable, he sat back and seemed to relax.

"Tell me about Lennon," he said in a conversational tone. I hadn't been certain of what I was expecting, but certainly not an opening for a chatty meet and greet. I sipped at my water, trying to decide if I should take his request at face value or try to stall until I was more certain of his motives. Surely he had more to do with his time than to arrange a private candlelit dinner *à deux*.

"What do you want to know?" I asked. He frowned slightly before pasting on that phony smile of his.

"The usual, I guess. Just making conversation," he replied. I decided to throw him a bone, as it were.

"Not much to tell. Born and raised in New London. UCONN undergrad, psych major. Last semester at UCONN Law. That is pretty much it." He was silent as Nick deposited a basket of bread and a saucer of seasoned olive oil in the center of the table, followed by a veritable trough of glistening pink shrimp, which he placed in front of me. It was almost too pretty to eat, with slices of lemon, sprigs of parsley, and a saucer of horseradish-infused cocktail sauce. There had to be a dozen shrimp! I looked up at Nick, who gave me a wink only I could see before plunking down a veritable tureen of onion soup sporting a one-inch thick layer of melted cheese. You certainly couldn't complain about the size of the portions here at Russo's. Nor the hotness of the waitstaff.

Roger reached for the breadbasket, when he suddenly let out a groan of protest.

"I'm not here to dip my bread like some peasant," he said, pointing at the olive oil. "Take that away and bring me butter. Not margarine, you got me?" His moon-shaped face was all blotchy, the passion for which he held his bread toppings evident for all to see. Nick nodded politely and scooped up the offending olive oil. As he turned to leave, he raised an eyebrow in my direction, communicating pity for me having to sit through a meal with a large, unpleasant man like Roger. I thought of all the rude diners I had put up with over the years. I feel you, is what I wanted to say. I've been right where you are, my friend.

I decided to not call Roger out for his over-the-top reaction to something so minor, so after allowing him to fuss and fume for another minute, I spoke up.

"Seriously, what did you want to talk to me about anyway?" I spread my arms out, taking in the elegant surroundings and the well-dressed customers. "What's up?"

He smoothed his napkin in his lap and waited until a bowl with a dozen pats of butter was placed in front of him. Liberally spreading a thick slice of bread with the butter, he studied me closely. "You got a text message last week," he said, and as we both knew it to be a true statement, I merely nodded. "It was from Glen, and it was sent to you in error." Again, this was old news. "Glen's an idiot," he continued, and I had no response, as it was a claim I could neither refute nor support. As far as I knew, I had never met Glen. I waited. He started to speak, stopped himself, then his words came out in a rush. "An opportunity presented itself, and I felt it bore further investigation."

I continued the process of freeing the fist-sized shrimp of their tails before dunking them in sauce and biting into them eagerly. Who knew such quality seafood could be found more than an hour from the coastline? Certainly not *moi*!

"After careful consideration, I determined it was a worthwhile endeavor. Do you see what I'm saying?" he asked. I thought of my grandma, who would have replied, "Yeah, sure. It's clear as mud," but I was busy chewing, so I gave a kind of "yeah, sure, please continue" gesture, which must have worked. Roger leaned in and dropped his voice to a whisper, a loud stage whisper, but still. "How do you feel about final exams?" I stopped chewing. How did I feel? The exams that would determine if I graduated in six weeks, and if I did, what kinds of job offers I might receive, if any, and . . . What the hell kind of question was that?

"Just peachy," I managed with a nearly straight face. "Why do you ask?" Oh no, not that grin again. No . . .

"What if I told you I could get my hands on the final exam for Con Law? In advance. No risk." I honestly had no clue what I thought he might say, but certainly nothing like this. I stared at him, speechless. Constitutional Law was a capstone course, dreaded by all students. The old, archaic cases it delved into were challenging to relate to, and the rumor mill was full of examples of students who had failed the course more than once. And the exam? One hundred percent of the course grade was derived from the exam. It was truly make or break. What the hell? He sat back and Nick appeared, balancing a tray carrying our dinners. I waited until there were steaming plates of attractively arranged food placed in front of us. Well, at least mine was looking fine. Roger's plate was dominated by a large blackened mass resembling shoe leather. As soon as Nick left, I leaned in to hiss at Roger.

"Seriously? Cheating? Like those Penn students last year who got caught and the Ivy League crew featured on *60 Minutes*? Are you fucking kidding me right now?" Roger's smile disappeared as quickly as it had surfaced, replaced with a look of disgust.

"How stupid do you think I am?" he said with a sneer. "I told you it was risk-free. There's no chance we could get caught. Like I said, I recognized an opportunity, did my due diligence, and am attempting to share what I have vetted as an exceptional chance to guarantee excellent grades in the most challenging course standing between us and our future. But if you're not interested, say no more. Let's just enjoy our dinners, and I'll drive you home. No harm, no foul." He sawed off a huge bite of his brontosaurus-looking steak and shoved it in his mouth, chewing enthusiastically.

I focused my attention on my meal but found I had no appetite and the food held zero interest for me. My stomach churned as I considered my course of action. Did Erin know about this? If so, why hadn't she warned me? If not, why was I being recruited and not her? Should I report Roger and Glen to the Ethics Committee? It was my word against theirs, but if it were ever found out and they could claim I knew about it, my future as a lawyer would be over before it began. The years of hard work, the sleepless nights, and the student loans—which would all come due whether I graduated or not. All for nothing. It would be easier to just stay silent, but what about doing the right thing? What kind of lawyer would I be if I ignored this? What would Randi do? I thought about it for exactly two seconds. Of course, Randi would already be scheduling an appointment to report this gross violation. She was fearless and self-assured, possessing the courage of her convictions. I hoped like hell that, down the road, I would be as well. But not today. I wasn't there yet.

The rest of the meal passed in strained silence. I pushed my food around, occasionally nibbling at a morsel of perfectly seasoned fish. Roger plowed through his steak as well as a baked potato the size of my head, covered and smothered with sour cream, bacon, and chives. He was wiping his chin with a beach towel-sized linen napkin when I realized he was speaking to me.

"Did you say something?"

He grinned as if we had been engaged in friendly conversation for the entire evening and gestured to the decimated remains on his plate. "I asked if you had a dog. If you might want to bring him a bone?"

I stared at him. He imagined I might have a dog in my barely one hundred-square-foot dorm room in an old Hartford brownstone. A dog who, judging from the bone in question, would have to be the size of a pony. Was he joking? Was he high? He responded to my silence.

"No, not in Hartford. I meant your place down on the coast. Old Lyme, right?" Again, I stared at him wordlessly, my confusion now replaced with a flicker of concern, then downright fear. How the fuck did he know where I lived? "I understand your summer housing plans have hit a rough patch. Will you be commuting from the shoreline for our group?"

I wiped at my lips with my own napkin, determined to hide my panic. It would do me no good to show him how much this conversation was rattling me. I was not about to discuss my living arrangements with this jerk.

"How do you know all this?" I asked. "Did Erin tell you?" But that was ridiculous, I realized immediately. I couldn't recall telling her much of anything about my life away from Hartford.

He gave an indulgent chuckle. "Surely you know by now our dear friend loves to gossip. If you want the world to know something, tell Erin, am I right?"

If he *was* right, then the real question was: How did Erin know all this? He still looked like he was waiting for an answer.

"No, no dog," I said with a shrug of my shoulders. "Allergies," I added, forcing a grin. Why was I explaining anything to this Neanderthal? His look was pure steel when he responded.

"Usually, people are allergic to cats, not dogs, but not you. Funny," he said in a tone that was anything but humorous. He knew about Randi and Eric's house, and he knew about Hobie? How? I tried to slow my breathing as I considered my options. This guy was a psycho, and he'd just essentially threatened me. I could call for a rideshare back to Hartford, or I could call . . . Who could I call? I wasn't sure if Erin had her own car or not. Randi was too far away, and Seth was even farther. Was this the sort of situation where one might contact one's father? I honestly had no clue. Was I being ridiculous? Was I overreacting?

Roger leaned closer and rubbed his fingers over the cuff of my black cardigan. I pulled my arm back quickly and saw he had plucked a gray hair from my sweater and was holding it up as some sort of proof. "Looks like you have a cat," he said with a grin.

"We should get going. I have an early morning," I said. "I'm letting my roommate know I'm on my way." I was actually sending the message to Randi, but he didn't have to know that. I read aloud as I texted. "See you soon. Roger Stevens is driving me home now. He's got a flashy yellow sports car and . . ." I stopped texting for a second. "What's your license plate?" He looked pissed but rattled off seven letters, and I dutifully added it to my message. "And send," I said happily. "Oh, wait," I added as I read over the text. NOTGILT. "Aren't you the clever one?"

Ignoring my jab, he placed his platinum credit card on the table, and seconds later Nick whisked it away. He returned a couple minutes later and placed the leather folio in front of Roger, who glanced at it, scribbled in a tip, and signed it hastily. Being the always vigilant former server I am, I glanced at the numbers, quickly realizing my dinner host was not only a cheating, conniving bastard, but a cheap tipper as well. He'd left a gratuity well below the range tonight's excellent service deserved. As Roger pulled on his sports coat, I reached into my bag, and my fingers found a crumpled bill I knew to be a twenty. I placed it as discreetly as possible next to my plate, earning a grin from Nick, who was starting to clear the table. Roger was already halfway toward the exit when Nick scooped up the cash and pressed it into my hand.

"Keep your money," he advised. "And don't worry about your friend. I've been doing great tonight, and one lousy customer isn't going to ruin that." I nodded my thanks and started to leave. "But I would take your phone number instead," he said, and I turned to him, flustered. No one ever asked me for my number, and I had a boyfriend, didn't I? Nick produced a slip of paper and a pen, and I found myself writing, all the while wondering just what in the hell I thought I was doing. I handed it to him, and he scanned it quickly before asking me, "Does this number have a name?"

"I'm Lennon, Lennon Gallagher," I told him solemnly, and he smiled. Not the practiced smile of a server who spent his evening groveling for tips, but the genuine smile of a handsome young man who looked like he spent his summers sailing in Newport Harbor and his winters skiing in Aspen. Neither of which I had ever experienced.

"Good to meet you, Lennon Gallagher. I'm Nick Russo, and I would like to take you to dinner sometime soon. Is it okay if I call you?"

I have a boyfriend. Well, I think I do, but he's kind of pissed at me and we haven't been getting along. And he was—is—my first boyfriend, but we've grown apart. And . . .

"I look forward to it," I said. "Wait, Russo as in Russo's?" I asked, gesturing around the restaurant. Nick gave me a sheepish grin before nodding.

"Guilty as charged, but don't hold it against me," he said. "You okay leaving with this guy? He hasn't had a drink while he's been here, so that's good. If you wanted, I could—"

I shook my head quickly. "He's a jerk, but a harmless one. But thank you for asking. Good night, Nick." I headed out to catch up with Roger, wishing I could stay and chat with Nick Russo instead. But I needed to put Roger in his place sooner rather than later, and there was no time like the present.

Chapter 10

During the drive back to campus, Roger tried to make conversation with me, but I wasn't having any of it. I nodded a few times when I felt his gaze focused on me instead of the road, but I didn't actually speak until he pulled up in front of my place. As I unbuckled my seat belt and prepared to finally escape the close confines of the small car driven by an oversized man who stank of onions and beef sweats, I spoke quietly, trying to sound calm.

"I want you to know there is no way on earth I would join you in this plan of yours, okay? Please, for both our sakes, let's not speak of this again. As of right now, I will probably stay in the group through exams. It's probably too late to find another group, but don't count on me for the law boards." He started to protest, but I held up a hand to stop him, quickly returning it to my lap as I realized how much I was shaking. "And one more thing. You may not have guessed it, but I can't afford to pay the monthly dues, and I wouldn't have agreed to join the group if I had known about them. Erin never said a word about this. We both know the library doesn't charge for the room, and I can bring my own chips. Going forward, we're not speaking of this, got it? As far as the others are concerned, I'm just another member, paid in full. Are we clear?" As soon as I said it, I realized how much it sounded like I was trying to blackmail him. I had practiced my little speech during the drive but had not meant it as a quid-pro-quo situation. I was about to backtrack when I caught sight of his shadowy face in the glow of the streetlights.

He was staring at me, and I finally got the full meaning of that expression "if looks could kill." He shook his head, and his glare of murderous rage transformed into one of . . . pity? "It's puzzling to me why you think for a single minute you are calling the shots. I'll decide if you can continue in the group, not you, sweetheart, and as far as the dues go, this month is on me. But you'll pay just like everyone else does going forward."

"What about Erin?" I asked, and Roger stared at me blankly. "Does she know about your scam?"

"That's not your concern. Just hold up your end of the bargain, and you'll be fine." How was that for a non-answer? I grabbed the door handle and attempted to open the door when I discovered the child safety lock was set.

"Seriously?" I said, and he smiled once more. He released the lock, and I scrambled to get out. Finally free, I heard him still speaking and sounding resolute, as if nothing bad had transpired between us tonight.

"I'll keep you posted on the delivery of the exam. I can't trust you to stay quiet, so you're in this whether you want it or not." I stared at him before slamming the door shut and bolting up the stairs. I turned my key in the lock, and finally I was safe inside the tiny, damp-smelling vestibule. I locked the door and, gulping for air, watched his car pull away from the curb.

•　　•　　•　　•　　•

As soon as I was safely in my room, I texted Erin.

WTF? Roger's crazy

I watched my phone, but my message wasn't read, not after fifteen minutes, so I sent another.

CALL ME!

Still nothing, so I went down the hall to the bathroom, brushed my teeth, and splashed cool water on my face. I felt antsy, out of sorts. I went back to my room and tried to read a novel I'd picked up at Randi's but found I was unable to concentrate. There was no way I could attempt to study anything tonight.

It took me hours to fall asleep, and then I missed my first class of the day because I forgot to set an alarm. Now I sat on my bed, staring out the window and clutching a mug of lukewarm coffee. The late April sky was gray and cloudy, a perfect match to the thoughts swirling around my head. I knew I should probably report what I knew to the Ethics Committee but I had no real proof of an imminent cheating scandal. It was only a "he said, she said" scenario at best. Roger was a well-spoken, prominent, respected member of the class and a legacy to boot. I was none of the above. I wasn't even certain *I* would believe me. Still no response from Erin, and neither text was showing as being read.

What the fuck should I do now?

I spent the morning wallowing . . . in what? Grief? Fear? Confusion? All of the above? I was nibbling on a leftover jelly roll someone had left on the counter of our communal kitchen, washing it down with hours-old coffee. I needed to figure out a better meal plan for the duration of my time here in Hartford. Ideally, one where I actually purchased and consumed my own food, but that involved planning and shopping and cooking—three activities for which I had neither the time nor the inclination. I crammed the last chunk of roll into my mouth and chewed as I raced back upstairs to get ready. I was due at the law firm at 1:00 p.m., and it was already half past twelve, so I would have to drive over, no longer able to spare the time for a twenty-minute walk.

I shoved some files and my phone into my backpack and checked my refection in the small mirror by my door. My hair needed cutting, my eyebrows were unruly, and I had purple circles under my eyes. I looked down at the white shirt and black pants I was wearing, the same ones I had worn waiting on tables at the Point. Noooo, was that a dusting of cinnamon or something even worse? I swiped at the spot on my upper thigh, succeeding in making it look even more prominent. I had no time to change, so I grabbed an ivory scarf hanging on the back of the door and tied it around my middle, effectively covering the damned spot but making it look like I was wearing a diaper or was totally unhinged or possibly both. Oh well, at least my legal brain was sharp as a tack after nearly three solid hours of restful sleep and a healthy power breakfast. *Crap.*

As interns were encouraged not to take up any of the few spots reserved for our clients and other visitors, by the time I found street parking, fed the meter, and raced half a block to the office, I was right on time to interview potential claimants for the lawsuit. I clocked in just inside the employee entrance and made my way to the lobby, where a line of folks had already formed. The other interns and I were working on the intake forms of potential claimants today as well as meeting with those we'd already vetted to address any of their concerns. I sat down at the first open table and quickly grabbed the printed schedule with the names of today's pool of potential claimants. While many filed online, there were a fair amount who chose to attend an open session like the one happening now. I cleared my throat as one of the staff members approached with a young woman wearing a stylish trench coat.

"Ms. Gallagher? This is Sara Hawkins. She's your 1:00 appointment. Ms. Hawkins, this is Lennon Gallagher. She will be working with you today. Ladies," she finished, doffing an imaginary cap before strolling away.

"Thank you, Leslie," I called to her. "Sara, it's nice to meet you. I'm not an attorney yet, but for all intents and purposes, I will act on your behalf, and anything you say to me is confidential."

If Sara had been able to do so, she would have scored a hat trick with her ability to roll her eyes, snap her gum, and look totally bored all at the same time. She cut me off quickly and took over the conversation. "I know how this works, so save your breath. It's not my first rodeo, but by the looks of it, it just might be yours. I was part of a suit against my homeowner's association last year. Let me save us both some time, and I'll tell you what I need you to know about me and my claim, got it?"

I nodded in amazement. This chick had some serious stones to come in here guns a-blazin' and telling me what she wanted me to do before she was even certified, but I was intrigued. A little put out, to be honest, but definitely intrigued.

"Hit me," I said, and she proceeded to lay out her thoughts on her right to be a claimant. She'd clearly done her homework, quickly convincing me her case contained the key elements to be included in the suit against Data Solutions: commonality, typicality, and adequacy. In short, she shared concerns and similar interests with other class members, which made her a suitable member of the class.

"What about—" I began, and she gestured around the crowded room.

"Numerosity? I'm fairly certain that's not an issue. Those cheap bastards screwed all their clients. I'm betting you'll have more than enough claimants to make your case."

Not bad. Not bad at all. I jotted down some notes on calls I needed to make to confirm a few details, and we scheduled a follow-up appointment for next week. After I confirmed our next steps, she stood to leave.

"You should consider a career in law," I said, only half-jokingly. She made a face.

"No way. Too many thieves and con-artists practicing law these days. No offense," she added and held out her hand.

"None taken," I assured her.

As we shook, she studied me closely for a second. Shaking her head sadly, she said, "There might be hope for you after all, Ms. Gallagher. But for the love of all that is holy, lose the diaper, would you?"

I glanced down at the scarf no longer covering the stain on my pants. Blushing, I promised her I would, and with a quick wave, she made her way toward the exit. If I were truly dressing for the job to which I aspired, I needed to go clothes shopping ASAP. My wardrobe was in desperate need of an upgrade.

I was trying to recall how much room there was left on my one and only credit card to determine if I could afford any new-to-me clothes, when my phone buzzed with a text.

Hey G. Hows yur day? Nick

Nick from last night? Cool! G? Did he send it to me by mistake? Was there a Gloria, Giselle, or Gillian out there waiting to hear from him? I decided to respond anyway.

Hi Nick It's me, Lennon.

The three bouncing dots appeared as I waited for him to say, "oh sorry, haha," but instead he wrote:

I sure hope so Lennon Gallagher with a G. Hows yur day?

What a loaded question! I couldn't even begin to describe the shit-show that was my day. Especially not to someone I'd just met.

Sorry, at work. Can't talk.

No problem. He added an emoji of a crocodile or an alligator… What the hell? I shoved my phone in my backpack and stood to shake hands with our next potential claimant. I would figure out what he meant later.

Chapter 11

Early the next morning, I heard from Erin. She called me as I was walking to class, and I answered quickly.

"Where have you been? I've been trying to reach you," I said.

"My mom called, and I went home. My little sister needed an emergency appendectomy," she said. My first thought was, 'and they needed you to perform the surgery?' I was stunned anyone would miss class right before finals. Even a top-ranking student.

"Wow, well, I hope she's doing okay," I said, and at Erin's mumble of agreement, I continued. "What do you know about the exam?" I brought my voice down to a whisper, and when she didn't answer right away, I wondered if maybe she hadn't heard me. "Erin?"

"You don't have to worry about that. They asked me, and I said no. Sounds like you did too. It's fine." Her voice was calm and made me wonder if I really was overthinking this situation. But how long had she known about this? And who told her I had refused to participate?

"Erin, I *am* worried. Roger basically threatened me, and I've gotten some weird texts. I don't really appreciate all this drama, you know?"

"Oh, Lennon, it's going to be fine. Trust me, I never would have invited you to join if I had known anything about a stolen exam. I found out the same time you did. We both said no. Case closed. I've got to—"

But I had more questions for her. "Hold on. What did you tell Roger about me? About the house down in Old Lyme? About Randi?" I refrained from adding, "About Hobie?" and I held my breath as I waited for her response.

"What? Nothing. I told him nothing. You're starting to sound paranoid, my friend. It's a simple misunderstanding. Got it?" I said okay, even though it wasn't, and she hurried on. "I've got to run. I'll see you tonight at group. Wanna go for ice cream after? We'll talk more, okay?"

She ended the call, and I made it into the classroom right before the door closed. I was relieved Erin had finally reached out, but I still couldn't believe she'd disappeared like that. But as I had no siblings, what did I know about how family members supported each other? Maybe I had a brother, I reminded myself. *That* would be awesome. I sat near the back and prepared to take multiple pages of notes over the next ninety minutes. I was fairly certain the professor would continue jamming in every possible fact and reference on federal income taxation we might need for the final as well as for the bar.

I was ready. Bring it on.

•   •   •   •   •

"The first rule of review group is you do **not** talk about review group," I whispered to Erin at the start of our session that night. This caused her to spit out the seltzer she was drinking and earned us a look of utter disdain from our leader.

"Girls, please. Try to control yourselves while we're here. Save your secrets for your slumber parties," he said, not bothering to mask his annoyance.

"You know he's picturing us having a pillow fight," I said.

"Yeah, and we're wearing baby-doll pajamas," she agreed, and I groaned at the image. *Ewww.* What a perv.

After just a week and a half of meetings, the rankings of the individual group members were already clear. At the bottom was

Chelsea, who had replaced Glen just in time for our initial meet and greet. To put it bluntly, she was not keeping up with the workload. Not even close. To be effective, we each were required to study on our own in order to prepare for these sessions. The main purpose of the group was to meet to test each other's knowledge. Chelsea never seemed to have her shit together. Although she was responsible for presenting on the topic of civil procedures before quizzing each of us this evening, she clearly had not done the reading, let alone prepared a discussion brief and follow-up questions. It was painful to watch but frustrating as well. The "weakest link" proverb came to mind. If Roger didn't do something and soon, I would be forced to add whatever chapters or topics she was assigned to my own to-do pile. I looked around, and it was clear the rest of the group shared my concerns.

Erin saw me looking and mumbled, "This is just so fucking tragic," and I nodded my agreement. A few minutes later, Chelsea ended her rambling and sat back, looking relieved her ordeal was over yet anxious about the likely fallout. She didn't need to wait long.

"That was not nearly the level of academic rigor I was anticipating, Ms. Turner," Roger began, looking more angry than disappointed. "We deserve your careful attention to detail; nothing less will be acceptable. I want you to take the weekend to reflect upon your efforts to date and come to Monday's session to share your thoughts on why you should be allowed to continue with this group. At that time, a decision will be rendered on your suitability to remain." He paused and, when Chelsea did not rise from her seat, continued on. "As for tonight, you should take your things and leave us while we move on to the work more expertly prepared by your classmates." Chelsea's face was frozen in shock upon being asked to leave. She slowly gathered her things and, before she slunk out the door, called over her shoulder.

"I'm really sorry, everyone. I'll get it together, I promise." You could hear a pin drop as we sat watching her go. Actions had consequences, but maybe a warning had been in order rather than expulsion. Regardless of what Roger said, I knew our group had just lost a member. After the door closed behind her, Roger looked around, studying each of us closely.

"Erin, you're up," he said, and she nodded. Sitting next to her, I could see how prepared and well-organized she was. Not just for tonight's talk, but every day. If Chelsea were at the bottom of the group when it came to her effectiveness as a contributing member, then Erin was definitely at the top. Her assigned topic tonight was recent court rulings in constitutional law, and she laid out the salient points in a clear and concise manner. Her explanations were spot on, and her delivery was such a marked contrast from Chelsea's. I found myself wishing I had gotten to know her better this past semester. When I made my way through the lecture halls lately, it was heartwarming to see her friendly face and welcoming wave as I took the empty seat next to her, reserved just for me.

Maybe I'd overestimated the challenge in giving up the whole 'lone wolf' role. I'd had some close relationships during my years in the system. We had been drawn together by fear and loneliness back then, living in group homes and desperately trying to find our place in the world. My early-stage friendship with Erin was different. We were busy young women with common goals and interests. And tonight, we had plans to go for ice cream, and I was looking forward to it.

The rest of the session passed quickly. After Erin's brilliance left us all wondering how she managed to make challenges to partisan gerrymandering sound not only interesting, but understandable as well, Justin, Sam, and I each presented on the first three amendments to the Constitution. The first ten amendments were referred to as the Bill of Rights, and Roger warned us repeatedly we would be expected to know everything about them if we wanted to pass Constitutional Law, arguably one of the most difficult required courses in the entire curriculum. Oh yeah, and the one with an exam available for purchase! I was honestly getting more than a little annoyed by how he kept saying, "If you want to pass the exam . . ." Of course, we did. Why else would we show up here twice a week to present, review, and be condescended to?

Justin handled freedom of religion, speech, press, assembly, and petition quite well, while Sam stumbled a bit on the second amendment. The right to bear arms was arguably a contentious topic these days. Mine was number three, the quartering of soldiers, undoubtedly the least litigated and most irrelevant of the ten. I think I managed to provide some historical context on why it was important to obtain the consent of the homeowner prior to sticking military personnel in private homes during wartime, but I had not come up with any quiz-type questions generating any real discussion. I expected some flak from Roger, but he seemed to be checked out at this point, so I concluded and we were done for the evening.

"Hey, Lennon, can you hold up a minute?" Roger asked as we started to leave. Erin and I exchanged a quick glance, and she jerked her head toward the doorway. I assumed it meant she would wait for me, so I slung my backpack onto the nearest seat and waited for him to conclude his conversation with Sam. As Sam had been only slightly more prepared than Chelsea, I could only imagine he was being given some sort of "shape up or get out" warning as well. I couldn't hear a word they were saying, but they sure didn't look happy. I could read body language like a pro, which was a terrific skill to have when you were desperate to survive in a fight-or-flight world. Getting yourself to a safe space, or at least one slightly less dangerous, required an ability to recognize the warning signs of tempers igniting, especially where drugs or alcohol were involved. More than once, I'd escaped a beating or worse based on my skills to sense trouble brewing. But of course, in an equal number of instances I had not been as fortunate.

As I watched, Roger and the much smaller Sam attempted one of those horribly awkward bro hugs. So wrong on all counts. As Sam turned to leave, I approached Roger. It was late, I was exhausted, and Erin and I were planning on stopping for ice cream. Talking with Roger was the only thing standing between me and a loaded waffle cone.

"What did you want?" I asked him, and he looked at me blankly. What a jerk! "You asked me to wait," I reminded him, and a look of recognition crossed over his face.

"Oh yeah, I've got something for you," he said with a sly grin. He reached into the ridiculously over-the-top leather briefcase he always carried, which probably cost more than my car, and pulled out a manila envelope. "As promised," he said and handed it to me.

I turned it over in my hands, looking for something to identify it, but I couldn't find a single word anywhere. "What's this?" I asked, suspicion clouding my features. His stupid grin turned conspiratorial as he leaned in closer to me. My jaw clenched as I tried to not breathe in his putrid-smelling coffee breath mixed with . . . something. Maybe whiskey? Through clenched teeth, I repeated my question.

"It's a copy of the Con Law exam. What did you think? It's hardly a birthday gift; besides your birthday's not for months, but by then you'll be slaving away at some law firm, billing eighty hours a week and earning six figures. Wham, bam, thank you, ma'am," he said.

He towered over me by more than a foot and was at least a hundred and fifty pounds heavier, maybe more, but right then I swear I could have ripped him a new one if given half a chance.

"That doesn't mean what you think it means, asshole," I growled, "and I've already told you I'm not interested. Take this exam and shove it up your cheating ass, and while you're at it, go fuck yourself." I tried to hand it back to him, but he raised his hands in a strange "can't touch this" gesture, so I dropped it onto the table between us. I pushed past him, every fiber of my being warning me flight was the only option. Despite being angrier than I could ever recall, this was not a fight I could win. I had to report this; he had left me no choice. He stepped aside to let me leave, but I wasn't surprised when he hissed in my ear.

"If anything happens, you're going down with me, you little bitch."

"Go to hell," I snarled back before I raced to the hallway, hoping to find Erin, but it was empty. Had she gotten tired of waiting, or maybe she'd stepped outside for some air? One glance out the window at the dark and stormy night and I figured she'd already left. No one would be out in this weather unless they absolutely had no choice. So much for ice cream.

Five minutes later, I let myself into the vestibule of my dorm. My canvas shoes were soaked through, as were my hoodie and jeans. I felt like a drowned rat, and I imagined I looked like one too. A quick glance at my image in the dusty mirror confirmed it. Yep, definitely a rat. The smell of damp carpet filled my senses, and I forced myself not to gag. I headed for the stairs up to my room. By the time I got inside, I was shivering. My teeth chattered as I stripped off my wet clothes and pulled on a thick fluffy pink robe. Probably the nicest thing I owned, a gift from Randi for no reason. I had one just like it in teal at her home in Old Lyme. I couldn't begin to count the number of nights (and quite a few days as well) I'd spent wrapped up in one of these robes. But tonight, I couldn't shake the damp cold infiltrating my body. A hot shower would warm me up, but the thought of trundling down the hall to the bathroom I shared with three other residents felt like too big a price to pay. I wrapped my robe tighter and crawled under the covers. Not wanting to seem too needy, I decided to pass on texting Erin tonight. I had taken the electric blanket off the bed last month since it was late spring by that point and stored it at Randi's. How much would I give to be able to switch it on right now and feel warm in minutes? Fifty bucks? Seventy-five? Instead of sheep, I counted cash in twenty-five-dollar increments. I believe I made it up to $1,125 before I finally fell into a restless sleep.

Chapter 12

An ambulance raced by the brownstone, and I came to with a start, hopelessly tangled in the bedsheets and the belt of my robe. I checked the time and saw it was not quite 11:00 p.m., which meant I'd only slept about an hour. I really needed to talk with Randi and admit to all the threats and cover-ups as well as the fact that, even though this situation had been going on for two weeks, I had done nothing to report it. Was I guilty of a cover-up? Probably so. But Randi and Eric were most likely in bed. I half considered texting Nick but realized our harmless flirtation could probably not handle this level of drama.

Ever since he'd explained the alligator image was code for "talk to you later," we had developed a short list of emojis we used to communicate. An alarm clock meant no time to talk, but an alarm clock with a number after it indicated a better time to talk. It was fun and silly, and I liked how he would ask me how my class went (I often responded with a stream of zzz's) or what I ate for lunch (salad—well, taco salad). But nothing would have prepared him for the news that in addition to being an oaf and a lousy tipper, Roger was also a cheat and a liar and was trying to drag me into his web of lies, which could get me expelled. Best to keep our chats light and breezy. But it was nice getting to know him, and it made me realize how much I missed having a friend who actually made time for me, saw me, and made me feel like I was important. If I were being honest, Seth hadn't made me feel like that for quite a while.

But he was still my boyfriend, with extra bonus points for being a night owl, and I suddenly felt a strong urge to talk to him. Was I feeling guilty over chatting with a guy I barely knew? Perhaps. But that was not something I could focus on right now. I found his name among my recent calls and dialed. He answered on the first ring, like he had been expecting a call.

"Hey . . . Lennon," he said, and I wondered if he had been expecting a call from someone else. It was hard to hear him over the background noise of a crowded bar.

"Hi, what's up?" I asked him. "Is this a good time?"

"No, I mean, yeah, it's fine. Let me just step outside," he said, and seconds later I was able to hear him clearly. "What's up?"

"Not much. It's been a long day, and I wanted to hear a friendly voice."

"And you called me?" he said with a chuckle.

"Yeah, go figure," I said. "Can I run something by you?" There was no response on his end, and for a second I thought he'd hung up on me.

"Yeah, I guess. What's up?" came his reply.

As quickly as I could, I told him about the study group, the weird texts, the dinner with Roger, and his threats. A couple times, I felt like I was losing him, not even the standard *uh, huh* or *seriously?* I stopped to catch my breath, and I heard him sigh. "What do you think?" I asked.

"You're bailing on me for this bunch of jokers? Are you fucking kidding me? Sounds like a great investment for your future," he added, not bothering to mask his sarcasm.

"Honestly, that's all you got? No advice, no thoughts on how to handle all this? Your only reaction is how this impacts you?" I couldn't believe he was being so selfish, so self-centered.

"You want my thoughts? Well, here you go. I think you're blowing this whole thing up, way out of proportion. I think you should let it go. Some classmates are cheating on an exam? Big deal. Shit happens, Lennon. Get down off your high horse and take a good look around you. This is the real world. Why you get so caught up in all this is beyond me. You're starting to sound like—" He stopped suddenly, perhaps aware he'd gone too far.

"Like who, Seth? Like Miranda Quinn? Is that what you were gonna say?"

"I just meant not everything is all that black-and-white as she seems to believe. Aww Christ, Len. Why are we arguing about this?" I wanted to say, "Yeah, we have plenty of other things to argue about," or, "Being like Randi in any way possible would be a dream come true for me." But I didn't. If we stood even the slimmest of chances to stay together, I needed to switch gears fast.

"Yeah, you're right. So how's your day?" I asked and was relieved to hear a chuckle from Seth. Crisis averted for tonight, but honestly, he was full of crap. I ran from drama; I never sought it out, but somehow it always found me.

He filled me in on the project consuming all his time at work and suggested we get together next week for the launch. He and two other colleagues were developing an app that apparently would change the global economy or something. I assumed for the better, but I honestly didn't understand any of the things Seth worked on. When I heard the term "cryptocurrency," it was like my brain exploded. I'm fairly certain he felt the same way about my work. I'd watched his eyes glaze over when I talked about custody issues and emancipated minors. But a launch party next week? I felt a sharp pain of annoyance threatening to make me lose it. Once again, Seth appeared to have no clue what was going on in my life. I tried to keep my temper in check as I set him straight.

"Next week? When the courts decide if our class action lawsuit will go forward and my paper is due on the gap between state and federal laws as they relate to our basic civil liberties? Next week, when the law firm will probably be deciding who they'll hire for the summer? And when I'll be skulking around searching for a new place to live. Do you mean *that* next week?" I heard a sharp intake of breath on the other end and knew my tone was probably sharper than I had imagined. But in my defense, are you freaking kidding me? The silence on the other end of the phone spoke volumes. We were right back where we'd left off the other day. Impasse!

"Forget I mentioned it, okay? What was I thinking? That I could actually have my girl *with* me, celebrating at a launch party?"

"Oh, will you just stop?" I begged him. "Why do you think guilting me into doing something I am incapable of doing is actually a good thing?"

"Nothing else seems to get through to you lately," he said, sounding more pissed off than ever. It made me feel so sad. What were we doing to each other? "Wait, what do you mean you're looking for a new place to live?"

"Oh, Seth . . ." I began.

"What?" he barked back at me.

"I feel like we're heading in two different directions," I said. "Ever since you moved to New York, it's like you can never make time for me. Like you don't even hear me anymore." Ugh, I hated the way I must sound right now. Like a whiny, clingy girlfriend. That was a role I never imagined I would play. But was that really the problem between Seth and me? Did a few hours on a bus or train really matter that much? Had our relationship, the one I'd always viewed as rock solid, run out of steam or, worse, gotten completely derailed? Seth broke the silence, sounding only slightly less annoyed.

"I just feel like I'm the lowest of the low when it comes to your priorities. Your classes, this class action suit, and now you're off on a wild goose chase to find your father."

"A wild goose chase? Seriously? That's all this means to you? I want to know where half of me comes from, the half that's hopefully not a crackhead who spends more time in a jail cell than raising her kid, and you can't see that? We weren't all raised by the perfect parents with a white picket fence, you know."

"You're taking everything I'm saying and twisting it to sound like some poor, misunderstood victim. And, oh yeah, all this manufactured drama bullshit getting caught up in some deep, dark classmate cheating crap. It's like you'll do anything to keep from focusing on us. And now you're moving? What the hell, Len? Where do I fit in? What do you have left for me?" I sagged against my pillow, feeling exhausted. My anger was gone, leaving a gaping hole of . . . sadness? Regret? What we said tonight couldn't be unsaid or unheard. What *did* I have left for him? I considered his question for a moment before answering him truthfully.

"I don't know, babe. I wish I did, but I don't. I am stretched pretty thin these days, and I don't always make time for you; it's true. But do you remember how it was during your last year here? Before you graduated, you were cramming for exams and interning at the firm in New London, and your dad needed surgery? Do you remember? Cuz I sure as hell do."

"Of course I do. I was there for all of it." Seth sounded like he was running out of gas. Clearly, he was as tired of this argument as I was.

"Look, we don't need to work all of this out tonight," I reminded him. "The next time—"

He cut me off. "The next time? Or maybe the time after that? Hell, I don't even know where we're going. Is there going to be an actual next time for us, or are we gonna drag this through the mud forever?"

His words stung, but he was speaking the truth. We had been in a holding pattern for a while now. "Where do you want *this* to go, exactly?"

"I asked you to marry me, or have you forgotten?"

"Oh please. We were together for like a year, and besides, we were naked at the time. Everyone knows naked proposals don't count."

"You laughed at me. How do you think it made me feel?"

"Wow, great time to pitch a hissy fit," I shot back. "I dunno how you felt. Hurt? Confused? Hormonal?" It was going from bad to worse, I realized.

"Fuck you. You're the one who says I never talk about my feelings, and when I do, you accuse me of being—"

"I *never* ask you to talk about your feelings, Seth. That's one of the things I always liked about you. I can keep my feelings all bottled up nice and tight, like any normal person. And you can do the same. Who says feelings should be discussed ad nauseum anyway?"

"Wow, really mature. That's why *this* is never going to go anywhere."

"What does *that* mean?" I asked, although I knew precisely what he meant. Where this conversation was heading. Of course I did.

"What do you think it means?"

"If that's what you want . . ." I began.

"No, that's what *you* want. So have it your way. Have a nice life."

I was too stunned to respond. *Have a nice life?* Did we just break up? "Seth," I started to say as I realized he'd hung up on me. I felt . . . nothing. Not sad, not upset, and okay, maybe just a little bit relieved. I stripped off my robe, punched my pillow back into shape, and slipped under the covers. I tried to rid my mind of worries about classes and exams and sadness over mothers who failed and fathers who bailed and boyfriends who didn't understand me. I pulled on my headphones and found some vintage Alanis Morrissette to get lost in. No one captured the pain of a breakup quite like her.

Chapter 13

The next couple days passed by quickly. It's strange to admit, but I didn't miss Seth. I thought of him on occasion, but not in the "oh, I have to share this with Seth" way or anything like that. More like a fond but distant memory of someone I used to know. I couldn't really be mad at him for pulling the plug. I'd known we were on the way out for quite a while, but we had both been too chickenshit to acknowledge it. I wasn't always the perfect girlfriend and could be less than understanding at times. We'd had a good run, but that was in the past. Maybe I was still in denial regarding the breakup, but I felt lighter and better equipped to handle the challenges ahead.

I clearly needed to focus all my attention on my studies. Our professors were apparently just now realizing their time with us was short, and they started cramming every bit of missed information into our oversaturated brains. I had been looking forward to the opportunity to review subject matter we'd covered earlier in the semester, but instead I found myself focusing on new material and trying to determine what would be on the final exam, included on the bar exam, or both.

Even though it would have lessened my workload considerably, never once did I picture myself scoring a copy of the purloined Con Law exam, but I did wonder who was participating. Was Erin involved somehow? It just seemed so odd how she had ghosted me the way she had. Having spent most of my life surrounded by untrustworthy sleaze bags, I generally considered myself a good judge of character—or the lack thereof. How had I misread what I'd hoped would be an actual friendship?

As far as the stolen exam went, in my mind there were no shortcuts in this life. I'd learned this at an early age, witnessing a whole line of family members and their friends caught up in get-rich-quick schemes and easy scores ending up with jail sentences or worse. Was cheating on an exam on par with robbing a convenience store? No, of course not, but you needed to draw the line somewhere. So, I studied. During my shifts at the library, I barely glanced up at classmates and faculty passing by the reference desk. Instead, I spent my time reading newly assigned chapters from the textbooks, reviewing my class notes, or quizzing myself using my now three-inch-high stack of handwritten flash cards.

Nick and I continued to talk regularly, and we texted several times a day. "I'm keeping you from your studies," he would tell me, and I always denied it. "I'm keeping you from writing," I would moan, and he would assure me the writing was going fine and not to worry. He told me very little about the manuscript, his "work in progress," only that it was a medical thriller, and I figured he would share it with me when he was ready. He was as busy as I was, taking shifts at one of his family's restaurants as needed in addition to his writing, as well as his true passion, mountain biking. Despite the fact the Greater Hartford area was not known for a mountainous terrain, there were a number of nearby peaks for him to enjoy for daytrips. I had agreed to go with him sometime as soon as I finished with exams. I hadn't ridden a bike since I had learned on a hand-me-down from a cousin when I was six and hoped riding a bike was actually like riding a bike and that I wouldn't embarrass myself totally.

Nick called me as I was walking to the library for my 5:00-11:00 p.m. shift. I loved hearing his voice.

"Hi, Nick, how're you doing?" I asked, trying and failing to tamp down my enthusiasm a bit. "I'm on my way to work."

"I hoped I would catch you before your shift started," he said, and I heard pans clanging in the background.

"Are you at North?" I asked, referring to the best known of the Russo Restaurant Group properties.

"Not tonight. They needed me downtown."

"All take-out, right?"

"Pretty much. The line is already out the door. I only had a minute, but I wanted to talk to my girlfriend." Girlfriend? I liked the way that sounded.

"Well, your girlfriend is walking into the library as we speak," I told him.

"Gator, babe. I'll reach out later," he said and ended the call.

I made my way to the reference desk, hung up my sweater on a hook on the wall, and settled in to what I knew would be a quiet evening. At this point in the semester, most of us had completed the term papers and case analyses that had plagued us for the past three years. We had moved on to memorizing our notes from class lectures and had less need for the voluminous reference books and periodicals on the shelves behind me.

I spent a couple hours happily reviewing and reorganizing my stack of flash cards, reveling in the peace and quiet I could always find in a library. When I was younger, I'd relied on the local library as a place of refuge, an escape from the drama and turmoil of life with the Gallaghers. My first library card had been like a magic ticket to a whole new world, and I had never forgotten that feeling.

My phone buzzed with a text. Randi!

'sup?

I grinned at that. Despite my regular advice, my friend loved to use terms she thought were still current, still in use. But thankfully, only on texts.

Not much playah? U? I shouldn't encourage her, but it was kind of fun.

Time to chat?

Sure thing

Seconds later, her face appeared on my phone. She was video messaging me.

"Hi, Len," she said. "I thought you might be at work tonight."

"Yeah, I'm here. It's so quiet."

"Calm quiet or spooky quiet?" she asked.

"Definitely calm quiet. I'm reviewing my flash cards."

"I won't keep you," she began, but I insisted I needed a break. "I just wanted to ask how the case was coming." I told her we had completed the discovery phase now that the testimony of the experts had been added to the report.

"It's in the judges' hands," I announced happily.

"That's great. Sounds like it's on track. Do you think it'll ever see a jury?" she asked, and I thought for a second before responding.

"If I had to guess . . . no, I think they'll settle. It's an open-and-shut—"

"There are no true open-and-shut cases, Len," she said. "You never know what the defense could be waiting to spring on you."

"But that will come out in discovery, right?"

"In theory? Yes, of course. But I've never seen a case without a surprise revealed during the final hours."

"That doesn't seem fair," I said, and Randi sighed deeply.

"No, but it's our justice system, warts and all, and it's still better than most. Anywho, what's up with bio-dad? Any more conversations?"

Hmmm. I hadn't told her yet about tailing him or his young girlfriend either. "No, but his office is fairly near to the campus . . ."

"Do you think that's a good idea?" Randi said. "He's the named claimant."

"I realize that," I replied rather testily. "I didn't say I was going to drop in on him, did I?" I had already decided I would probably postpone any meetings with Michael until classes were over and, technically, my internship too. No one had said anything about extending my time at the firm, so I assumed it was not going to happen. As if she were reading my mind, Randi posed another question.

"Have they made any announcements about summer placements?"

I groaned. "No. I keep hearing it will be soon. But there's something I've been meaning to talk to you about." I watched as she sat up straighter, laser-focused on what I had to say. So I told her about the text I'd received in error, the threats to keep quiet, and how Roger kind of freaked me out. I watched her as I talked, her expression morphing from one *of* mild concern to alarm. When I finished, I waited for her response.

"What are you going to do?" she asked. *Whaaat?* No advice from the sharpest legal mind I would ever encounter?

"You tell me. What would you do? Should I have taken the exam and turned it in?"

She sighed and shook her head. "As you said, you have no proof, and it sounds like Roger is pretty well connected. He could just deny everything, and you would be in possession of the stolen exam. Will your friend Erin back you up? Maybe if you reported it together, it would be taken more seriously."

"Maybe. I don't know, but next time I talk to Erin, I'll see what she thinks. I'll keep you posted." I held back my concerns about not having a place to live and how Seth and I had broken up. Those were issues for another day. "Hey, so I gotta split. If I sent you a gator emoji, what would you think?"

"As long as it's not an eggplant," she replied. "To be continued, dear one." She knew me well enough to not bother trying to get any more out of me tonight.

"You got it. Love you," I said, knowing it was the truest thing I could say.

"Love you more, babe. Stay safe. Talk soon."

The next couple hours passed by slowly, and I found myself watching the clock, never a good thing to do when time was literally standing still. Right at eleven, I hopped up, grabbed my sweater, and called good night to the cleaning crew, who were just arriving. They would lock up when they were done, so I was free to head out and hurry home. The moon was low tonight, I noticed, and the streets before me were fairly deserted. I moved along at a quick pace, but I felt safe despite the late hour. I was about to cross the last intersection before my building when a I heard a car idling behind me. I started to run even before I realized it was Roger. I raced up the brownstone's steps, juggled my keys in the lock, and burst into the tiny vestibule. I turned the deadbolt and, my heart pounding, watched as his yellow car drove slowly down the street. *Message received, psycho.*

Chapter 14

I slept fitfully, and despite several cups of coffee, I was exhausted when I arrived at work the next day. "All hands on deck," Cal called out as I exited the elevator on the seventh floor. "I need everyone in the conference room. There's been an important development on the case. Cancel any evening plans. We're working straight through," he added and hurried off. If memory served, we had a forty-dollar dinner stipend anytime we worked late. Maybe a hearty pasta dish I could make last for two additional meals? With my meal plan in place, I walked into the conference room.

What I found there was nothing short of pure chaos. It looked like a bomb had gone off in a room generally so sleek and pristine it could be on the cover of *Lawyer's Monthly*—if such a publication actually existed, and I, for one, could only hope it did not. I stared in horror at the scene in front of me.

The large mahogany table, which probably cost more than an associate's annual salary, was covered in a chaotic mix of papers, some crumpled, others stacked haphazardly, with coffee stains and half-eaten snacks scattered across the surface. A few chairs were pushed askew, with one tipped over, as if someone had left in a rush.

On the whiteboard, remnants of brainstorming sessions were visible, with colorful markers scribbling ideas and diagrams, some of which were faded or crossed out. The floor was littered with discarded printouts and wrappers, and the air carried a faint scent of stale coffee mixed with a whiff of something unidentifiable. I pegged it as fear. But why?

"Where have you been?" shouted a red-faced older man I recognized as Cal's boss. Russ something. What was he doing here, and more importantly, why was he yelling at me? I looked behind me, just to be sure. Yeah, I was the only one standing in the doorway.

"Don't just stand there gawking," he continued. "We need to gather copies of the depositions." Man, if there was anything I truly detested, it was not having any sense of what the actual fuck was going on. Read the room, I told myself. There were several paralegals in the far corner of the space, looking through electronic files and tapping away on their laptops, while two of my fellow interns were combing through boxes of paper folders. One of them, a guy named Mark, looked up at me with an expression of utter desperation. I mouthed, "What's going on?" but he just shook his head and looked back down at his keyboard. I watched as Cal came rushing in, and I put out a hand to stop him before he sailed past me into the maelstrom.

"Cal, what's going on?" I whispered, and he looked at me, seeming surprised by my question. He leaned in and whispered to me through clenched teeth.

"The case is dead in the water, that's what. Where have you been?" Again with that question.

"I was due here at one, and I arrived early." Like six or seven minutes, I might have added but chose not to.

"I sent you an email at seven this morning," he responded, seeming more tired and less angry, which was good for me.

"But I'm not supposed to access company email from home on an unsecured line. Why didn't you send me a text?" I was confused, as that was clearly the preferred method of communication between us.

"Apparently, I delegated that task to the wrong intern. Mark," he said loud enough for him to hear. Mark looked up briefly, shrugged, and mouthed, "I'm sorry."

"So what's going on?' I repeated, anxious to get back to the crisis at hand. Cal motioned for me to join him back out in the hallway. He looked exhausted. Hell, everyone did.

"Someone dropped the ball, Lennon. Screwed the pooch, fucked up—" I held up a hand to stop him from sharing any more colorful ways to communicate failure. He nodded briefly and started to explain.

"We were done with discovery. We exchanged documents with Data Solutions and their defense team. All the claimants testified in depositions. We finalized the interrogatories and submitted the expert testimony reports. We were done." He stopped as if trying to recall if a step had been missed. I had been part of the discovery process almost from the beginning, and suddenly I felt a sense of panic causing my heart to pound and my palms to sweat. Had I screwed the pooch? Maybe I . . .

Cal was studying me intently, shaking his head. "I can see where that brain of yours is going with this, but it wasn't you, Gallagher. It was way above your pay grade." I felt somewhat relieved , but the problem still existed, even if it wasn't mine. How would this affect Michael, as well as Sonny's family and *S.C.* and *T.B.* and all the other claimants who were counting on us to make things right?

"Anyway, the defense team read through every word of the interrogatories. Every comma, every typo, the spelling of the claimants' names, middle initials. Seriously, when this is over, we need to look at hiring their fact-checkers away from them. But the bottom line is they found several discrepancies. Red flags that were ignored or swept under the rug. Essentially, information—actually, more like warnings—that if acted upon by the claimants could have prevented the whole situation."

I was stunned, but I tried to make sense of this new information. "What you're saying is Data Solutions experienced minor problems possibly visible to our clients, and it's our clients' fault for not collectively reporting them, and now that it's a big problem, Data Solutions is not responsible?"

Cal nodded slowly. "They would put all that a bit more eloquently, but in a nutshell, yeah, you're right. They filed a motion to dismiss first thing this morning. I need you to focus on the lead. Kelliher. You're the only one I trust. Read through every word of his initial interviews and compare them to his depositions and finally to the interrogatories. Look for anything that's off. A date, a name, anything that might contradict his earlier statements. I need them by 9:00 p.m. Got it?" As it was only half past one, I assumed it was doable.

I nodded, then asked, "Was he the only one?" I breathed easier as Cal explained there were issues with six of the claimants, but as the named participant, Michael's files were the most critical. We could probably excuse other claimants with cause, but not Michael. Without him, it would mean starting from scratch, and I doubted we had the support of the senior partners to do that.

I headed over to where my peers were hoarding the files. I figured I would begin with the paper trail and work my way up. Mark saw me coming and flushed a deep crimson.

"Sorry, Lennon. When I got here for my shift at nine, it was already a madhouse. If Cal says he told me to get you in here, well, he's the boss. But I honestly don't remember him telling me. Anyway, sorry."

"No worries. Can you grab the Kelliher files for me, please?"

"We figured they were saving them for you," he said. "Grab a seat, and I'll bring 'em over."

•　　•　　•　　•　　•

Seven hours later, I was certain of only three things: pasta primavera was delicious when piping hot and only slightly less so when lukewarm, the human spine was clearly not designed to remain in a hunched-over-the-computer pose for hours at a time, and last but not least, Michael Kelliher was totally legit. His claim was consistent from his initial questionnaire, his audio, video, and written testimony, and from the depositions and the interrogatories in his file. I read, listened, and watched every word, and there were no errors, no red flags, and no concerns when it came to the named claimant. He may well be a shit of a husband, but his claim was as squeaky clean as it could be. And I was even more convinced this man was indeed my bio-dad. I typed up my notes and emailed them to Cal.

I wondered why Cal insisted on tasking me with this. Had the defense team identified something I'd missed? I stood and stretched, my eyes gritty and my bladder full to bursting. First things first. I went to the restroom, and as I washed my hands, I splashed cold water on my face. It felt so refreshing; I did it again. I found my pasta in the fridge, and after a nuking it for a minute, I ate what was left, scraping the sides of the plastic bowl to get every last savory bite. I would have to ask Nick about Russo's pasta primavera. So good!

Then I went in search of Cal. He was bent over his own keyboard, typing away. A new résumé, perhaps? If this mistake was as big as he'd warned me, heads might roll, and I assumed his would be among the first. I did that weird "knock, knock" thing people say instead of actually knocking and walked into his office. It was tiny compared to the senior partners' digs, but it was furnished with chic, timeless pieces of furniture. It was immaculate, not a stray paper or file out of place, a marked contrast from the conference room I had been working in all day. He looked up warily, then smiled at me.

"C'mon in, Lennon. What a trooper! What can I do for you?" His face was a bit flushed, and his eyes were bright and slightly glassy. A bump of coke, maybe, or just fatigue?

"Sorry to bother you, Cal. I just wanted to ask you about Michael. Um, Kelliher, the named claimant."

"I think it's safe to say at this point you probably know him better than anyone at the firm. Your report was clear and concise. But what did you want to know?" *Man, you have no idea just how well I might actually know him.* But he looked concerned, and my suspicions about drugs vanished. Still Cal. Cool guy, good boss.

"You asked me to review his files, and as my report indicated, I didn't find a single issue or concern. Was there something the defense team found suspicious?"

He immediately shook his head. "No, not on Kelliher, but there were a handful of others needing to be addressed. We will be removing six claimants from the case first thing in the morning." I must have continued to look confused because he continued. "I wanted you to go through his claim carefully one last time, just to make sure. You're the best we've got, Gallagher. I knew if you signed off on him, we were good to go."

I allowed myself a momentary flush of pride before continuing. "What about the defense's motion to dismiss?"

"The judge vetoed that after our conference call just now. Once we offered to remove the six claimants and we showed there was no material damage to the case as a whole, the motion was denied."

"Wow, that's good news," I said, and Cal nodded.

"It was touch and go for a while there, but it looks like we pulled it off. Thanks to all of you. And speaking of the team, most of your crew has gone home. Do you need a ride?"

"Oh no, I walked. It's only twenty minutes or so. You don't have to—"

"Nonsense. That's what car services are for." He grabbed his phone and pressed a few numbers. "Yeah, it's Cal from Myers, Stone & Johnson. Need a pickup ASAP for one of our superstars, Ms. Lennon Gallagher. Yes. Hold on. What's your address?" he asked me, and I told him. He relayed it to the dispatcher, then nodded. "Ten minutes. Black SUV. License plate WV-232 with livery plates," he confirmed and hung up. "All set. You got the plate and all?"

I nodded, but I still had a question. "Um, so I was wondering how, I mean, if, um . . ."

Cal understood my concerns. "It's all paid for, including the gratuity. You can just sit back and relax. You worked hard, and you deserve a little comfort. We appreciate you, Lennon. Now go grab your stuff. Your car will be down there in just a few minutes."

I thanked him and left his office, relieved he knew how hard I worked and how much the case meant to me. I hoisted my backpack over my shoulder and took the elevator down to the lobby, and as I made my way to the exit, I spotted the biggest, blackest, shiniest vehicle I'd ever seen. A good-looking uniformed driver greeted me.

"Ms. Gallagher, I'm Joseph, and I have the pleasure of driving you home this evening. Shall we?" he added and opened the door for me. I slipped into the back seat, which was about the size of my mattress and twice as plush. With help from Joseph, I discovered bottles of sparkling water, assorted high-end snacks, and a DVD player. I wished the ride home was longer.

As if reading my mind, Joseph turned to me. "So you're my last pickup tonight. What do you say about taking the scenic route? I'll get the overtime, and you can load your backpack with all the goodies. How does that sound?"

"It sounds like a win-win to me, Joseph. Let's do it." My five-minute ride home took closer to thirty minutes, and after watching four Miley Cyrus music videos in a row, I filled my backpack with bags of apricot-glazed cashews, organic trail mix with cranberries and walnuts, and tiny squares of the richest dark chocolate I'd ever tasted. Joseph opened the door for me and waited until I got my front door unlocked.

"Good night, Lennon Gallagher," he called.

"Good night, Joseph," I managed to get out. "Thanks for the ride." Damn. Chocolate throat. I twisted open one of the six bottles of sparkling water I'd also grabbed and swallowed half of it as I climbed the stairs.

Free dinner, a car and driver, *and* pricey snacks. I could definitely get used to this.

Chapter 15

The next morning, I called Randi. She hadn't left for work yet, and I was able to fill her in on the latest regarding the lawsuit against Data Solutions.

"You were right," I said. "About the surprises." Silence on her end. "Randi?"

"I didn't hear you," she said. "Must have been a bad connection."

"All I said was there were surprises."

"No, the other part."

"Oh, got it. You just want to hear me say it. You. Were. Right. Happy?"

"Tickled pink," she replied. "What do you have going on today? I need to attend a meeting in Hartford this morning. Do you want to have lunch afterward?"

"Of course," I agreed, and she said she would reach out with a place and time.

I checked my phone, surprised Erin still had not texted. I could understand her wanting to take off the other night and not wait around for me to receive my verbal beatdown from Roger, but a call or text would have been welcome. I was hoping to talk to her about my need to move next month. She was renting a bed and bath in a large private home close to campus, and I wondered if she knew of any vacancies. I sent her a quick text.

Hey U good?

I waited a couple minutes before getting up to stretch, listening as my bones creaked and groaned. When all of this was over, I vowed to get into better shape. I had always been thin, but that didn't mean much when it came to fitness. Maybe I could train for something after I graduated. Like a mini-marathon or maybe a 5K, depending on how long that worked out to be. I looked down at my phone. Still nothing. I typed quickly, realizing I needed to be out the door pronto if I was going to make it to my first class on time.

See you in class

Five minutes later, a personal best, I'm fairly certain, I was dressed and out the door, hurrying down the sidewalk to the classroom building. I slid into an empty seat just as the lights started to dim and today's slide presentation on the disadvantages of irrevocable trusts began. I found myself paying less attention to the material being presented and more on the audience. Even in the dim light, I could spot the place where Erin usually sat, but as far as I could tell, there was no Erin and no empty seat reserved for me. I switched on my phone again and saw nothing. No return text from Erin. Both my earlier texts showed as delivered, but apparently neither had been read. I shoved my phone back into my bag and tried to focus on the presentation. My mood slowly improved as the lights came on at the end and I could scan the room looking for Erin's curly red hair tied up on her head with a brightly colored scarf. On me, it would look stupid, but she was tall and stylish and managed to pull off any number of accessories or outfits. No sign of her. She must have slept in this morning.

I decided to join the crowd in the first-floor cafeteria, hoping there was money in my account. The whole time Mom—I mean, Charlene—was in prison, I made sure her commissary balance was always in the black. There I was, hustling for tips at the age of sixteen, all so my mother could eat her weight in peanut butter cups. Not fair, you say? Yeah, I hear that.

I picked up a tray and began the slow circle around the perimeter of the lunchroom. I was starving but also aware I was meeting Randi in a couple hours. Just a quick snack, I told myself, debating the merits of heading home and brewing a half pot of coffee to tide me over. But the precut slices of carrot cake looked so delicious. Decision made, I grabbed one and poured coffee into a large takeout cup and headed to the cash register. My balance covered my purchase, and I found an empty table with a single chair. Perfect. I inhaled the cake and sipped coffee while scrolling on my phone. I was feeling fidgety, and it made me think of Michael Kelliher. I wondered how he was, what might be going on with the case, and if he actually was my father. Part of me hoped he was and I could get to know him and meet his son, my half-brother. *That* would be something. Maybe I would finally feel connected to someone besides Randi and her family. Maybe I would resent Charlene a little bit less for some of the bad decisions she'd made over the years. But if Michael was cheating on his wife of fifteen years, with an extremely young woman, did I really want him in my life? What was wrong with men?

I took the stairs two at a time to my next class. Surely, Erin would be there in our usual spot, waving to me, saving me a seat. I scanned the middle section to the left and saw her red curls peeking out from under a cap like an old-timey newspaper boy might wear. But then I noticed the seats on either side of her were occupied. I recognized the cute guy with the shaved head to her left, but who was this woman sitting to her right in *my* seat? I made my way over and found her in the middle of a spirited conversation with her new friend. I stood nearby waiting awkwardly to be waved over. For the woman in my seat to excuse herself and find her own damn place to park her ass. But there was no wave, not even the slightest sign of recognition on Erin's part. The lights started to dim, and I looked around for an empty seat, finally moving closer to the front. I slid into an open aisle seat just as the professor started his lecture.

Today's seminar dragged on interminably, and although we concluded at the usual time, I felt as if I were glued to my seat forever.

By the time we were filing out of the auditorium, there was no sign of Erin or her new friend. I decided to skip texting her right now, even though I wanted to ask her what the hell was going on. I stopped briefly in the ladies' room before stepping out into the fresh air and double-checking the address Randi had sent me earlier. According to my phone, I was only seven minutes from the restaurant, so I ambled along slowly, realizing it was the first time in several days I didn't feel the need to rush. It was nice, normal, I guess—not that I would recognize "normal" if it bit me in the ass. The day was bright and sunny, and I was going to meet my favorite person in the world for lunch. That was more than enough.

•   •   •   •   •

When I arrived, Randi was already seated at a table in the corner by the large picture window overlooking the restaurant's terraced outdoor seating. She waved me over, her face glowing when she stood to hug me.

"How nice is this?" she asked. "Getting to see you mid-week, midday?"

"It doesn't suck," I replied. "Thanks for making the time to get together."

Randi studied me closely. "Of course," she replied. "Tell me about him."

I blushed, delighted to have the chance to share what I knew.

"Well, Nick's great. Super nice, but I'm not sure—"

"Nick? I thought his name was Ronald or Richard or something," she said, looking confused.

I felt a flush creep across my cheeks. "Wait, oh, sorry. You mean Roger, who heads up my review group. I'm sorry, I thought you meant—"

"Who is Nick?" she asked, and when she trained her sharp green eyes on me, I had no choice but to spill.

"He waited on us at that restaurant Roger dragged me to. His family owns it and several more too. He's a writer—well, he writes, not published yet, but he's working on a novel. It sounds pretty interesting, I think. But yeah, he's real smart, graduated from Wesleyan last year. Dual major: poli sci and English lit. And he lives in a tiny house, like the show on HGTV, 380 square feet and he designed it himself. It's on a secluded piece of land on his family's estate. That's what he said. Family estate. I haven't been there, but he told me, and I looked it up on Google Earth. It's so cool." I looked up to see her gaze softened considerably, and she looked . . . fascinated.

"You like this guy. You really like him."

I do, I do, I wanted to shout, but instead I stared down at the menu in my hand, unsure when I'd gotten hold of it. Had it been here all along?

"It's not like that," I started to protest, but she wasn't having it.

"What's going on with Seth? Did you guys break up?"

I nodded slowly. "Yeah. He asked me to come into the city for some opening."

"That bastard. What on earth was he thinking?" she said, feigning outrage.

"Not you too," I moaned. "How the hell am I supposed to drop everything and toddle off to Brooklyn for some techie launch party?"

"If you really wanted to, you would find a way," Randi countered, and I slumped back in my seat. She was right. I had offered up a reasonable-sounding excuse, but honestly? The thought of joining him had never occurred to me, not even for a second.

"It hasn't been working. Not for quite a while," I explained. "We fight all the time, and he's convinced he's the one trying to hold this whatever-it-is together, but he's not. I'm just wicked busy, and if I bomb out this semester, I'll have to repeat classes, and then I'll need to start paying off my loans. And I'll be dead broke and worse off than I am right now. Which is pretty bad, don't you think?"

"It's not good," she agreed. "Do you think there's a way for you two to get past this?"

"I don't see how," I said. "I don't have the bandwidth to smooth things over and make nice, you know? And I honestly don't even want to." The words were out of my mouth before I realized it. But they were true, I knew that much.

"I think we should order food before we get asked to vacate the premises," Randi said, grabbing her menu and gesturing to mine, which I was still gripping with all my might. We perused the offerings before deciding to go with bowls of New England clam chowder and a large order of crab cakes. Perfect! The server left with the menus, and I considered starting with a slice of fresh bread spread lavishly with butter when I recalled Roger's big hairy paw doing the same. I closed my eyes for a second to try to erase the image when I felt Randi's hand cover mine. "You okay, hon?" she asked softly, and the tears I'd held back all morning finally let loose. And, Randi being Randi, she let me cry, all the while holding my hand and keeping me safe. Was I crying for the end of my relationship with Seth or the fear of Roger exacting revenge on my skinny ass or because I was afraid I would never know who my father was or because I was bone-tired and emotionally starved and Erin didn't want to be my friend anymore? Yes, all that.

The server placed steaming bowls of chowder in front of us and, catching the end of my sobs, asked me, "Are you okay, miss?" in a voice indicating he hoped I was and if not that I would lie and say I was.

"I just found out my husband's getting released early from prison," I said in a shaky voice. "Overcrowding. Praise the Lord." He glanced at Randi before looking back at me.

"Well, that gives you and your mom something to celebrate," he replied with a forced grin. "Let me go check on those crab cakes," he added and sprinted away from us. Randi was shaking her head at me.

"You're incorrigible," she told me, barely hiding her smile. "Now tell me more about Roger. What's his endgame?"

While we dug into our chowder and I enjoyed a piece of crusty bread sans butter, I told her how he'd made it clear that, like it or not, I was part of his devious scheme. How Erin had disappeared and how she'd ignored my texts this morning. I almost added how she hadn't acknowledged me before class, but I still felt hurt and I didn't want to revisit it. Still too soon.

"Tell me again about the exam. Did you accept the envelope?" she asked, and I thought about her question for a split second.

"Did I accept it? No, I mean yes, he handed it to me, and I took it before he told me what it contained. Then I tried to hand it back to him, and he was like, "No way," and I dropped it like it was hot and told him to fuck off. I already told you that."

"And what about your friend? Where was she in all this?"

I was confused. "My friend? You mean Erin? Well, I thought she was waiting for me in the hall. We were supposed to go for ice cream. But I must have kept her waiting too long, and it was raining, so she left."

"And since then, nothing, right?"

I could see the wheels turning inside that brilliant mind of hers, but I was not clear on where she was going with this line of questioning.

"Objection, Counselor," I said. "Relevance?" But Randi didn't smile at my attempt at humor. She looked dead serious.

"How close are Erin and Roger?" she asked as a large platter of miniature golden crab cakes was placed between us along with small plates, wedges of lemon, and bowls of cocktail and tartar sauces. I grabbed one and popped it in my mouth before realizing how piping hot it was. I reached for my water just as our server left us with a "Watch out, the crab cakes are really hot" warning. *Yeah, thanks for that!*

As soon as the pain subsided, I leaned forward in my seat. "Why are you asking about Erin and Roger? She thinks he's a total tool, just like I do." Randi dunked half a crab cake in the cocktail sauce before stopping to study it closely. I waited until she bit into it, chewing reflexively before continuing. "Seriously, Ran. You can't think Erin has anything to do with this whole mess, do you?" Randi's delay in responding only lasted a few seconds, but I knew this woman. They hadn't called her "Quinn for the Win" in the state's attorney's office for nothing. There was always a point to her questions, and her instincts were spot on. *Crap, crap, crap.* "Ran?"

"I'm sorry, hon, but I think it's likely there is a connection between Roger's threats and Erin's vanishing act. It's just too much of a coincidence, and you know I—"

"Don't believe in coincidences," I finished for her, and she nodded.

"So you have never seen any sign of a connection between them?" she probed, and I shook my head, all the while racking my brain for something to disprove her theory and coming up empty.

"Roger runs the show," I explained. "He assigns topics to each of us to review and prep for the next session. We take turns presenting our topics to the rest of the group before quizzing them on what we covered. Erin's are always perfect—concise, clear, and informative. Even the questions she asks us are brilliant. Why would someone like her resort to cheating?" I honestly didn't believe she could be involved, but Randi wasn't wavering.

"Why does anyone do anything?" she asked. "Because they can or they need to or simply because they get a perverse thrill in getting away with something. But I have another question for you, and I want you to think about it, okay?" I nodded slowly before she continued. "Tell me this: Did you know Roger before you met him in your group? Had you ever seen him before?"

I thought about it for a moment but came up blank. "No, I don't recall ever seeing him before our first study session."

Randi nodded before asking, "And what about Erin?"

"Yeah, we were friendly. I told you that. We sat together in class and grabbed coffee a couple times. She was always nice, and she asked me to join the review group," I added.

"Don't you think it's awfully odd that after three years of classes and time spent on campus, you're suddenly approached with a fail-safe plan to score a copy of an exam from someone you have never met?" Randi asked. *What?* I was gobsmacked, as my grandma used to say.

"Um, maybe because I joined . . ." My voice trailed off. Randi had a point. Why would someone like Roger, with all his connections, want to bring me into his circle? Why would he trust me?

"Hear me out on this, Len. Don't get pissed, okay? But the other question needing to be answered is about Erin. What's her angle, huh? You said she's popular, smart, pretty? Why—"

"Why would she waste time on a loser like me? Is that what you're trying to say?" Randi looked crestfallen, and I knew deep down she had not wanted to hurt me. But still.

"That's *not* where I was going with that, Lennon, and you know it. My question is: With only a few weeks left in the semester, why does a pretty, popular, smart young woman suddenly have the need to make a new friend? Why would she pursue you now? And why would Roger trust you enough to tell you about his plan? Try to be objective and tell me what you're thinking."

I tried to take myself out of the equation and look at this weird triangle between Roger, Erin, and myself logically. I spoke slowly at first, speeding up when I started to see things more clearly.

"Regarding Roger. Why would he pick me, hell, *target* me to be part of his plan? Not financial, that's for sure. I've heard students pay hundreds, even thousands for an advance exam. I certainly could not have afforded it. And as far as my grades, I am ranked in the top ten of the graduating class, have been since 1L. In a perfect world, wouldn't he pick someone with average or even below-average grades? And a big checkbook? What makes me such low-hanging fruit?" Lost in thought, I paid no attention to Randi until she leaned in and grabbed my hand.

"What?" I asked.

"You said it before. You're broke. That's it." She was beaming at me, and I couldn't figure out why.

I knew my head hurt, and I wondered if she had time for coffee and where the hell our waiter had disappeared to. "Please tell me what you're talking about. My brain is fried."

"Here's what I'm thinking: Roger is about to join the family business and chase ambulances all day. He's under pressure to perform in his last days prior to graduating, but he's got a lot on his plate, and he hears about a sure thing. A way to guarantee his last semester study time can be cut back and garner excellent results. But he sees himself as too good to get his hands dirty. So he recruits—"

"Glen," I say excitedly.

"But Glen makes the mistake of telling you, and Roger finds out, and now Glen is gone."

"But why continue to pursue me?" I still didn't see the connection.

"Two things," said Randi. "Glen already alerted you something was up, and you're certainly bright enough to have dug deeper and discovered the truth about the exam. And two, who better to throw shade at than a scholarship girl with a mother in and out of prison? No offense."

"None taken," I said. In hindsight, I really was an easy target to pin a crime on. Thanks, Char!

"I think we've got it," said Randi. "That's the reason he won't forget about the text you received in error. He's using you as insurance."

"But the question remains, what are we going to do about it?"

"We need a plan, hon. This has to be reported and sooner rather than later. And we need something proving you had nothing to do with procuring the exam in the first place and that Roger is the ringleader." She checked the time on her phone. "I've got time for coffee if you do," she added, and I nodded. I had nowhere I needed to be, and time with Randi was always well spent. We ordered, and the server appeared a couple minutes later with a tray of coffee and a huge slice of what appeared to be a chocolate torte.

"Congratulations on your good news," he said, placing the plate in front of me with a flourish. "On the house." I was confused until I saw Randi mouthing the word "prison" in slow motion. Of course. Early release for the imaginary felon I was married to.

"Bless you," I said in what I hoped came off as heartfelt, and he beamed at me before hurrying off to fetch our bill.

Randi sipped at her coffee as she eyed the cake. "Is there anything you wouldn't do to score free dessert?" she asked. I dug into it before pushing the plate closer to her.

"Probably not," I said. We polished off every trace of the cake before sitting back and finishing our coffee.

"What now?" Randi asked, and I thought about her question before I responded.

"I'm just going to continue prepping for exams, finish my paper for the tax course, and try to wrangle a couple extra shifts at the library circulation desk," I said.

"What about Roger?" Randi asked. "Or Erin?"

I shook my head sadly. "I don't know about Erin. I see why you think she's involved, and you're probably right. But for now, I am going to avoid the two of them like the plague," I decided. "No more study group for me." I held up a hand to stop the protest I saw coming. "I already know how important it is, and I will make best efforts to see if there are any last-minute openings for bar review groups after exams are over." Honestly, the one member of the group I felt I could learn from was Erin, and all indications were that she would be MIA for the duration. Not to mention facing Roger was just not something I felt I could handle. And to what end?

As I now had nothing on my schedule for the rest of the day and no group to prepare for, I talked Randi into going shopping, reiterating my need for a decent wardrobe if I planned to be noticed in a good way during my remaining time at the law firm. We walked to a consignment shop a few blocks away, and I scored big-time. A gorgeous black blazer, two lightweight sweaters in neutral tones of gray and taupe, a black pencil skirt accentuating my slim waist and giving the illusion I had hips, black dress pants with no stains, and a couple sleeveless tops that would provide much-needed pops of color.

"You need shoes," Randi said, looking down at the canvas slip-ons that were my go-to's if flip-flops or Doc Martens might not be right for the occasion. I groaned, and we perused the extensive shoe selection. I unearthed a pair of scuffed-up black pumps needing a quick coat of polish in order to look only slightly worn. I paid the five dollars plus sales tax and added them to my bag.

"What about . . . ?" Randi began, and I groaned in protest.

"No more shopping," I begged. "We've been at it for hours." She checked the time before letting me know we had left the restaurant a mere fifty minutes earlier. "Well, it sure feels like hours," I said.

"You didn't let me finish," she said. "I was going to ask you about your bio-dad." I flushed a deep red. I had been thinking a lot about him lately but still hadn't decided how or even if I wanted to proceed. After I'd seen him with his girlfriend, I had tossed the coffee cup I planned to have tested for DNA. The last thing I needed in my life was another person to let me down and ultimately break my heart.

"I think I need to get through exams and the last two weeks of classes before I decide if I should travel down that rabbit hole," I said.

"Look at you, prioritizing your shit like a real adult," she said, swooping in for a hug. Without me even realizing it, we arrived at the parking lot where she was parked. "Do you want me to drive you home?" she asked, and I shook my head.

"I'm going to get my steps in and enjoy this nice day a little longer." I hefted my shopping bag and adjusted my trusty backpack. "Thank you for always being there for me, Ran," I told her. "You're the best. And give a hug from me to your sweet hubby too. I love you guys."

"We love you too. And feel free to bring Nick around sometime. We need to meet this writer/waiter of yours." The very idea left me tingling in all the right places. Yes, spending time with Nick was definitely in order.

I waved and started off down the street. Despite my purchases and heavy backpack, I felt lighter than air. Screw Roger and screw Erin. I would ace my finals without any help from either of them.

Chapter 16

The next time I showed up at the law office for my shift, I was surprised to see Michael Kelliher's name on my schedule for 2:00 p.m. As the lead claimant, I would have thought he'd have been fully briefed and up to speed by now. I had a couple appointments between now and then, and I imagined I would be asked to meet with a walk-in or two if time allowed. I stood and studied the small crowd in the lobby. Most of today's visitors were sitting on the folding chairs provided, but a few paced back and forth, clutching folders or printouts of some sort. I zoned in on a familiar-looking figure, and when he turned, I realized it was him. Michael. Quite tall, medium build, sandy hair, clean-shaven. He noticed me at the exact same time, and broke into a wide grin. He nodded happily at me, and I found myself smiling right back at him. Then, remembering I was an attorney in training with no good reason for grinning like a fool, not to mention the fact he was a lying cheater, I nodded briefly before breaking off eye contact. I sat and fiddled with the various folders in front of me until the clerk showed up and introduced me to my first client.

The next hour passed fairly quickly, and I'd amassed several pages of notes to input into the database. I tried carefully to "under-promise and over-deliver," as Randi repeatedly counseled me to do, but couldn't resist going the extra mile for the clients whose situation appeared particularly dire. Data Solutions had truly screwed these people over with its careless disregard for their private information, and we were charged with trying to make them whole again. When my 2:00 appointment was escorted to me, I glanced at the wall clock and saw it was 2:13. Not too bad, considering.

"Hello, Ms. Gallagher," Michael said with a smile not quite as wide as the one he'd flashed at me an hour earlier.

"Please, it's Lennon," I corrected him, and his smile grew a bit more forced. He studied me for a moment, a quizzical look on his rugged face.

"I wasn't aware your name was Lennon," he said, his eyes briefly scanning my laminated nametag. The one which identified me as L. Gallagher, University of Connecticut Law School, Class of 2025.

"That's me," I said, trying to appear professional, all the while wishing I could bounce up and down in my seat. *It's me. Your long-lost daughter. I'm just a few years younger than your girlfriend, but what the hell? Beggars can't be choosers.* A brief look of confusion passed over his handsome face as he tried to recall . . . something. A long-ago night with Charlene, playing Beatles' songs on the jukebox, or maybe—

"What's new with the case?" he asked, all businesslike, and the moment where we might have gotten closer to the truth about my humble beginnings passed. I fumbled with my folders, finally unearthing the one labeled with his name. I scanned the top sheet, where an update was typed in. I read over it quickly, nodding with satisfaction.

"Well, it looks like a good deal of progress has been made," I began. "Let me share with you where we're at. Our investigation is complete, as is the research we've done on relevant laws, precedent, and current regulations. The class has been determined as viable. We have filed our formal complaint in court, outlining the claims being made, and the defendants, Data Solutions and CEO Susan Greenley, have been served with summonses and the detailed complaint. An initial conference was held earlier this week, and Judge Robert Edwards set forth schedules and discovery." I looked up to find him watching me closely. "Am I going too fast?" I asked. "Or using too much legal jargon? I can explain—"

Michael held up a hand to stop me. "No, I'm good. You're doing great."

"We filed a motion to certify the class. Strictly pro forma, that's all standard, and naturally, the defendant's counsel will file opposition." I was nodding as I recited the process that, up until this point, had been all theoretical, something pulled from a frightfully expensive textbook or an obscure journal. But this was real, happening right now, and I was proud to play a role, however minor.

"And what happens after that?

"We were required to share what we have with Data Solutions—the depositions and interrogatories. Those are the answers to written questions submitted under oath. Then we compiled and filed the expert testimony at close of business yesterday."

"What about the response from the defense team? Are all the claimants solid? Any new issues?"

"There's really not too much else I can tell you, I'm afraid. The judge has our report, as does the defense. Now it's hurry up and wait," I said with a shrug.

"Just like the military," he quipped, and my ears perked up.

"Did you serve?" I asked.

"I did," he said with a touch of pride. "I enlisted in the army as a way to pay for school. After basic training, I was sent to infantry school and got deployed to the Middle East during the Gulf War."

"Cool," I said. "Um, thank you for your service." I was pleased I may actually have a relative who served in the military. Most Gallagher men liked to brag they were lovers, not fighters. So gross. I looked up to see Michael watching me expectantly. He cleared his throat before speaking.

"I appreciate your time, um, Ms. Gallagher. I'm just trying to take it all in. We're actually doing this, yeah? I've had my doubts, but you are getting it done. Do you think the case will ever go to trial?" Michael asked, and I thought about my answer. A large percentage of cases like these were settled out of court. It really depended on the strength of the case and the depth of the pockets on the part of the defendants. Data Solutions was a newer company and served clients throughout the New England states. While they had insurance for this type of situation, it might not be sufficient to cover our demands.

"If you're asking me as your lawyer, I'll withhold my opinion for now," I said.

"How about as my friend?" Michael asked, looking hopeful. *Or as your daughter?*

"I would be surprised if we didn't settle this before, I don't know, my birthday, maybe?" At his confused look, I clarified. "Oh, sorry, it's in October. The 5th. I think it's also the day I should hear about whether or not I passed the law boards, which I'll take this summer. Lately, I think of every event as happening before or after my birthday. I'll be twenty-five."

Michael grinned, looking like he had a secret he was dying to share. "They say everyone born in the first week of October was probably conceived on New Year's Eve." He ran his fingers through a thick lock of sandy hair. "I know, too much information, right? My son, John, is always on me for oversharing," he said with a rueful grin.

I surprised myself by asking about his son. "What's he like? John, I mean. Is he um, tall, like you?" Michael's smile spread across his face. I could clearly see the pride he felt for his son.

"Tall? Yeah, he's nearly my height at thirteen, so we might be looking at a full-ride basketball scholarship. He's amazing on the court. And he's a smart kid too. Makes first honors every semester." A parent proud of their kid, on and off the court. Can you even imagine?

"That's terrific. You must be so proud." Why was I belaboring the point? We get it. "Maybe-my-dad" is proud of his kid, and he's clearly an excellent, loving father. What. Ever!

"What about your folks? They must be proud of you, studying to be a lawyer and all." I flushed and looked down at the legal pad in front of me. Was this my chance to find out if my instincts were spot on or if it was just a case of wishful thinking? I still couldn't make eye contact with him, but I decided I would go on a short fishing expedition. Maybe something would click.

"Well, here's the thing. I grew up in a series of foster homes. My mom had a substance abuse issue, and she was locked up on and off for years. Even when she got clean, it wasn't a good environment, you know?" I dared to take a look at him and was surprised to find his kind eyes watching me closely. No sign of the "damn, I'm sorry I asked," look I often saw when I opened up about my past. He nodded his understanding.

"I'm sorry you went through that, Lennon. It must have been really rough."

"Yeah, it was," I agreed. "She's clean now, I guess. Maybe clean-adjacent. She still drinks, and she smokes weed sometimes, but no needles or crack pipes, so there's that."

"You know you're not responsible for her, right? I hope she stays clean-ish, but either way, it's not on you." I read enough Al-Anon pamphlets to know he was right, but it didn't make it any easier.

"Yeah, I know, but I'm all she's got. My grandparents are gone, my aunt flaked out on us years ago, and everyone else is doing time in prison or living far away. Nice, huh?"

"None of us grew up with perfect families, but you've had more than your share of dysfunction. Can I ask about your father? Is he in the picture?"

I felt a flash of anger as I considered the irony in his question but tamped it down. "I don't have a father. He dumped my mom when she told him she was pregnant with me," I said with barely a trace of the bitterness I was feeling and waited to see his reaction. It wasn't guilt or resentment he was feeling, just sadness for me and my mom.

"That must have been very traumatic for you, Lennon. Growing up, knowing how he—"

I cut him off, suddenly certain I did not want to hear any more on the subject of my conception.

"It's fine; it's whatever. How did we get off topic so quickly?" I caught sight of the admin assistant heading my way, escorting a middle-aged woman with the stoniest expression I'd ever seen, and knew my time with Michael Kelliher had far exceeded the standard appointment. He must have realized it as well, as he started to gather up his papers and prepared to leave.

"Thank you, Lennon, for your help today and for trusting me with what you're dealing with." He slipped a business card to me with a nervous grin. "Since most of my clients don't trust me enough to spend a forty-five-minute hour with me anymore, I suddenly have loads of free time. If you ever want to talk, give me a call. No charge, off the record, just a friendly chat. All evidence to the contrary, I'm pretty good at what I do," he said. "Thanks again." He smiled at me right before he turned and made his way through the lobby. I watched him go with a touch of something . . . hope, maybe? Even if he wasn't my dad, I felt like another conversation would be worthwhile.

I stood to greet Virginia Greenwood, my 2:40 appointment. The clock read 3:04. A quick glance at her file confirmed she was forty-four, single, and formerly employed as the youth director at a Catholic church in a nearby suburb. She had been fired by her employer when it was revealed she had been treated for a number of sexually transmitted diseases over the past ten years.

"Thank you for coming in, Ms. Greenwood, and I apologize for the delay. How has your day been so far?" I asked and watched as the expression on her face started to thaw just a bit. Maybe I had some social skills after all.

Chapter 17

The pressure of all the work required in my final semester was definitely starting to get to me. Whether I slept four or five hours or a miraculously restorative eight hours, I woke each morning alternating between feeling drowsy at the sound of the alarm on days I still had early classes and super focused at dawn on days I could sleep late before showing up at the law firm for the afternoon. Today was a class day, so naturally I barely heard the alarm. I stumbled around, gathering up my shower stuff and slowly making my way down the hall. Where was Roger with that amazing coffee when I needed him? I wondered, knowing I wouldn't risk ever laying eyes on him again, not for all the coffee in the world.

Minutes later, I was back in my room feeling slightly more human, pulling on underwear and a sports bra, hurrying so as to not miss a stop for coffee if the communal pot in the lounge was empty. Of course it was, I discovered minutes later, not-so silently cursing the jerk who had chosen to not make another pot after draining this one. The fact that it was frequently me who failed to make more seemed totally irrelevant at the moment. I grabbed my backpack, slipped on a sweater, and headed out the door. The line at the coffee truck wasn't too long, and I made it into my classroom with minutes to spare. Minor victories!

Out of habit, I looked around for Erin's head of long red curls but came up empty. I sat a few rows back from where we used to sit together and alternated my time between sipping mediocre coffee, checking my phone, and watching for Erin. I realized several minutes later I should have spent my time reviewing my notes this morning as it was Professor DaSilva's habit to continue the dreaded practice of cold-calling from our first year. And today, his first victim was yours truly. Students were warned repeatedly to be prepared to be called on in every class. Most faculty retired the tortuous process of calling on random students after the first year, but not all. Although some professors would give advance notice of "your day," most didn't, including Professor DaSilva.

"Ms. Gallagher, can you please share your thoughts with the class, along with any fresh insights into recent examples of Supreme Court cases being overturned?" His voice boomed, and I felt a sense of panic wash over me. Damn. Of all the days. I began to flip through my notes after taking a final look around to see if Erin had joined the class. Nope, apparently not. "Ms. Gallagher, if you please," he added, and I heard a chuckle from a few seats over.

"There goes the curve," one of my classmates said with a laugh. I honestly couldn't blame him. A standard grading curve dictated the percentage of A's, B's, and C's which can be given, so grading and class ranking are big deals. I'd just looked the other day, and was thrilled I was currently ranked at seventh. Not too shabby, considering I was one of 129 students. The top ten percent was generally considered to be more than adequate to garner offers from the most prestigious firms.

"Here goes nothing," I mumbled to myself before standing and reading aloud from my less than meticulous notes. I stumbled a few times when I struggled to read my own writing, but not enough to garner the ire from the podium, and sat down, relieved and feeling strangely exhilarated. Imagine if I were truly prepared, I told myself. And next time I would be.

Knowing I had done all I needed for today's class, I let my mind wander far from the intricacies of case law onto more pleasant matters, starting with my graduation in only three weeks. Randi had offered to throw me a party, but I wasn't sure how that would work with the ceremony in Hartford and the party eighty miles away in Old Lyme. It was just far enough to make it a challenge for Randi and Eric to host. Not to mention the fact I only had tickets for four guests. I had always assumed it would be Seth, Randi, Eric, and Charlene. Seth had said he would borrow his dad's car to pick my mom up and bring her to Hartford, but that was clearly not an option any longer. So much for more pleasant matters. When Charlene was part of the equation, you could guarantee there was going to be a problem.

At least I could keep my room on campus through commencement. If I got the offer to stay on at the law firm for the summer, I would need to buckle down and find a place somewhere. I knew I could stay with Randi, but the gas and the commute would be too much to deal with for more than a week or two.

All around me, my classmates were getting up, gathering books and belongings, and chattering about plans for the weekend, which ranged from sleeping, getting wasted, bingeing shows on Hulu and doing laundry. All but the getting wasted sounded good to me. When your mom was a junkie, you either joined them on the dark and twisted road or walked the straight and narrow. There was nothing in between. A buzz signaled an incoming text, and I fished my phone from my backpack.

It was the law firm in West Hartford I'd interviewed with several weeks earlier.

Good morning, Lennon. We would appreciate the opportunity to speak with you again soon. Please call our office to schedule an appointment at your earliest convenience.

Deb Saunders, Managing Partner

Colby, Graves & Coyne ~ Attorneys at Law

That firm specialized in environmental law, and it took me a moment to recall exactly why I'd applied there in the first place. Oh yeah, Erin had recommended them to me because that was where she had interned last fall. They were one of the firms I'd seen at a career fair held on campus over the winter. Randi had suggested I go—well, actually, she'd insisted I go to network and practice my pitch. I had attended, slunk around grabbing up business cards as well as pens, travel mugs, tote bags, and more. I had literally been like a kid in a candy store because some of the firms offered fancy chocolates and mints, all free for the taking. Had I talked to a single recruiter or junior partner or whoever they would send to these things? No, I had not. But I had gone back to my room with loads of freebies, made myself almost sick on chocolate, and salvaged three business cards from the firms with the best loot to apply to. So yes, CG&C had gotten my vote mainly because they'd had the forethought to order customized Stanley tumblers and full-sized Toblerone bars. That would really be a fun anecdote to share at their holiday party if I got hired there. Would they offer Erin a job as well?

I walked home slowly, enjoying the warm sun on this beautiful spring day. I lifted my face to the sky to try to drink it all in, but my slower pace caused the young man behind me to crash into me. I heard him mumble "dumb bitch" as he hurried away. Unlike many of my fellow Zoomers, I never walked around with a phone in my face or a pair of AirPods in my ears. Where I grew up, you could get yourself killed like that, or more likely mugged. This neighborhood was clearly a step up from the mean streets I was familiar with, but old habits were hard to break. I kept my phone in a front pocket whenever I was walking and my backpack held tight to my body. I grasped my keys in my hand like a weapon, ready to slash, stab, or maim whoever looked at me sideways. I was always vigilant, always on guard. You did what you needed to do to get by.

I was climbing the steps to my brownstone when I got another text. Nick!

Hey G! Howz yur day?
Great. Got a 2nd intrvw!
Sweet. Where?
W. Hartford. CG&C
Cool. They gave u the Stanley mug, yeah?

This guy was definitely a unicorn. He remembered things I told him, even the stupid things. I hurried inside, raced up to my room, and jumped on my bed. I wanted to give him my full attention. I leaned back against the headboard and let my thumbs get to work.

Yeah, and chocolate too. What r u doin'?

Not much. U free on Fri? Dinner?

Yes, I was, and if I wasn't, I would be.

Yeah, sounds good.

C U @ 6

Chapter 18

It was early Friday evening when Nick and I picked up a pizza at the little place on the corner near my dorm. Our plan was to hang out in the lounge area, consume said pizza, and find a movie to watch. I was feeling comfortable with him, like I'd known him a lot longer than the two weeks since we'd met. He was easy to talk to, and despite his busy schedule, our conversations never felt rushed or like he was crossing off something from a to-do list. Just the opposite from most calls with Seth. For months, it felt like he had wanted to be anywhere in the world besides chatting with me. And since our argument, we hadn't spoken at all, and I had no energy or desire to try to track him down. And do what? Apologize? Plan a trip to visit him in Brooklyn just so we could spend an entire weekend arguing? At least that's what it felt like we would be doing. So instead, I was going with the flow and trying to have a little fun on my one night off from studying or picking up a shift at the law library. We were just two twenty-somethings eating pizza and hanging out.

We turned onto my block, chatting companionably. I held the square pizza box in front of me while Nick carried a large reusable shopping bag loaded with soft drinks, chips, and a half gallon of mocha chip ice cream. A sudden movement on the steps leading to my front door caught my attention, and I instinctively stepped backward, sensing a threat of some sort. Nick shouldered the bag and placed a protective arm in front of me. But it was only Seth. My ex-boyfriend Seth, looming large and frowning at the two of us. He was swaying slightly, and his big brown eyes were glassy, unfocused. Was he drunk? And what was he doing here?

"Seth, what the hell?" I said, feeling guilty and more than a bit surprised. "Why didn't you let me know you were coming? I would have . . ." Would have done what? Cleaned my room? Not invited a new friend over? He glared at me.

"Would have done what, Len? Not scheduled a hot date the minute my back is turned?" His face contorted into a sneer. "Who the fuck is this?" he asked, his words slurring just a bit. "Who the fuck are you?" he asked Nick, who was standing by quietly, taking it all in.

Nick smiled, a tight smile like someone with impeccable manners might offer to an incredibly rude person. "Nick Russo," he said with a nod toward Seth. "I'm a friend of Lennon's," he added. "I'd shake your hand, but I've got soda and ice cream, so . . ."

Seth scoffed. "A friend of Lennon's? Nice try, player, but my *girl*friend doesn't have any *guy* friends."

I was growing impatient, and our pizza was getting cold. "Seth, you should have called before coming all the way up here. Nick and I were going to have pizza in the lounge. I guess you could . . ." I glanced at Nick, and he nodded almost imperceptibly at me. "Do you want to come in for a bit?" He must have taken the bus to Hartford and then scheduled a rideshare here to the campus. He wasn't falling down drunk, but he wasn't much of a drinker, and I knew it wouldn't have taken much to get him to this point. I wasn't sure if he could make it back to the bus station in his condition.

"And ruin your romantic evening?" he protested. "Now why on earth would I wanna do that?" Oh, for God's sake. I climbed the stairs to where he stood and glared at him.

"Come in and have a slice. Stop being such a jerk. You come in too." I motioned to Nick. "C'mon." I stomped up the stairs, and Nick followed closely behind Seth. The three of us made our way into the large open room where residents shared meals, watched TV, and hung out. Notoriously deserted on weekends, I expected there couldn't have been more than a few of us sticking around this weekend despite the proximity of final exams.

I found some paper plates and napkins and set us up at one of the round tables in the center of the room. I placed the pizza in the middle of the table, popped the top off a can of soda, and pulled up a chair. I watched the guys circle each other like jungle animals about to pounce.

"Sit," I commanded, and they did. For a while, the conversation was kept to a minimum as we each consumed a couple slices. It was a pretty good pie, but the lump in my throat made it difficult to swallow. Why did Seth have to pull a surprise visit tonight of all nights? Should I ask him to leave? And do what? I wondered. It was a three-hour bus ride back to New York. But this was Seth. It would be rude of me to ask him to leave, but what was the alternative? I wasn't going to sleep with him, of that I was certain. I supposed he could sleep on one of the couches here in the lounge and I could drive him to the bus station first thing in the morning. And what about Nick? I didn't plan on sleeping with him either. At least not tonight. But hopefully soon. That is, as long as he felt like a girl with all this baggage was even worth it. *Crap.*

The guys were eyeing the two slices left in the box, and I waved my hand at it. "Go for it. I'm done," I assured them. I finished my soda, trying to decide what would happen next. Movie, friendly game of poker, duel to the death at midnight? This was not the sort of thing that ever happened to me.

Wiping his mouth with one of the napkins, Nick chugged down the rest of his drink before leaning forward to address us.

"Should we find a show to watch?" he asked, a friendly smile on his face. "What streaming services do you have, G?" Seth winced at Nick's casual reference to the first initial of my last name. "I have been looking forward to watching the latest *Yellowstone*. You with me?" Nick and I had discussed our mutual enjoyment of the series earlier in the week.

I nodded enthusiastically. Anything to break up the tense atmosphere. I hopped up and crossed the room to where the large-screen TV was mounted to the wall and found the remote. Within seconds, the latest episode of *Yellowstone* was playing, so the three of us got comfortable, or as comfortable as we could, with Seth on the couch directly facing the TV and Nick and I each occupying one of the recliners on either side. Nick grabbed another soda and the bag of chips and settled right in, watching the opening scene with interest. Seth looked bored to tears, and I hoped his obvious lack of interest didn't spoil Nick's enjoyment. I tried to pay attention to the show, but I was still worrying about whatever would happen next.

Time passed, and other than a handful of comments from Nick on the borderline sociopathic Dutton family, the only sound in the room came from the well-placed speakers. Until I heard a new sound, something out of place but oh so familiar. I looked over at Seth to find him sleeping soundly, flat on his back and snoring softly. I glanced at Nick, who heard him too. He crossed in front of the couch, heading toward me.

"They're so cute when they're sleeping," he said without a touch of sarcasm or guile. That was the moment when I knew. Nick Russo was a good sport. The kind of guy Randi always encouraged me to seek out. "Looks fade," she had said, although her husband Eric was still a total smoke show, "and a sense of humor is terrific, but sometimes you might not feel like laughing. A good sport, on the other hand? Someone who won't piss and moan when plans change or when their team loses or McD's runs out of Shamrock Shakes? Find yourself a good sport, Lennon. And be one too." Not that she'd ever actively encouraged me to break things off with Seth. I knew for a fact she liked Seth quite a lot. But honestly? He could be a bit of a whiner sometimes. If buses ran late or traffic built up, or he couldn't reach the person he needed to talk to in two minutes or less . . . "Quit your whinging" my grandma would always say, usually to my mom. Charlene? Not a good sport. No surprise there.

Seth took that opportunity to roll over on his side with his back to us. Nick and I smiled at each other, and he perched on the arm of my chair. He leaned in closely, asking me, "Can I kiss you? Just one kiss?"

I nodded, and he pressed his lips to mine, and I felt the most delightful tingle starting with my lips and running down to most every other body part. Man, this guy was a good kisser! He pulled away smiling and, with a nod in Seth's direction, made himself comfortable once more, sitting across from me. He grew quickly absorbed back into the show, but he was smiling, and I knew he was thinking of our kiss. I sure was. Seth rolled over again and started snoring in earnest. We were an hour into the episode with only minutes left, but it seemed like a good time for an intermission. Nick hit the pause button before standing and stretching. His T-shirt rose above the waistband of his jeans, and I caught a flash of pale skin and toned abs. I wondered how it would feel to run my tongue over—

"I should probably get going," said Nick, sounding like leaving was the last thing he really wanted to do. Same!

"I'm so sorry," I said. "You asked me out, and now our whole evening is ruined." I gestured toward Seth, who was now lying on his back, snoring softly. "He barely drinks," I said with a hint of an apology in my tone. "I have no clue what got into him."

Nick shrugged in response. "He got his heart broken. It's too bad, but it happens, right?"

I nodded slowly. I wasn't certain about the broken heart bit, though. More likely a bruised ego. Seth had been argumentative and cool toward me for the past couple months. I honestly wondered if he even cared about me any longer.

"Well, I'm just sorry you got caught up in all of this," I said, feeling unsure what to do next. I wanted to head off to the quiet and solitude of my room, but there was an intoxicated ex-boyfriend sleeping on the couch and . . . someone looking at me with a gleam in his eyes.

"Tell me something," he said, taking a step closer to me. I nodded, and he moved closer still. "Do you want to get back with him?" I shook my head. No, no way. "Do you want me to call you tomorrow?" he asked, and I nodded, slowly at first, then with enthusiasm. Yes, yes, I did want that. He smiled and nodded in agreement. "How about I leave you to clean up this mess, and I'll drive our friend here to the bus station and make sure he gets on board. Damn good thing he's not driving. Then tomorrow, I'll call you and we can make a plan to get together. What do you think?"

I nodded again before speaking up. "That sounds great, and thank you. I don't know how—" Then Nick's arms were around me, and he kissed me. Gently at first and then with a fervor I found thrilling. God, he smelled so good, and his lips were like silk or cotton or silky cotton. It was heavenly. I let out an audible groan of protest when he pulled away from me.

"I've been wanting to kiss you like that all night. That first kiss from earlier? Just wanted to see if you were into it. You're not easy to read," he added, in a way that made me think he liked that about me. "Now let me make good on my promise." He walked over to the couch, where Seth was now struggling to sit up. He looked fairly calm, just a bit disheveled. I wondered if he'd seen us kissing just now.

"C'mon, man, I'm gonna get you to the bus station. Get you back home. How's that sound?" Seth looked confused at first, then shook his head vigorously.

"Nah, don't bother. I'm not going anywhere." He looked at me, hope in his eyes, clearly thinking I might ask him to stay. I shook my head.

"You need to go home, Seth," I told him in a tone I hoped brooked no argument. He nodded, knowing it was impossible to argue with me, to change my mind. He started texting and walked toward the vestibule, clearly intent on his phone. I watched him, feeling both relieved and sad, before turning back to Nick. "Thank you again. Tonight was . . . um, not sure exactly what it was, but the pizza was delicious."

He grinned back at me, his hazel eyes sparkling. "You know what else is delicious, G?" he whispered in my ear. "Your lips," he added, and a new round of tingling left me feeling more alive than I'd ever been.

In a move totally unlike me, I whispered back, "I can't recall ever being so turned on before," and I brushed my lips ever so softly across his cheek as he gazed at me, delighted. But before he could respond, Seth came back into the room.

"C'mon, man, the bus to Middletown is gonna be boarding. Not that anyone cares, but my sister is gonna meet me there, and I'll stay with my folks tonight. Let's go," he insisted, not willing to make eye contact with me. I approached him slowly, warily. His outburst had frightened me earlier, but I hoped he'd calmed down after passing out for a while. I put my hand on his arm as he started to turn and leave the room.

"Take care of yourself, Seth," I said, and he nodded gruffly, pulling away in case I decided to hug him.

"You too, Len. You too," he said and left the lounge. Nick gave me a thumbs-up before hurrying after him. I watched them go, relieved but very sad. Our relationship had been circling the drain for a year, but neither of us had been able to call it. Was it all for the best? I didn't know for sure, but it probably was.

As I gathered up the discarded pizza crusts, soda cans, and napkins, I looked around the deserted common room, with its cushy couches and more shabby than chic carpets. I had spent many nights in here watching TV and eating leftovers. Tonight was the first time I had invited a date to join me, and look how that turned out. There's always next time, I thought, and I found myself hoping it happened soon. I turned off the lights and climbed the stairs to my room. Just as I unlocked the door, a text came in from Nick.

He's on the bus, G. All set.

Thank you so much Nick. And again, sorry.

Got your back babe. Sleep well Call u tom.

It had been a very confusing evening overall, but one thing was crystal clear. I really liked Nick Russo having my back.

Chapter 19

Nick called me midmorning on Saturday, and we chatted for a while, drinking our coffee and making plans to get together next week. I hung up feeling excited and motivated to get my work completed.

I spent the rest of the weekend preparing for the dreaded Con Law exam with short breaks for the good things in life, including doing a load of laundry, lest I run out of clean undies calling my mother to get the latest updates on her meetings with her parole officer and her steady string of doctor visits; texting with both Nick and Randi; and running out for donuts, tampons, and fast food. My healthy diet regime was clearly on hold until I graduated, moved out, and found a job.

Currently, I was sprawled out on one of the lounge's comfy sofas, reviewing my notes. Despite all the thoughts about my future swirling around in my head, I felt clear, focused. I was going to graduate soon, and everything else would be resolved or not. It was difficult to believe it had been three years since I had started here. The first year had been tortuous (pardon the pun), the infamous 1L comprising the foundation courses: Contracts, Torts, Civil Procedure, Criminal Law, Property, and more. The Lawyering Skills course where we learned legal thinking and writing, research, briefing, and motions had been one of my favorites. It was a lot of work with many assignments and large briefs to research and write, but for the first time, I could truly imagine the actual work of lawyering and how future-me would spend my days. From then on, I was hooked.

It was the second year of law school when I started to have doubts about my choice to become a lawyer. Suddenly, I was faced with choosing electives and considering a suitable internship. I had to admit I loved the structure of the first year better. My childhood years had been pure chaos shaped by where I was sleeping at night, if I attended school or not, and who I was responsible to on any given day. In order to survive, I had adapted my own set of rules and guidelines. I'd tried to fit in with my classmates, unwrapping a PB&J at the lunch table, turning in homework, and finding relatively clean clothes to wear each day. It had been a constant struggle, but I'd deemed these things to be my top priority: a packed lunch, completed assignments, and suitable clothing. I hadn't always succeeded, but I'd wanted my exterior to be beyond reproach, even if inwardly I had been a whirling dervish of stress and anxiety.

Staying with family was always a wild card as there was little or no privacy or even space to do homework or study. I learned to survive on four to five hours of sleep each night and copious amounts of caffeine, skills that came in very handy today. I was always being sent to the corner store for cigarettes (Grandma), tampons and other feminine products (Aunt Kelly), or beer (Charlene). The same clerk who'd sold ten-year-old me a jumbo box of maxi-pads never questioned me when I returned the next day to purchase a six pack of Bud Light.

I had craved routine back then and rarely found it. College and especially law school were a huge relief for me. Structure, requirements, a roadmap for success. I thrived when I knew precisely what was expected of me. My focus had always been family law, and after checking out the many other options available, I'd returned to my original choice. I could empathize with families torn apart by poverty, addiction, and mental illness, and I hoped it would make me a better lawyer. Randi herself had personally experienced none of those issues, but she was one in a million. If I aspired to be half the advocate she was, I needed all the help I could get.

For today, I was pleased to complete an outline of topics for review and three dozen brand-new handwritten flash cards. If I could enlist my neighbor Jimmy, a 2L student, to work with me tonight, I would be in great shape.

· · · · ·

First thing on Monday morning, I dressed in a pair of leggings and a Harry Styles *Night Changes* T-shirt. In lieu of coffee, I sucked on a few caffeine-infused lozenges and headed out. It was time to face the music and seize the day. I was prepped, wired, and desperate to get past this. In the 2L and 3L years, the grading for many courses rested solely on the final exam, reportedly done to mimic the pressure of sitting for the bar exam. This particular form of torture resulted in a lot of pressure to complete outlines after each class and keep up with the work. I was reasonably confident I would do well, although that didn't always mean getting an A. With the curve mandate in place, there were very few A's awarded for each class.

I entered the classroom and signed in, scanning my student ID card. I found a seat near the back of the large room and watched as students continued to trickle in. Other than a few nods of recognition, there were no attempts at conversation, as everyone appeared to be focused on the task at hand.

I'd heard stories of students wearing adult diapers to avoid time-consuming and very much frowned-upon bathroom breaks. Looking around at the other students, I wondered how many were wearing Depends or whatever. I saw a number of students I recognized, but there was no sign of Erin's red hair. As I watched, I saw the large outline of a man whose bulk and shuffling gait could only belong to Roger Stevens. Don't look this way. Go sit over there, I begged silently. Oh crap, he saw me. He headed straight for me and took a seat one row over. He gave me a conspiratorial wink before opening his laptop and logging onto the university Wi-Fi. Smug bastard. I gave him the finger as I pretended to scratch my head, but the moment was lost since he had been staring at his screen. Ass-hat!

I logged in to my account with the software the university utilized, which prevented any other programs from being accessed once the exam was downloaded. The link was now live, so I hit the download button and, as soon as I could, pressed start. I was always happy to work directly on my laptop and submit electronically. My handwriting was crap, and it was easier to update and edit my responses. I quickly skimmed over the exam to get a sense of the different stories or "fact patterns" provided. For each, I would need to read through the content carefully, identify the issues, state the rules of law, apply them, and then arrive at conclusions for each issue spotted. It was about what I had expected. It was go-time!

At the halfway point, I was feeling good about my progress, as I regularly checked the clock to monitor how much I had completed against the time left. One and a half hours in and I was partway through the fourth of six pages. I wanted to leave time at the end to go over everything for typos and missed questions, so I continued at the same pace, glad to not have to leave my seat for a bathroom visit. I soldiered on.

Eighty-five minutes later, I felt like I had done all I could. In the last fifteen minutes, I had fixed a few typos, filled in a couple blank spaces, and nodded appreciatively as I reread some of my responses. I saved my work, hit submit, and closed my laptop. I was surprised to see so many empty seats around me. I was so focused I hadn't even noticed the mass exodus that had taken place. I looked over, and naturally, Roger's seat was empty. I hoped I'd done well, but either way, I didn't regret my decision to steer clear of the stolen exam.

I gathered my things and gave a few quick nods to the remaining students seated near me. I signed out, again using my ID, and left the room, just as I heard one of the three proctors call out it was time to hit submit on the keyboard.

I stopped at the bodega on the corner and treated myself to a large coffee and a breakfast sandwich I rescued from its spot under a heat lamp. I sipped the acrid coffee that must have sat on the burner for hours, but I didn't mind. It tasted like victory to me. Now I just had to wait to get the results. After a couple bites, I tossed the dried-out sandwich in an overflowing bin but held on to the coffee as I walked home. I imagined stripping down to the basics and sliding between the sheets, having time to relax, and even sleep. The rest of the day was mine, and I intended to squander every moment.

Chapter 20

I slept for a couple hours and woke feeling rested and ravenous. I popped down to the lounge, dug around in the back of the freezer, and found the package of stuffed shells I had hidden several weeks earlier. A few minutes in the microwave and dinner was served! I swirled the contents around in the small black plastic container, trying to merge the ice particles with the sections that were steaming hot. A very disappointing meal, but it satisfied my hunger pangs for the time being. I went back upstairs, popped on my headphones and listened to some vintage Taylor while I stripped my bed and remade it with clean sheets. Then I started tidying up, hanging up articles of clothing and emptying the trash into the bin out back. I found a few clean cardboard boxes by the dumpster and used them to start packing. It was only a half-hearted effort, but I emptied my drawers and closet of my winter hats, scarves, and sweaters and felt like I had done something productive.

By midafternoon, I had already started checking the portal to see if grades were posted. Since our exams were graded by a slew of teaching assistants, we students expected a fairly fast turnaround. I'd developed the habit during 1L of checking early and often. Refresh my browser, then check again. By early evening, I was getting discouraged before I remembered Professor Chan was old-school and had said grades would be also be posted on the bulletin board outside her classroom. She had even provided us with unique codenames to protect our privacy. I checked my notes. There was mine: **XJKK567**. Random, but whatever. Maybe there was a problem with the server, but I could still see the results first thing tomorrow if she posted them.

I slept fitfully, waking on a regular basis to check the portal. Just before 6:30, I'd had enough of the waiting. I checked the portal one more time, and there was a new announcement from the registrar's office. Yes! I opened it quickly, feeling the stirrings of fear beginning to form. What the fuck?

Grades for yesterday's LS673 Constitutional Law exam are currently being reviewed. Final results are pending. You will be notified when this matter is resolved.

I started to panic as I reread it. Maybe there was a follow-up email? I scanned through my inbox, which was shockingly free of pleas for funds and offers of free sex from bored housewives (my first name earned me loads of those) and found an email from the provost's office sent an hour earlier. I opened it quickly. What the hell was this?

To: L. Gallagher

You are hereby requested to appear before the Ethics Committee today 5/19 at 3:00 to discuss the results of the exam which you submitted on 5/18 at 10:56 AM.

Dean R. Atkins, Co-Chair

The Ethics Committee? Was I being accused of cheating? Oh crap, crap, crap. My first thought was to contact Roger, which I immediately decided was just plain stupid. It was only 7:00 a.m., and I wondered if the exam results would be posted for the rest of the class. Were a group of my classmates crowded around the board, scanning the scores, and seeing a zero posted next to my name? Of course not, everything was coded for privacy purposes. But would they all be guessing at the identity of their classmate with a big fat fucking zero by their code? Oh my God. This was bad. Really bad.

As I pulled on a pair of jeans from the top of my pile of dirty laundry and grabbed a hoodie to wear over my sleep shirt, I debated my course of action. I could check the list, double-check if I had received a grade, and then . . . melt down? Demand an official recount?

Just go, I told myself, slipped into a pair of plastic flip-flops, and grabbed my keys. I flew out the door, hearing it slam shut behind me, and hurried down the hallway. Quiet for a weekday, but classes were over and most of the folks who lived here studied late into the night. I dashed down the steps of the brownstone and hit the sidewalk at a dead run, tossing possible scenarios of how this would play out. Would I be expelled? Given a failing grade for the course and need to retake it in the fall? That was thousands of dollars in tuition and fees I did not have. Maybe a slap on the wrist? By the time I made it to Churchill Hall, I was panting with exhaustion but mostly fear. All these years of hard work, sleepless nights, and debt up to my eyeballs, all for nothing? It wasn't fair, I told myself as I peeked around the corner to the hallway leading to my classroom. Empty. Great, I could scan the board, see what it said, and plot my next move. I moved cautiously down the hall when I heard a voice.

"Hey, Lennon. Here to check the grades? What a ballbuster of an exam, am I right?" I looked up at a pair of smudged spectacles and a spectacular case of bedhead, and then it hit me. Like an unwanted blast of dreadful. Coffee breath. Stale and putrid. If I wasn't so intent on checking the results before going to hide out, I would have gagged. Andrew Something . . . Thomas? Did it really matter?

"Hey, Andrew," I said. "Yeah, what a ballbuster." Idle chitchat? Never, but especially not today. I could see it now. Andrew reporting to the rest of the class about my behavior that morning. *She was in a hurry. Like she knew she was guilty and didn't want to talk to anyone. No, Andrew,* I corrected him silently. *You wanna know why I don't want to chat? Did you ever hear of a toothbrush? No? I didn't think so.*

"How do you think you did?" he asked, all conversational and chatty. I mentally rolled my eyes, imagining what I could say to him if

I were so inclined. *I think I fucked up, man. Pretty sure they're gonna toss my ass out of here later today. Byeeee.*

We were only a few steps from the board as I considered my response. "Hard to say," I said with a shrug. "I never—"

Andrew cut me off as he read from the paper tacked to the middle of the large corkboard. "Well, don't hold your breath," he said with a chuckle. "No results yet."

"Seriously?" I said, pushing past him to check for myself. But there it was: a lone flyer thumb-tacked in the middle of the corkboard with a bold black font.

The results from the yesterday's exam are being withheld, pending a thorough investigation. Students will be notified as more information becomes available.

Professor N. Chan, JD

It seemed like it wasn't just my test results that were in question.

"So, Andrew, did you get an email this morning?" I asked. He smiled at me before shaking his head.

"An email? Yeah, Lennon, of course I did. I read it while I was watching a movie on my Betamax and playing a game on my Atari. Boomer alert." His face glowed with laughter as he continued his diatribe on outdated habits from the 90s or whenever. I was so done with this conversation. I gave a wave I hoped came off as dismissive and turned back the way I had come. Nothing more to do here today.

"Hey, Lennon, I'll send you a friend request on MySpace, okay?" he called after me, and I resisted the impulse to flip him off as I broke into a run.

Back at the dorm, I made a quick pit stop in the lounge area and was delighted to find a freshly brewed pot. I found a cup I was fairly certain was mine and poured, allowing the rich fragrance to fill my head. Maybe it was just some sort of glitch preventing the grades from being displayed, I thought as I sipped contentedly while scrounging around for something. Hadn't I hidden a packet of gas station donettes somewhere not too long ago? I pulled a chair over to the counter and, standing on my tiptoes, managed to find my partially buried treasure. I hopped down and proceeded to unwrap the dry, tasteless little morsels and bit into one quickly. Essentially artificially sweetened sawdust, but what can you do? If I got kicked out of here later today, I would learn to cook real food or at least buy it at the grocery store. With the minimum-wage job I was going to be needing to find and soon, these would be a real treat reserved for weekends or special occasions.

I plopped down on the chair, sipping my coffee and inhaling the donettes, picturing a big, hearty breakfast served up by Randi and Eric. Randi would be devastated when I told her. I had vowed to wait until eight to call her, so I bided my time with my sad meal. Picturing something, anything besides this. Even a gluten-free repast at the home of Seth's parents would be better. Well, that ship had clearly sailed. They liked me, welcomed me into their home and all, but probably warned Seth's younger sisters not to *be* like me. Stay in school, keep curfew, practice piano.

Oh hell, it was twenty minutes to eight. I'd certainly called Randi earlier for a whole lot less. I waited as the phone rang and rang again before—

"Len. We were just talking about you. It's early. What's up?" Hearing her voice, picturing her in a robe the exact twin of mine, sitting at the kitchen island in her beautiful home, drinking coffee with her wonderful husband . . . It all felt just a bit too much, and for the second time in a week, I burst into tears.

•   •   •   •   •

Randi had insisted we needed to prepare for my appointment with the Ethics Committee and would be heading my way shortly. Meanwhile, I was to prepare a timeline of every contact I'd had with Roger and the other members of the study group. Beginning with Erin's rather sudden transformation from classmate to casual friend, the mistaken text from Glen, Roger's bullying when we first met, to the sessions themselves, the creepy dinner, and so on. I took screenshots of everything and, using the calendar in my phone, noted the exact dates and fairly accurate times for everything. I had no witnesses to corroborate my claims of bullying and threats, as Roger had never treated me any differently than anyone else. He was an equal-opportunity creep who used sarcasm and fear to intimidate us and keep us in line. His threats on the consequences for not cooperating weren't in writing nor had they been made when anyone else was nearby. I would have to get every detail down if I wanted to convince the committee of my innocence. And damn it, I was innocent.

I worked in the lounge area, notes and legal pads spread out everywhere, and I felt like I was making good progress. I was typing the details into my tablet when Randi showed up just before ten armed with a large thermos of coffee and a bag containing . . . aaahh, French crullers, my all-time favorite. We hugged briefly, and she unloaded everything before pouring cups of steaming coffee for each of us and selecting a large flaky pastry. She took a huge bite, washed it down with a gulp of coffee, and sighed with satisfaction.

"Whatcha got?" she asked me, and I ran through my hastily assembled timeline.

"I'm certain the dates and times are accurate," I told her. "If I left something blank, it means I'm not sure about the exact time, but the dates are solid."

"How about screenshots? Or any photos of your study group?"

"No photos, but yes to the screenshots. I've got the text messages between Glen and me as well as the ones between Roger and me."

"What about with Erin?" Randi asked, and I groaned.

"We don't know for sure if she's part of this," I said, although the evidence against her was looking pretty solid.

"You don't know what someone might do, Lennon. I'm looking out for you here. Everything is on the table until it's not, okay?" Her tone softened. "Let's not rule anything out at this point." I nodded, and we got back to work, fleshing out my account of all that had occurred since the day I'd first joined the group.

"I'll play devil's advocate," Randi said after several minutes passed. "Ms. Gallagher, you claim to have rejected the exam in question when it was offered to you by Mr. Stevens. But you later contradict yourself by admitting you accepted the exam when Mr. Stevens gave it to you. Can you please explain your actions for the record?"

I took a deep breath and let it out slowly. You got this, I reminded myself. I hadn't done anything wrong, except, of course, not reporting the matter to the very committee that had summoned me today. "When Mr. Stevens held the unmarked manila envelope out to me, I accepted it. It was an automatic response. But when I asked him what it was, and he told me it was the copy of the exam he had mentioned, I tried to give it back to him, but he wouldn't take it, so I dropped it onto the table between us. I told Rog—Mr. Stevens that I wanted no part of this."

Randi was nodding happily. "Perfect. Always answer the question directly. No need for embellishment. Simple, straightforward. If you don't understand the question—"

"Ask for clarification. Got it," I said.

We talked about some of the other possible questions I could be asked, and I added a few more notes to my file. Randi was reading over my shoulder and nodding to herself.

"Do you have access to a printer?" she asked.

"Yes, but it's at the library a couple blocks away."

"How about this? It's just after one. Email me the timeline and the screenshots and then you go and put on one of your new outfits. I'll borrow your access card, go to the library, and print everything out. I'll meet you back here, we'll tie up any loose ends, and you'll be good to go. Sound like a plan?"

I nodded, trying to hold back the tears threatening to fall. What had I ever done to deserve this woman? She always had my back, no matter what. I pretended to search through my backpack to find my access card so she wouldn't see how emotional I was. There was no time for tears today.

"Here you go," I said, handing her my card. She winked at me as she slipped it into her jacket pocket.

"It'll work out, hon, I know it will. Don't worry, okay? Now go get cleaned up, and I'll be back in a bit." She gave a quick wave and headed toward the door. I watched her go as I gathered up the cups and napkins from our snack. I was still apprehensive about my meeting this afternoon, but having talked through all the possible scenarios with Randi, I felt prepared to take on whatever they had for me.

Chapter 21

I sat outside the provost's office later that afternoon. The row of worn wooden chairs with slightly uneven legs communicated loudly and clearly this was not a desirable place to hang out at any time of the day. If you were here, perched on one of the rickety seats, you had to have done something pretty bad. I smoothed my black skirt with palms slick with sweat before I sat on my hands to keep me from twitching and gnawing at what was left of my fingernails. I had my notes, as well as the timeline Randi and I had prepared in my backpack, but we'd decided I should not offer up anything before I knew more about the situation. I couldn't imagine this meeting being about anything other than the stolen exam I had been offered, but you could never be too sure. The door to the office opened, and a man's head popped through, looking around the hallway before lighting on me.

"Ms. Gallagher. Please join us, won't you?" he called out, opening the door wide and motioning me in. There was another man sitting at a round table in the corner as well as a couple familiar faces belonging to Professor Chan and her teaching assistant, Alex. The severity of the situation truly registered for the first time. They hadn't gathered all these people together for a simple misunderstanding or concern. This was the big-time, for sure.

"I'm Dean Atkins," said the man who'd ushered me inside. "And this is Dr. Brennan, our provost, and of course, you know Professor Chan and Mr. Taylor from your class. Let's get started, shall we?" On rubbery legs that couldn't possibly support me much longer, I went and sat in one of the two open chairs. No one was making eye contact with me, I noticed, except for Alex, the TA, and the sense of dread I'd been experiencing hit me anew. I placed my backpack on the floor and resisted the urge to dig for my timeline and my notes. I would wait and see just how bad it was before I produced my evidence.

Dean Atkins cleared his throat before addressing me. "Ms. Gallagher, a situation has come to our attention that determined the need for today's meeting. I hope you know how much we appreciate your willingness to join us on such short notice."

"Yes, sir," I responded quickly.

"Well, there is no sense in beating around the bush. This meeting is in reference to the Constitutional Law final exam you submitted yesterday morning for Professor Chan's class," he said before pausing. *Here it comes.*

"Did you have advance access to that exam prior to entering the classroom yesterday at," he stopped to glance at his notes, "7:48 in the morning?" He scrutinized me carefully as he waited for my response. He didn't need to wait long.

I answered without hesitation. "No, sir, I did not."

"You're saying you did not receive an unauthorized copy of the exam before yesterday?" he pressed.

"No, sir, I did not," I repeated.

"Did you provide another student with an unauthorized copy of the exam?"

I tried to hide my annoyance at this line of questioning. "No, sir," I managed between gritted teeth.

The dean was shaking his head at me. "Then how can you explain this?" he asked, producing a grainy photograph from the file in front of him and handing it to me.

I barely stifled a gasp when I caught sight of the image. There I was, accepting a large manila envelope from a shadowy figure. If I hadn't known for certain it was Roger Stevens, I honestly might have not recognized him. His hulking frame and moon-shaped face were obscured. But how had anyone taken this photo? The only person who could have been responsible was . . . Erin, who had been waiting for me out in the hall. Of course. Erin, my friend, who had ghosted me right after photographing me in what appeared to be a truly compromising position. From this angle, it could be argued I was delivering an advance and illegal copy of a final exam to an unknown accomplice or accepting it from him. Either way, I was screwed.

"It's not what it looks like," I began, realizing that was what guilty individuals always said. "No, I'm serious. I did take the envelope when it was offered to me, but I didn't know what it was. As soon as I did, I attempted to hand it back, but um . . ."

"What you are telling me is that this photograph shows you returning the envelope, *not* delivering it to the other party. Is that correct?"

"Yes, exactly. I tried to give it back, but he held up his hands and wouldn't accept it, so I dropped it on the table and left."

"Can you identify the person in the photo? The one who gave you the envelope and then wouldn't accept it?" Snitches get stitches, I thought, stifling a nervous giggle.

"It's Roger Stevens," I said and saw the knowing glances shared by everyone except for Alex, who was in the midst of an in-depth study of the dark hairs springing out around his wristwatch. Was he counting them? That really was a nice watch he was wearing. Looked expensive, but had to be a knockoff right? TAs didn't make much money. How many exams did he need to sell to afford a watch like that?

"So Mr. Stevens is the person who offered you an advance copy of the final exam?"

"Yes, sir, he is."

"Based upon the image in front of you, who do you think could have taken the photo?"

I didn't have to think twice about my response. "The only likely person is Erin Cooper, sir. She was there that evening, and from her vantage point in the hallway, it's the only logical explanation. She did it, I'm sure."

"And where is that envelope now, to the best of your knowledge?" the dean asked, and I shook my head.

"I don't know," I answered truthfully. "When I left the room, I believe it was still on the table where it would have landed." I was following the suggestions Randi had made and which I knew to be the best course of action when being interrogated. Answer the question. Keep it simple. Don't embellish. But part of me still wanted to assure them I was innocent and was clearly being set up for some unknown reason. I squeezed my hands together in my lap and focused on slowing my breathing, grateful my new blazer hid the flop sweat pouring off my body. I stifled a shiver and tried to focus.

Dean Atkins had more questions needing to be answered. I leaned forward, attempting to demonstrate I would give him whatever information he needed to prove my innocence.

"How well did you know Mr. Stevens prior to him offering to cut you in on the exam?"

"I met him right before the first study session I attended. If I can just . . ." I pulled my notes from my bag and scanned them quickly. "It was April 23rd just before 5:00 p.m." I described how he'd cornered me by the vending machine and asked me about the text I'd received earlier in the day. I saw the dean looking through his own notes before looking up at me with a confused expression on his face.

"What text are you referring to?" he asked.

"I'm glad you asked that." I passed out copies of the screenshots I'd taken from the first text Glen had sent me in error, as well as the "whoops, my bad" text and the one I'd received after I'd gotten home that evening. The one instructing me to not tell anyone. I noticed Alex studying his copy with avid interest, seeming overly concerned about what the messages might contain. Clearly, he was the source, the one who had secured a copy of the exam and sold it to Roger. As a teaching assistant, he would have access to the professor's files. It had to be him. I just needed proof.

"Do you understand why you were asked to come in today?" Professor Chan asked, and I thought about my answer. I was about to say "no, ma'am" when I decided to plead my case.

"I assume it's because you believe I am guilty of cheating on your exam, Professor Chan," I said. "But believe me, I did not cheat. I was offered an advance copy of the exam, and I refused. I realize I should have reported this incident to the committee. I have no excuse for my lapse in judgment, but honestly, I did not believe I would be able to prove it. I studied long and hard for the exam. I'm a strong student, and even though I rarely speak up in class, I'm an excellent test taker." I took a breath before continuing. "I have never cheated in your class or any other class. And that's the truth."

Dean Atkins spoke quietly to Dr. Brennan while Professor Chan looked lost in thought as she rifled through the file in front of her. Alex was studying his fingernails as if he'd only recently been made aware they contained all the secrets of the universe. He was going to go down for this. He had to.

After a silence quickly heading toward awkward, the dean spoke up. "We are still at the information-gathering stage. We will be investigating the incident, but this close to graduation, we need to tread carefully. Do you understand?" I started to nod again before realizing I did not understand. What was happening here?

"I'm sorry, but I don't understand. Will this affect my ability to graduate?" *Me, me, me. It's all about me.*

The dean cleared his throat and met my eyes. "Your exam grade is being held up for now, Ms. Gallagher. There have been conflicting reports as to the identity of the student who accessed a copy of the exam and sold it to their classmates, and at least one report points the finger directly at you."

I drew in a sharp breath, certain I had heard him wrong. But all eyes were on me now, even Alex's little piggy ones. I swallowed hard and willed my bone-dry mouth to form words. "I have a right to face my accusers," I said. "Who is saying it was me?"

"This is not a court of law, Ms. Gallagher," the dean said. "As I said, we are at the beginning stages of our investigation. We will advise you if we need to question you any further." He started to stand, and I knew my time was up, but I could not let it go.

"But what you are not saying is I could be expelled. Kicked out, after all my hard work. I can't believe this. It's not . . . right." I felt close to tears, and that was the last thing this dreadful situation needed, me ugly crying, with tears and snot flying everywhere. I stood and gathered up my notes, shoving them in my backpack. I needed to get out of here fast.

"We will be in touch, Ms. Gallagher," the dean said, and I mumbled my understanding as I crossed the room. I was already through the door when I heard Professor Chan calling my name. I turned and saw her approaching, so I stopped in my tracks. Now what?

She caught up with me and motioned for me to keep walking. We were out in the empty hallway when she gestured for me to follow her into the ladies' restroom. She spoke softly but urgently, and I strained to hear her.

"I know you did not cheat on my exam. And they know it too."

"Then why?" I asked, thoroughly confused.

"You scored a perfect one hundred," she said. "Well done."

I was shocked and even more confused. That alone might make it look like I had cheated. But . . . ?

Professor Chan was smiling now. "I made several last-minute revisions to two of the cases. At first glance, they would be hard to spot, but they were actually quite significant. We questioned the three students who submitted answers to an earlier version of the test. They identified and analyzed issues no longer included and completely missed the new ones. The dumbasses didn't even bother to read the revised cases." She shook her head, a look of disgust marring her elegant features.

"So, if I answered the correct exam, why is my grade being held up? Am I going to be expelled?"

She did not hesitate. "As the dean said, one of the students claims you sold them the exam. They also said you knew it would be revised but did not divulge that information."

"But why?" I asked before the realization came to me. "The seller would know whoever bought the stolen exam might do just what they did. Prep answers for the wrong questions and not take the time to check, and they would get caught and expelled. But why me?"

"Whoever sold the exam would benefit financially," Professor Chan reminded me.

"Of course, and I'm the scholarship kid with a mother fresh out of prison. Who better to blame?"

Professor Chan glanced at her watch before looking back at me. "I need to get back in there, Lennon. I promise I'll do everything in my power to get this resolved as quickly as possible. For now, just lay low and try to be patient."

I nodded my understanding. "Thanks for being straight with me," I said. "For what it's worth, I think you're a really good professor and I learned a lot in your class."

There was a gleam in her eye as she asked me, "Enough to want to join the department and teach law?"

I shook my head. Never in a million freaking years. "Sorry, no," I said. "Family law is what's right for me."

"I expect great things from you, Lennon Gallagher." She patted my arm, turned, and hurried out. I sagged against the wall. I sure hoped she was right.

Chapter 22

I took my time walking home. I was amazed to see from the huge clock on the admin building that it was just after 4:00 p.m. Had I really been in there for only an hour? I tried to unpack all I had learned today. Roger and two other students had submitted answers to an earlier version of the exam. When questioned, at least one of them (it had to be Roger) said I sold them the exam. But what was Alex's role? He had to have taken it from Dr. Chan's file, then delivered it to Roger, knowing it would get sold to other students. Erin had taken the photo of me accepting the envelope from Roger, but why? Was she one of the three students who would be suspended and not be able to graduate? Was a photo of me some form of insurance so they wouldn't take the fall on their own? An opportunity cooked up by her and Roger to cast a wider net of suspects? A chance to cut a deal if either of them could provide more names? If she wasn't one of the three, it made no sense, unless she just wanted to get rid of me, a student she saw as competition. Either way, she had befriended me and betrayed me. With no regard for my feelings, she had been willing to throw me under the bus. I hadn't seen that coming, and I wondered why I had let my guard down with her. I would need to be more vigilant, resume my earlier ways, and build those walls back up. I couldn't trust anyone.

As I climbed the stairs to my room, my phone buzzed. It was Nick.

Hey G- Any chance you're free for dinner?

Were these walls meant to keep me safe and secure from Nick as well? I had no reason to doubt his sincerity and genuine interest in me, but then I hadn't doubted Erin either. Clearly, my judgment was off. Better to be safe . . .

Raincheck. Swamped with work. Lennon

After a minute, he sent his response.

No worries. I'll reach out later.

I read his response and tried to imagine how he was feeling right now. Clearly, he couldn't expect I would be available whenever he felt like seeing me. I barely knew this guy, and I was at the end of a stressful semester and had a ton of to-dos on my plate at the moment. I couldn't sit around moping and worrying I had hurt his feelings. But I did. I listened to my playlist and stared out the window for over an hour, trying to decide if I would head out in search of real food or try to pillage the lounge for leftovers. Or continue to sit here and stew. Crap, now I wanted stew. Lamb stew. I had very few memories relating to family dinners. At least not happy ones. But I do remember my grandma's homemade lamb stew. *Mmmm.* Bubbling on the stove, it made the whole house smell amazing. And the flavor! Slivers of onions, celery and carrots, chunks of potatoes, and lamb so tender it would melt in your mouth. Decision made, I grabbed my keys and headed out the door.

•   •   •   •   •

Half an hour later, I sat in the lounge and happily devoured tender, thin-sliced lamb topped with creamy sauce and wrapped in pillowy-soft pita bread. The Shawarma Empire had come through for me tonight. I hadn't resolved anything regarding the Ethics Committee or Erin's betrayal or the way I'd left things with Nick, but I felt more optimistic somehow. Like I was better equipped to deal with all of this on a full stomach. Satisfied, I gathered up the wrappings and used napkins and went to toss them in the large trash bin. Which was already overflowing! I added my trash and lifted the heavy bag from the bin, tightening the drawstring, and heaved it over my shoulder. Then, for the very first time in two years, nine months, and a few days, I carried it out back to dump it in one of the large receptacles provided. Look at me, I wanted to shout. I'm adulting my ass off here, people. Chuckling to myself, I tossed the bag over the top and listened when it made a satisfying *thunk* as it came into contact with the other trash bags. My work done, I spun around and came face-to-face with none other than Roger Stevens. What the hell? I tried to make my way around him, but his baseball mitt-sized hands shot out and grabbed me by my arms, lifting me off my feet as I struggled and tried to fight him off.

"Let me go, you fucker," I screamed. He tried to cover my mouth, and as soon as his hand came into contact with my face, I bit down as hard as I could, eliciting a scream from my would-be captor. His fingers raked across my face and pain shot through me when he dropped me on my ass in order to examine his boo-boo. Gritting my teeth, I pulled myself upright, frantically searching for a way to escape. His uninjured hand grabbed me again, and he pulled me close to him, angry and snarling like a wounded bear.

"You worthless cunt. Do you know what you've done? Do you have any idea what sort of trouble you've caused me? My father is ready to disown me. They're threatening to kick me out of school. All because you couldn't keep your fucking mouth shut." Drops of spit flew out of his mouth as he ranted, and he began to shake me like I was some sort of rag doll. I pulled back as far as I could, raising my left knee and thrusting with all my might, hitting him squarely in the family jewels. He howled, doubling over in pain, and let go of me in order to cup his injured privates. As I turned to run, I heard the sound of clapping, like a golf clap on steroids. I looked up to see Erin standing near the gate, a wide grin across her face. She waved me over to her, and after checking to make sure I had temporarily incapacitated my attacker, I limped slowly toward her.

"What the fuck, Erin?" I snarled at her. "Were you just gonna let him kick the shit out of me? How could you?"

"From what I could see, you were the one doing all the kicking, darlin'. Although you should have them check out the scratches on that pretty face of yours. But don't worry, I would have stepped in if I thought you needed my help. Sisters before misters, am I right?"

Oh please, that was rich. "What are you doing here? Did you come with him?"

Erin looked disgusted at the very idea. "No, but I followed him. He stopped by my place to bitch me out, blaming me for bringing you into the group in the first place. I told him to get fucked. He took off like a bat out of hell, and I just knew he was heading straight to you. And here we all are. Oh, and I called the cops. They're on their way."

"A phone call to me would have been nice. A heads-up to let me know I was in danger." The fight-or-flight rush of adrenaline had left me feeling shaky, and the sharp pain radiating from my tailbone had traveled up my spine. All I wanted was a long hot shower or a soak in a warm tub. Roger was still whimpering, now curled in a fetal position. What a big baby!

"I did call you," Erin said. "Like twenty minutes ago. You didn't answer, and I figured you were still mad at me."

I stared at her, amazed. "Mad doesn't begin to cover it, *darlin'*. You lied to me, and you hurt me . . ." The lump in my throat refused to go away, and I turned away from her, knowing I was ready to cry.

The police sirens that were a constant in this neighborhood grew louder. It sounded like they were . . . Holy shit, two cruisers with lights flashing pulled into the parking area, followed by an ambulance. Erin hurried over to explain the situation to the officer exiting the first vehicle. I watched in amazement as Roger was questioned, read his Miranda rights, and got himself carried off on a stretcher. The medics approached me next and, after questioning me and checking my injuries, called for a second ambulance. Erin sat with me while we waited and I was grateful for her company.

• • • • •

Two hours later, I was released from the hospital. No sign of a concussion had been found, so after the police took my statement, the detective in charge of the investigation offered me a ride home. I gratefully accepted, asking about Roger's arraignment as we pulled up in front of my building.

"Should be at the Pearl Street Courthouse as early as 8:00 a.m.," the young woman replied. "I can pick you up," she added, but I thanked her and said I would get there on my own.

I collapsed in bed after hobbling painfully up the stairs. While I was waiting to be examined, I had reached out to Nick, and he and I had been texting back and forth this whole time. I wanted to let him know I was back home.

I'm home About to crash

He replied in an instant.

I wish you would let me pick you up
You should see my bedside manner

It was tempting, but no.

Raincheck. Just need sleep
G'night G I'll reach out tomorrow

I set my alarm for 6:30 to allow time to get cleaned up before I called for an Uber to the courthouse. I fell asleep quickly thanks to the muscle relaxant they had administered in the ER.

A few short hours later, I dragged my bruised and battered self to the shower. It hurt too much to brush my teeth, so I settled for a quick gargle with mouthwash instead. My wet hair remained plastered to my head because I was unable to lift my arms to try to get a comb in the general vicinity. I pulled on the most comfortable clothes I could find and stumbled down the stairs to wait for Terry in a red Subaru.

The courthouse appeared fairly deserted as we pulled up several minutes later. I thanked the driver and limped slowly up the stairs, slipping through the heavy oak doors behind a trio of young women all chattering away. I made it through security after only a cursory glance at the contents of my backpack and asked the first guard I saw which courtroom I needed to be in. I got directed to number seven, and I slipped inside and watched as Roger was led in through a side door and presented before the judge sitting way down in front. He was limping and looked as if he'd had the proverbial shit kicked out of him. And he had! I made my way to an empty seat in the first row and settled in to watch. It was over very quickly. The judge read a list of charges, including assault and battery and reckless endangerment. He concluded by asking Roger how he pled, and there was a brief pause before a husky voice replied, "Not guilty." He sounded a lot less sure of himself than he usually did, and I imagined a night in jail would do that to a person. Roger's attorney requested bail be set, and before I knew it, Roger was being led back through the door, probably to his holding cell while his release was processed. As I stood, a wave of dizziness hit me, and I held on to the back of the bench as I waited for it to pass. A few minutes later, I was out on the sidewalk, caught up in the bustle of pedestrians hurrying to work. The air felt wonderful compared to the stuffy confines of the courthouse, and I realized I was famished. I entered the next coffee shop I saw, grabbed a stool at the counter, and ordered. My butt hurt like hell, but seconds later I was sipping a decent cup of joe and, a few minutes after that, attacking a large platter of French toast drowning in maple syrup. It was delightful.

Chapter 23

When I got back to my room, the first thing I did was call Randi. She was walking into a courtroom down in New London, but I managed to give her a condensed and well-edited version of Roger's visit and his subsequent arrest. She ended the call with a terse, "To be continued, Len," and I knew I would eventually be grilled by the best lawyer I'd ever known.

The next call was a tricky one, but after my third cup of diner coffee, I had decided it was a must. I dug around in my backpack and found the business card I was looking for, leaned back against the headboard, and dialed.

"Dean Atkins's office," a brisk, no-nonsense voice answered.

"Good morning. My name is Lennon Gallagher, and I'm—"

"I'll put you right through, Ms. Gallagher." A couple clicks, then the dean's booming baritone.

"Good morning, Ms. Gallagher. I was expecting your call. How are you doing? I understand you suffered quite the ordeal last evening."

What the hell? How did he know about last night?

"Um, yes, sir. I'm doing fine, just fine. I'm calling to—"

"All has been resolved. Your friend explained everything. We're releasing your exam grade, and your record is clear. We'll be seeing you at commencement very soon."

My friend? Now I was thoroughly confused. I had landed on my ass last night, so why was my brain all scrambled? "I'm sorry, sir. Maybe I did suffer a concussion after all. What friend are you referring to?"

"Why, Ms. Cooper, of course. She left my office not a half hour ago. She explained how she had been tricked into taking a photo of you receiving an envelope from Mr. Stevens."

Stunned by what I was hearing, I realized it was my turn to speak. *Say something!* "Oh yes. Tricked . . ."

"Apparently, she believed it was some sort of romantic gesture on Mr. Stevens's part and he had hoped you would open it and, well, I guess jump up and down or something and say 'Yes, I'll marry you, Roger.'"

"I'm sure she was surprised when I refused to open the, um, proposal, huh?"

"Yes, at least until he arrived at your dorm last night. She explained how the two of you were drinking tea and chatting when Roger came barreling in and attacked you. Then she called 911 and he was arrested. She was shocked to find out later what the envelope had actually contained. She said he was a loose cannon, and you were glad to be rid of him."

"Well, she got that right. So as far as the stolen exam . . . are the three students, um, expelled?" I wanted to ask if Erin was one of them, but based on this conversation, I had to assume she was not. How had she managed that?

"Well, that is, of course, quite confidential. But I'm sure the rumor mill will be buzzing despite our best efforts. If there's nothing else, then, I have a meeting to get to."

"Sure, yes, sir. Thank you, sir. Goodbye."

I went back and forth, then decided to text Erin.

Creative fiction much? Yur quite the storyteller.

Her response came immediately. **Yur a badass. He's a cunt.**

Hmmm. **Thanks.**

CU soon.   

I stared at my phone for a couple minutes before powering it down and tossing it on my nightstand. Surely, all this would make much better sense after a nap. I crashed hard and slept for several hours and woke feeling much better. Achy and sore, but restless, eager to do something. I assumed Randi was still tied up in court, so I reached out to Nick.

Went to arraignment then French toast. Off the hook at UCONN. U?

Three dots appeared right away. **Feeling better? I heart f toast.**

I was about to respond with a suggestion that maybe we could have breakfast sometime, but he beat me to it.

Up for dinner tonight?

Oh boy, was I ever. Play it cool, I told myself. Hard to get. Oh, fuck it. Life was too short to play games.

Yes. When? Where? I waited as the three bouncing dots did their thing, then finally . . .

How's 6? I'll come to you

Sounds great. See you soon

I considered adding a heart emoji, but before I could, he "loved" my last text. I had a very good feeling about the night ahead, ripe with all sorts of possibilities.

My doubts about letting myself be vulnerable had lessened since last night. I still wouldn't completely trust someone like Erin, but I needed to believe I was a good person, someone who was worthy of being loved. Being cautious didn't require I live like a hermit. I had a good feeling about Nick, and spending time with him was the best way to find out if I could learn to trust him completely.

I had plenty of time to fix my hair and makeup and pick out an outfit to wear. He hadn't said where we were going, but I figured I couldn't go wrong with a pair of dark-wash, straight-leg jeans, a plain white T-shirt, and my blazer. It was technically our third date, if you counted meeting at his restaurant when I was with Roger as our first date and the pizza debacle with Seth in the lounge as the second. And wasn't the third date the one where you . . . ? I grabbed my shower stuff and hightailed it to the bathroom. Time to primp for my second-ever third date.

•   •   •   •   •

Right at 6:00 p.m., the buzzer rang, and as I stepped into the cramped vestibule, I could see him through the filmy glass panels. Had he gotten cuter, or was it my imagination? I opened the door eagerly. Nope, definitely even cuter. He was dressed casually in jeans and a dark green Henley shirt with the sleeves pushed up, revealing well-muscled forearms. His hair color was lighter than I recalled, or maybe he had gotten it cut. Either way, he looked so handsome, and I was thrilled at the thought of spending the evening with him.

"Hi, Nick," I said, and he smiled back at me.

"Hey, G, you look amazing. I'm glad you could get together tonight. You feeling good?"

"A little sore, but I'm fine. It's great to see you," I told him. "So where are we heading?"

"It's a little out of the way, but I think you'll like it. Are you all set?" I nodded in agreement, and after locking the door behind me, I followed him out the door and down the steps. In one pocket, I had a wallet containing my license, a twenty-dollar bill, and a card that might have another twenty-dollar credit available, and in the other, my phone, housekeys, and a tube of lip gloss. I was good to go and ready for most any occasion.

"I parked over here," he said, indicating a late-model sedan wedged into a tiny parking spot between two SUVs. He opened the passenger's door for me and, after I was seated, closed the door and headed over to the driver's side. He started the car, and it was so quiet I thought it had stalled. At my look of surprise, he shrugged. "Electric," he said, and I leaned back into my seat, marveling at how relaxing a car ride could be when the car was not huffing and puffing all the time. He pulled out into traffic and expertly navigated his way through the congested downtown streets.

"So how did today go?" he asked. "The arraignment?"

"He was charged and released on bail, but I gotta say it was very satisfying to see his smug, fat face looking all sad and broken. Prick," I added.

He gave my hand a quick squeeze, a grin on his gorgeous face.

"Glad to hear it. So what happened at the school? You said you're off the hook?" He reached for my hand again. Sweet! I took the opportunity to explain how Erin had come through in the end, and we both had a good laugh at the thought of Roger and me getting engaged.

"Are you telling me I might have a chance with you?" he teased. "Now that old Rog is out of the picture."

"I think your chances are quite good," I told him with a smile. This was already the best date I had ever been on, and we hadn't even gotten to where we were going yet!

We found street parking and walked half a block to what appeared to be an abandoned storefront. There was a small sign that said *Nari's*. I was surprised when Nick led me into a dimly lit room totally devoid of any décor or charm but smelling heavenly. An older woman wearing pink scrubs and a colorful apron nodded at Nick, and he said something to her I could not understand. I followed the two of them to the only empty table. The other dozen or so diners were speaking in low voices and appeared to be enjoying their meals. I assumed the food had to be good as there was no ambiance whatsoever, save for a strand of string lights left over from Christmas.

"You are full of surprises," I said. "How did you find this place?"

"I'm fairly certain it found me," he said with a grin. "Okay if I order for both of us?" he asked as the woman approached carrying a small pad of paper. She reached up and pulled a small pencil out of her elaborate updo, greeting us in a language I'd never heard before. I stared in amazement as Nick responded in what must have been the same dialect as the woman smiled and nodded at him. The two went back and forth a couple times, conversing before she nodded a final time and disappeared behind a curtain to what must be the kitchen.

"You speak Chinese?" I asked Nick, who shook his head.

"A little Cantonese, but that was Korean you just heard." He shrugged as if coming to a place like this and ordering a meal in a foreign language was an everyday occurrence. "If you're wondering, I ordered us soup and sandwiches."

A young boy came by with glasses of water, silverware rolled in heavy linen napkins, a steaming pot of tea, and two little cups. Nick said something to him, making him laugh, and I marveled once more at this fascinating man I'd had the good fortune to meet. He was sweet and funny, and man, was he ever hot. He poured me a cup, and I breathed in the steamy floral fragrance.

"Jasmine?" I guessed, and he nodded.

"Blended with citrus, I believe," he added and took a long sip. I followed suit. Mmmm. So good.

Minutes later, we were feasting on kalguksu, a chicken soup with zucchini, carrots, and mushrooms, and banh mi, crispy baguette sandwiches stuffed with meats and pickled vegetables. Nick explained both dishes and assured me he'd ordered everything "not too spicy for first time here" girl.

"I like it spicy," I assured him with a wink, even though my tongue felt like it was already on fire and a fine sheen of perspiration coated my forehead and upper lip. He grinned at me, and I noticed he appeared to be cool and comfortable.

"Challenge accepted," he said and waved the young boy over. Nick spoke quickly, and after a quick glance in my direction, the boy gave a thumbs-up and disappeared behind the curtain, returning quickly with a small bowl of something brown and chunky. He placed it on the table between us and hurried off.

"What is this?" I asked.

"Kimchi," Nick said in reverent tones. "It's the very definition of spicy."

"What do I do with it?" I asked, and he leaned toward me, using his chopsticks and scooping up a portion of what looked like a mixture of vegetables.

"You eat it," he said and gasped a little as the flavors exploded in his mouth. "Christ, that's hot," he managed while reaching for his water and downing it in one gulp. "Seriously, G, you don't have to try it. I was just teasing you."

"Challenge accepted," I said with mock gravity. I speared the smallest amount I could and popped it in my mouth. "For the love of sweet . . . Are you kidding me right now?" I downed my own glass of water and held out my empty glass to be refilled by the boy who stood watching from nearby. He said something to Nick, who smiled and nodded. The two did some weird fist-bump bro thing before the boy disappeared again.

"What is that?" I asked. "And here I thought jalapenos were the spiciest thing on the planet."

Nick shook his head and downed more water. "Kimchi is a popular Korean side dish, made with salted and fermented vegetables. There are countless different recipes, but I like it here because its super flavorful but not usually a five-alarm fire. My young friend must have been having a go with me." He looked up, and we saw the boy watching us from behind the curtain. Nick shook his fist at him. "I'm on to your tricks, Chul," he said in English with a wide grin.

The woman in the brightly colored apron approached, and once more Nick spoke her language. She nodded briskly and called out something to our young waiter. He carefully stacked our dishes and carried everything off on a tray. He returned a few minutes later and placed a glass bowl between us. I stared, mesmerized by the artful arrangement as well as the recognizable ingredients.

"Don't tell me, let me guess. Shaved ice, fruit, and what looks like beans?"

"Very good. This is bingsu and it's a real treat; even the beans are sweet," he added, noting my confusion over the unusual pairing. "And these," he said, pointing to the small plate of rice cakes that had just arrived, "are tteok. Very chewy, not spicy."

"I trust you," I said and sampled both desserts. The shaved ice was cold, sweet, and tangy and took away some of the residual burn from the dinner. The rice cakes were simply delicious, especially when followed by a second cup of tea Nick poured for me. "This has been such a fabulous meal, but are you really not going to tell me how you found this place?"

His gaze grew thoughtful, and it seemed he was thinking of something sad. He shook his head as if to clear his thoughts and looked at me. "I guess it's technically mine," he said.

"Yours? What, you mean this restaurant?" Now I was confused. He seemed embarrassed as he began to explain.

"A long time ago, my parents hired an au pair from Korea. Her name was Lily, and she was the most delightful young woman I'd ever met." He shook his head again. "But keep in mind, I was only eight and hadn't met very many young ladies. But Lily? She was special. She lived with us, drove me back and forth to school, did homework with me, fixed me a snack every day after school. She even took me shopping for school supplies and presents for the birthday parties I went to." He smiled at me, but it was a sad smile.

"But what does that have to do with the restaurant?" I asked, but I was already starting to sense what he was about to say.

Nick's hazel eyes glistened with unshed tears, and right then I began to fall in love with him. This was a man who was not afraid to express his feelings, and I was hooked. Maybe I hadn't been closed in, on emotional lockdown for all these years when it came to romance and intimacy. Maybe, just maybe, I had never found someone I felt comfortable enough with to share my feelings. "Lily came to us when she was eighteen. The agency where we found her had a strict one-year policy, but she became a part of the family, so my parents paid off her contract and hired her as a full-time employee, got her medical benefits and all that. It wasn't like one of those situations you hear about where she wasn't allowed to . . ." I put my hand on his to stop him. He didn't owe me any explanations.

"What happened to Lily?" I asked, and he took a sip of the now tepid tea and closed his eyes. "It's okay, you don't have to . . ." but he started talking.

"When she turned twenty-one, she went out with some friends to celebrate her birthday. They were crossing the street, and a drunk driver hit her. Lily died at the scene." He wiped at his eyes with his napkin. "What a waste!" he added.

I reached for his hand again. "Oh, Nick, that's so horrible. That must have been so traumatic. You were what, eleven?"

"Yeah, it was a shock for all of us. It was the first time anyone I knew died. Anyone young, I mean. We notified her family in Korea, and my parents paid to have Lily's mother fly here for the service. She stayed with us for a while and ended up getting an apartment of her own. She found work as a cook in a couple local spots."

I thought about the woman who had seated us, who appeared to run the place. "Wait, are you telling me that's . . . ?" Nick nodded.

"Mi Cha is Lily's mother," he said. "I wanted to help her out, so last year we found this space, and she got it up and running." He looked around proudly. "I have been around family restaurants my entire life, but this place is my favorite." I remembered the small placard near the door when we'd arrived.

"So does Nari's mean Lily's?" I asked, and he nodded.

"Yes," he said simply, and we held hands across the table and were silent for a time. I wanted to take his pain away, to make it disappear. I couldn't recall feeling so connected to anyone. Ever. I felt like I was . . . home, but not like any place I had ever known.

Chapter 24

Mi Cha, or Mimi, as Nick called her, never brought us a check, but I saw him slip a few bills to young Chul, and as we left, he placed an envelope on the table. He caught me watching him and smiled, putting a finger to his lips.

"Mimi's too proud to charge me for dinner, but I like to help her out when I can." I squeezed his hand, and he squeezed back. On the short walk back to the car, he pulled me closer to him.

"There's something I've been wanting to do all night," he said, a crooked grin lighting up his handsome face. He leaned in and whispered in my ear. "If it's okay with you, G."

Kiss me. Please kiss me. And he did. If it was possible, it was even better than the kiss we had shared last week in the lounge, my ex-boyfriend passed out and snoring just ten feet away. That kiss was more exploratory, like "*Hmmm*, what do we have here?" Tonight's kiss was more "I see you, and I want you," and believe me, it was mutual. When we finally came up for air, my lips actually missed his and my legs were the consistency of rubber.

We walked arm in arm to the car, and after we buckled up, he turned to me. "Do you want to come home with me?" he asked, clearly hoping I would say yes. And I did say yes. Sort of. I was kind of flustered, you might say.

"Your, um, tiny one, you mean?" I stammered before groaning after I realized what I had said.

"I'll let you be the judge," he said, stifling a laugh. "But I do try to overcompensate in other ways. So is that a yes?"

I struggled against the confines of my seat belt as I leaned over to whisper to him. "That's a yes."

All the way to his house, he talked about his childhood, expressing gratitude for his parents and their willingness to allow him to pursue his interests over the years, including mountain biking in Colorado on several occasions and hiking through the Alps with a friend at the age of eighteen. "I really had to pay for that one," he added. "Not financially, but I had to agree to go to cooking school in Milan the following summer."

I stared at him in amazement. "Cooking school? Where did that come from?"

He suddenly looked uncomfortable and focused all his attention on the road as he answered me. "It's a rite of passage to us Russos, you might say," he said with a shrug. "It's in our DNA. But hey, enough of that. We're here."

Pulling onto the grounds of the Russo family home, I gasped at the enormity of it all. Rolling hills, pockets of densely packed trees, and a long and winding road taking us right through it. Nick caught my eye. "Twenty-three acres," he said casually, "but much of it's wooded." After several minutes, he parked beside an adorable tiny house featuring a wraparound porch and gray weathered shingles. It was perfect, just miniaturized down to the last detail.

"Home at last," he said and came around and opened the passenger door for me as if he had been doing it his whole life. He had a certain grace and the kind of personality that would shine on a country club golf course or a hole-in-the-wall Asian restaurant. What the hell was he doing with me?

"You get the five-second tour," Nick told me as he took my arm and led me inside. The interior lighting must have been voice-activated or maybe motion-sensitive because the whole space was suddenly bathed in light. I looked around, totally enthralled by what I was seeing. If modern design and functional living had a baby . . . Yeah, just like that. It was stylish with a compact layout featuring large windows for loads of natural light. I stared out, entranced by the sight of the sun quickly disappearing behind the western hills.

"Magical," I told him with a smile.

"Magical," he agreed, his eyes focused on me. I felt a thrill, a warmth spreading through me, turning my heart to mush. At the risk of seeming too eager, I forced myself to look away and focused on the space's unique design. Still standing in the doorway, I took in the open living area featuring a sleek sofa in a nubby teal fabric, flanked by a pair of cream-colored wing chairs. A live edge oak coffee table I imagined could do double duty as a space for dining sat on a plush carpet. Ahead of me, I could see a well-designed kitchen featuring minimalist cabinetry, what appeared to be high-end appliances, and an island that fit perfectly in the space.

"Bathroom's in there," Nick pointed to a door on the left, "and up there is the sleeping loft," he said, indicating a set of stairs leading to a loft area. "Do you want something to drink? I have sparkling water, herbal tea, seltzer."

I shook my head. "No, I'm good."

He approached me and placed his warm hands on my shoulders, studying me closely. "I would very much enjoy having you stay the night, but how do you feel?" he asked and waited for me to respond. I leaned closer to him and kissed him lightly on the lips, pulling back just long enough to whisper, "Oh, hell yeah."

"I'll meet you upstairs," he said with a flash of that grin of his, and I hightailed it to the bathroom. It was sleek and modern with a walk-in shower and high-end finishes. And loads of plush soft towels in a variety of sizes, all in a rich teal. I rested my warm forehead against the cool tile, trying to control my breathing. You got this, I told myself, but I was having second thoughts. Not that I didn't want to sleep with him, because I did. But was it too soon after Seth? Probably. And was it likely Nick would run for the hills when he discovered I was hardly more than a feral alley cat with a smart mouth and social skills possibly on par with an employee at the DMV? Definitely.

But I wanted this. I wanted him. I splashed some water on my face, spread a tiny ribbon of toothpaste on my finger, and ran it over my teeth. When I was done, I cast an appraising glance at my reflection, noting my flushed cheeks and sparkling eyes. I couldn't do anything about the scratches and a bruise from last night's mishap. I tousled my short, dark hair and grinned. "Get some," I told myself and went to climb the ladder to Nick's sleeping loft. I found him lying under the covers—naked, I presumed—and looking good enough to cause me to shed my own clothing and slide in next to him.

"Hey, you," he said. "I was beginning to think you changed your mind."

"No way," I assured him. "I'm exactly where I want to be."

•   •   •   •   •

Nick was attentive and gentle, and I felt comfortable with him from the start. As we explored each other, constantly delighting in what we found, every kiss felt electric, each caress an instant connection. He was so expressive, so confident in his lovemaking, I found myself letting go of my insecurities about my body and letting him know what I needed, what I wanted. I felt beautiful and desirable, powerful yet vulnerable. We stayed up until dawn, making love, talking, and eating bowls of granola with coconut milk. Would I have preferred Cap'n Crunch and whole dairy? Well, certainly, but it was fine. More than fine. It was great. At the risk of sounding kind of cheesy, we just . . . fit. It was like we were made for each other. All the chats and texts we had exchanged made being with him feel safe but thrilling as well. Had I found a place where I made sense? A person I made sense with? At one point in the night, Nick had murmured, "You're home with me, G," and I knew he was right.

After a couple hours of sleep, I woke to the feel of a rough tongue and the odor of bad breath, followed by the sound of panting. I opened my eyes and found myself staring into a pair of big brown eyes.

"Danny Boy," I called out, and the magnificent animal wriggled with joy, delighted by the sound of his name. I allowed him to continue licking my face and sniffing me happily. Seconds later, Nick's head appeared at the top of the ladder.

"G, I'm so sorry. Danny, you know you're not supposed to be up here," he said, sounding only half-serious. "C'mon, boy, let's let our guest have some coffee first, huh?" He placed a tray on the floor in front of him, then bounded up the last few rungs. Danny approached the tray, and after giving the coffeepot and mugs a thorough sniffing and realizing there were no treats for him, he hopped back up on the bed, curled himself into a ball, and closed his eyes.

Nick poured two cups and came back to sit next to me on the edge of the bed. "I really am sorry," he said. "He's just not used to me having company." *Hmmm.* That was interesting. I decided a smart-assed comeback was not needed in this instance.

I took a sip of the coffee. "Heavenly," I murmured. "He's fine. I've never been woken up by being licked," I said.

Nick cocked an eyebrow as he studied me closely. He started to say something, then stopped, shaking his head. "No, it's too easy," he said with a laugh. He leaned in to kiss me, and it was the kind of kiss that made my toes curl. It was the kind of kiss that made me want to pull him back into bed and replay some of last night's highlights. But he was already dressed and looked like he wanted to say something else. I sat against the cushy headboard, sipped my coffee and listened. "I went up to the house earlier to get Danny. My folks and I share custody. My dad was on a call but said he needed to talk to me about something. To come back in an hour. So Danny and I took a walk here to see you. I've got to get back up there soon. Can you sit tight for maybe an hour, and I'll finish up and drive you home? Or if you can't stick around, I'll call for a ride for you. What do you think?"

"Um, well it's early, not even eight yet. I don't have to go in to work until one, so yeah, I can stay for a while, I guess." I didn't have anything to read or study, so maybe I could . . .

"There's loads of books on the shelves downstairs," he said, "and there is a TV." Danny chose this moment to rejoin our circle of two and sprawled out, his head in my lap. I got an idea.

"Can I take him for a walk?" I asked. I'd never had the pleasure of walking a dog, and it suddenly seemed like the best thing I could do right now. Nick studied me closely.

"He's a good boy, but if he sees a squirrel or a rabbit, he's off like a rocket."

"Now that I know there might be rabbits, I really want to take him," I said, and Nick agreed.

"I let him off the leash sometimes, but there's a den of foxes nearby this spring and the kits are still getting acclimated. Danny can be a bit of a distraction," he said, and I promised I would hold on to the leash with all my might.

"We'll be downstairs," Nick told me and picked up his dog. Turns out although Danny was quite adept at climbing up the ladder to the loft, he needed to be carried down.

I slipped into my clothes from last night and brushed my teeth with a brand-new brush Nick had laid out for me. Minutes after Nick left the house and started walking up the path, I set out the other way with Danny Boy.

So here I was walking a large golden-coated dog around the grounds of a lovely country estate. If Char could see me now, she would totally freak out, I thought with a smile. I could clearly picture her telling me, "Girl, you stick with him, you hear? He might be half Eyetalian, but he's rich, so don't fuck it up now." Just then, it felt like my shoulder was getting yanked out of its socket. A trio of baby rabbits darted across the path about fifty feet from us, and Danny took off after them like the rocket Nick had warned me about. He pulled me along with him as we chased the bunnies to the edge of the woods.

"No, Danny," I scolded him as we both stood there, me gasping for breath and Danny clearly puzzled at the disappearance of his three new playmates. "C'mon, boyo," I said and pulled him with me to the path. I didn't have my phone on me, and I had a crap sense of time, but I figured we should be heading back. Danny had let off some steam, and I was feeling pleasantly spent myself, so we took our time making our way back to the tiny house.

We arrived to find Nick sitting on the deck, clearly happy to see us. He came down the steps and, after patting Danny on the head, wrapped me in a big hug. He released me long enough to kiss me, a slow, sweet kiss I doubted I could ever grow tired of.

"I could get used to this," he said with a grin. "You, me, Danny Boy, our own little family." *Danger, danger!* My brain waves were going haywire. Family? My face must have given me away because Nick let out a chuckle. "Don't worry, G, I won't rush you into anything, I promise."

"It's not you, it's me," I assured him. Over the last few weeks, I had told Nick a great deal about my jailbird mother, my missing-in-action father, and the string of foster homes ranging from pretty bad to completely dreadful. It had been easy—well, sort of easy—to share over the phone or via text messages, less so when I could see his face. Although in his defense, he was a lot less prone to looks of shock or sadness or anger than the few other people I'd trusted with my crap. That's what always got me. School counselors, doctors, group home administrators—they all say they want you to open up and give them all the sad-ass details of your fucked-up life, but when it came down to it, after a few gasps or looks of horror in response, I would just shut down. "You can't handle the truth," I'd wanted to shout at them and expose all their good intentions as fraudulent.

"I know, babe," he said simply. And despite his upbringing and his lord-of-the-manor lifestyle, I believed he really did.

"You in a hurry? Want more, um, coffee?" he asked, giving me a look that said he wanted me, not coffee. I agreed happily, and we scooted up to the loft. Nick lifted the ladder so, try as he might, Danny was unable to join us.

Last night's lovemaking had been passionate but slow, relaxed, like we had all the time in the world to learn what the other person wanted. This morning was more frenzied, almost rushed, as if time were running out. It was all quite fabulous, and the only thing I wanted was more.

Chapter 25

As I was getting dressed in last night's clothing for the second time that morning, I remembered something. "How did your talk with your father go?" I asked Nick. "Was it just a chat or—" I stopped as his expression grew serious and he began to fiddle with the cord on his hoodie. Had I hit a nerve? "Nick?" I began, but he pulled me in for a hug.

We ended up sitting cross-legged on the floor, facing each other, our knees touching. He seemed embarrassed by what he had to say, and I assured him he could tell me anything. That whatever it was, I would support him. All the while, I was thinking to myself, "Please don't be something bad."

"You know how I said I went to cooking school in Milan one summer?" he asked, and I nodded.

"You said your parents let you go backpacking in the Alps if you went."

"I didn't tell you the truth, G. Not the whole truth. And now it's too late." I felt the first prickles of fear start to form, and I studied him closely as I asked him what was too late. "Cooking school was already on the table. It was a given, kind of like a rite of passage. I was able to negotiate the Alps trip as a bribe for being a good sport about it."

I was now thoroughly confused as I saw how upset he was getting. It had happened five or six years earlier, and I couldn't imagine what it had to do with today. "Spell it out for me, Nick. I can handle it. What's going on?"

"I have to go to Italy this summer and finish cooking school. I'll be gone for six months," he said flatly, and I felt myself start to panic. Six months wasn't all that long, but we had only just started seeing each other. What would . . . ? "But it gets worse," he added. "When I'm done, they want me to open the next Russo's restaurant out in San Francisco or possibly Los Angeles." I fell against him, too stunned to cry. He held me close while I struggled to slow my breathing. Finally, I straightened up and spoke.

"Nick, I'm so sorry . . ." I began, but he shook his head.

"I'm the one who should be sorry, G. I should have, I don't know, eased into it. I had no right to just hit you with all of this. You've shared all your family drama and everything you've been through with me, and I've led you to believe I've led this happy, privileged life. That I'm the king of the frigging castle. That's on me, babe. And I'm sorry. Truly."

"But why cooking school? And why now?"

He explained how his parents had always had a plan for him, one that included his finishing cooking school before opening a brand-new Russo's on the West Coast. He'd been granted a three-year reprieve after earning his degree in order to complete the novel he was working on, get published, and establish a writing career. If that didn't work out, he had to finish the culinary degree, join the family business, and earn his place in the Russo empire. The deadline had seemed plenty long enough to Nick until today, when his father told him his time was up. There was a spot reserved at the same school Nick attended previously. In less than six weeks, he would be moving to a family villa outside of Milan and going to cooking school.

"I feel like I've led you on, G," he said. "I shouldn't have let things get this far. It's not fair to you to wait for me to return from Italy. And I can't expect you to move to California next year either."

"I'm a big girl," I assured him. "It'll be okay," I lied as I gathered up my things. This was too much to unpack all at once. I needed some space to process everything. "Can you take me home now? I've got to get to work."

Nick told Danny to be a good boy and we left, driving fast along the narrow paved road toward the surface streets leading to the highway and the three-story brownstone I would call home for just a few more weeks. "I'm sorry," I said finally, more to break up this awkward cone of silence that had taken over than to express actual regret. What did I have to be sorry about? I was in shock, had no time to prepare for this kind of news, and I couldn't think of anything else to say.

I stole a glance at him and watched the way he stared resolutely at the windshield and the way he gripped the steering wheel, his knuckles white with tension. And his taut jawline, just lightly covered with a smattering of pale stubble. I leaned over and placed a hand on his right leg.

"It's okay, Nick. We can figure something out, if you want to, I mean."

He loosened his grip on the steering wheel long enough to grasp my hand in his. "I want to, G. More than you can possibly imagine," he said, not even trying to hide the catch in his voice and the tears pooling in his hazel eyes. And I believed him.

•   •   •   •   •

Nick dropped me home just after eleven. With all that had already happened today, I felt ready to hop in bed and go to sleep, but I needed to get dressed, pick up something for lunch, and be at the office by one. But how, with all the thoughts swirling around in my sleep-deprived brain, was I supposed to manage all that? The news Nick had shared with me left me reeling. I needed to talk through this. There was only one person who could help me work this out. Still dripping from the shower, I wrapped myself in my favorite robe, quickly towel-dried my hair, and padded back down to my room. Once inside, I grabbed my phone and hit one of my recently called numbers.

I leaned against my headboard and settled in, hoping like crazy I didn't get voicemail. It rang several times before I heard a familiar voice.

"Hey, you okay?" At the sound, I could feel my resolve slipping away. Maybe this wasn't such a good idea. "Lennon, talk to me," Nick said. "Please."

I let out a breath and I talked. And Nick listened to me, really listened. I told him how sad I was his family had this plan for him, how disappointed I felt. "You don't want to be a chef, and you don't want to manage a restaurant. I just don't understand this."

"It's really pretty simple. I made a promise, G. I have to live up to it," he said, sounding impossibly old and tired. Resigned. Yes, he sounded resigned. "And I'll be home by Christmas. Maybe the California plans won't even happen. My cousin is supposed to be scouting locations, but who knows? It might not be . . . all that bad." I couldn't argue with him any further. I needed to accept it and move on. I couldn't bear the thought of losing him, but the time we had left together was so short, and I didn't want to waste it by being upset.

"Let's try to have some fun and really enjoy ourselves before you've got to head out. Deal?"

"Deal," he said, and we made plans to get together later in the day. I ended the call and dashed around to get ready for work. What were the chances? Girl meets boy, boy travels to Italy to fulfill family promise, girl . . . ? To be continued.

Chapter 26

Despite my need to keep my head in the game, I felt out of sorts that afternoon at the law firm. I filed briefs, typed up notes, and generally performed my duties, but my thoughts were elsewhere. There was still so much to do, so many loose ends to tie up. I needed to resolve the "Who's my daddy?" issue sooner rather than later. And commit to a study schedule for the upcoming bar exam. And find a job. And spend some time with my mother. Her texts had morphed from whiny to downright hostile over the past week. Oh yeah, and spend as much time as humanly possible with my new boyfriend so he doesn't fall for some hottie in Milan. And just where the hell was Milan anyway? My phone buzzed when a group text came in.

I want everyone in the conference room right away. Cal

I looked around to see my fellow interns powering their computers down and gathering their belongings. We were used to shuffling between open desks and never left anything behind. I followed the other interns into the seventh floor conference room and grabbed a seat closest to the door. I looked around me, noting the neat and orderly décor, the shocking lack of snacks and bottled waters. This must have been a very last-minute decision to have us meet in here.

Cal looked around the room at the seven of us, smiling as he began to speak. "It has been an exciting semester, and I want you all to know how much everyone here at Myers, Stone & Johnson appreciate your efforts and hard work on what is shaping up to be a fifty-million-dollar class action settlement." There were gasps and cheers, and I sat there stunned while everyone started high-fiving each other. Cal held up his hands to silence us. "The claims administrator reached out to us with that figure only an hour ago. We are speaking with the claimants, starting with the named claimant, Mr. Michael Kelliher, to get their take on it. As it is quite close to what we had originally projected, I believe it is safe to say we will accept their offer." I grabbed my phone and quickly punched in the numbers, dividing the huge amount by the 189 approved claimants. On average, they would receive just over a quarter million dollars for their pain and suffering. But I recalled the structured settlement model which created a wide range of claimants based upon real or perceived damages, injuries, and what was referred to as status. Simply put, some claimants would receive significantly more than others. After legal fees and court expenses, it was likely the former youth minister might receive fifty thousand and Sonny Leone's estate possibly ten times that amount. What about Michael? I wondered. For the first time, it hit me. The timing of these unrelated events. He might receive a six-figure settlement just in time to learn he had a long-lost daughter looking for her share. But of course, I would never do something like that. He would need every bit of that money to rebuild his practice and provide for his family. His real family.

Cal was losing me now, and I only half listened to his explanation of the formulas used to calculate how each claimant's percentage had been determined. We had gone over all that weeks ago. I guess now that there was a dollar amount, it was more compelling, but still. My mind continued to wander until I heard him say the words "summer interns." Now he had my attention.

"All that being said, the partners and I have decided we will offer summer positions to two of you." I could feel my heart start to race. If they offered me full-time employment, I could stay in Hartford, study for the bar, and see Nick. "The focus will be on communicating with the claimants, disbursing payments, and closing down the case. We have extended the offers, and I'm pleased to tell you Mark and Allison have accepted. Please join me in welcoming the newest members of MSJ, Attorneys at Law." Another round of clapping, high fives, and back-slapping congratulations ensued. Apparently, I was the only one in the room shocked into silence.

I glanced over at Cal, determined to learn why, after all the praise he had given me and the confidence he'd shown in me, I was passed over in favor of stupid Mark. Allison was a no-brainer. If I were a gambler, I would have bet on her to be picked. But Mark? Puhleeeze, he couldn't even be counted on to text me to come in early when he was asked to do so. I happened to catch Cal's eye and raised my eyebrows in what I hoped was a "What the fuck, dude?" look, but he smiled and shot me a quick thumbs-up.

I stuffed whatever was on the table in front of me into my backpack and prepared to leave. Cal was already on his phone and heading out into the hallway. I turned and crashed right into Mark, the hot-off-the-presses new summer intern who would probably be paid a thousand dollars a week to file crap no one cared about and shake hands with the claimants as they received their settlement checks. The job that should have been mine.

"Cool, huh?" gushed the brightest legal mind to ever grace his parents' living room. I studied him closely, taking in his too close-set eyes, his wispy mustache that didn't stand a chance in hell of ever growing in, and his flushed red cheeks. I know people who live in glass houses, etcetera, etcetera, but he literally looked like he was twelve years old. Poor dumb-ass kid.

"So cool," I shot back at him, trying to match his perky tone and missing by a mile. "Congrats, Mark. Have a great summer." I turned to leave, but he stopped me with a question.

"What are your summer plans?" he asked, looking like he actually cared about my answer. I thought about it for a moment. Study for the bar. Try to keep myself from murdering my mother. Establish a relationship with my maybe-dad. Get to know Nick better before he left for Italy. All that, but no matter what . . .

"Hang out with my friends down at the shore," I said with a grin. "See ya, Mark. Good luck."

I headed for the back staircase, wanting to avoid all the false gaiety that would surround my fellow interns as they rode the elevator together one last time. An excess of high fives, bro-hugs and other gestures of bonhomie would be on display in addition to the *call me's*, and *stay in touches* that were well-meaning, but who were we kidding? By the time the ink dried on our diplomas, most of us would forget about this place. Still, it irked me, actually pissed me off how Cal never attempted to talk to me today. To wish me well or ask me about my plans. I guess it proved my point about the fleeting nature of most relationships, especially professional ones.

As I walked across the lobby to the exit, I pulled out my phone. Might as well access the excellent Wi-Fi service for the last time. A text message from Nick:

Big News Call me!

What might his big news be? I was attempting to resign myself to the fact he would be leaving in only six weeks. Maybe his parents had granted him an extension to stay all summer?

Another text. From Cal:

Thought you would be pleased. We need to talk.

Now I was really confused. Pleased about the settlement? Of course I was. Pleased about Mark taking my summer slot? Not so much. Although in hindsight, and with a little reality check, the work he would be doing over the summer sounded fairly dreadful. Sticking checks in envelopes. Offering coffee and Danish pastries to claimants while the real lawyers reviewed their settlements. So maybe I had dodged a bullet here. But still. What was there to talk about? I checked my work email one last time on the secure network. Several emails in my inbox, all but one of which should have been caught by the spam filter. But the last one? The one that had come in this morning at 11:47 a.m.? That's the one I opened now at 5:14 p.m. It was from Cal.

It was brief and to the point. And I'd nearly missed it.

The attached job offer entitles you to a lifetime of hard work, long hours, and questionable co-workers. Please accept and join us at MSJ. Calvin Hodges, Esq.

.   .   .   .   .

As soon as I got home, I called Randi. I forwarded the job offer to her, and we spent an hour going through it word for word. MSJ was planning to launch a family law division to better serve the needs of the community. I would come onboard as a first year associate, reporting to an as yet unnamed director. Neither Randi nor I could identify any restrictive language or red flags. The starting salary was more than competitive, and the perks and benefits package were fabulous. There was even a signing bonus, which would be enough for a deposit as well as first and last month's rent for an apartment. Of course, I would be required to pass the Connecticut bar exam, preferably within the first year of service. Once I did, there would be a twenty-percent bump to my salary.

"Should I accept it?" I asked Randi.

"Hell yeah. Sign it and send it back," came her immediate response. So, I did.

Then, despite feeling faint with hunger, I called Nick to share my news. I would be working in Hartford after all, so once I found a place to stay, we could spend the time he had left together. His phone rang several times before I heard his voice.

"Hey, it's Nick. Can't pick up. You know what to do. Later."

"Nick, it's me. I have news and sounds like you do too. It's 6:30. Call me."

I put down my phone and went to read over the job offer I'd left open on my computer. I considered calling my mom, but it was probably happy hour somewhere, so maybe not a good time. I was salivating over the benefits list when there was a knock on my door. Jamie, maybe, or Sasha reminding me to find a new place to live and to get the hell out of here. I pulled open the door to find Nick, carrying a huge bouquet of flowers and a wide grin.

He swept me up in a hug, and we crash-landed on my bed. Rose petals went everywhere, and then he was kissing me. I pulled back just far enough to study his handsome face and those kind eyes and oh so kissable mouth.

"I have great news," I managed to say.

"Me too," he said. "You go first."

"I got a job. I'm staying here in Hartford."

Nick's grin grew even wider. "I got a publisher. I'm staying here too."

•　　•　　•　　•　　•

It was much later in the evening when I finally learned the details about Nick and his novel, *Clinical Trial,* a medical thriller about a mountain-biking pediatrician who stumbles upon a Big Pharma drug conspiracy. I had assumed he was working on the first draft this whole time, and he had let me think that way. But the truth was he had already found an agent, an ambitious young woman who was the older sister of his college roommate. She'd submitted a query to one of the Big Five publishers last year, and they'd expressed interest in seeing it when it was completed. For the next seven months, he had worked on the book, gotten feedback from several beta readers, and hired an editor to make sure the final version was as good as it could be. The whole time since we'd met, he had been waiting to hear if the publisher was going to move forward, and today he'd learned they were. Next year, on April 18th, *Clinical Trial* would be published.

"When are you going to tell your folks?" I asked as we sat in the lounge eating takeout from the Chinese place around the corner. I spooned more noodles onto my plate and slurped them hungrily. Nick was expertly wielding a pair of wooden chopsticks to spear jumbo shrimp and peapods directly from the carton. "And just sayin', but Mimi's food is much better than this."

Nick nodded in agreement and finished chewing, clearly deep in thought. He had been working on this book for about the same amount of time as I had been enrolled in law school. I was so excited for him.

"I'm thinking of heading up to the house tomorrow. Catch my dad before he heads out to play golf. Probably as good a time as any to get him and Mom at home."

"How do you think they'll take the news?"

Nick thought it over for a moment before responding. "My mom has always known I was not cut out for the business. She will probably cry. Great big tears of joy. My dad is a different story. It's been this thing between us for years, and he's too stubborn to let it go. Honestly, I think he will be relieved he won't have to force the issue. Wanna come with?"

"To meet your parents? Yikes. I don't know. It's kind of soon, isn't it?" I was possibly making a much bigger deal out of it than it was. But as I had only "met the parents" one time in my life, it felt big to me.

"Up to you, babe," he said. "I do want you to meet them, but if you're not feeling it, that's cool. I don't want you to do anything that makes you feel uncomfortable."

There was that good sport I was quickly falling in love with. I knew I shouldn't compare, but I couldn't help thinking how irritated Seth could get if I begged off on a social engagement. I felt like I was a constant disappointment to him if I didn't want to hang out in a sports bar with his friends for hours on end or attend every function his large, extended family threw, from one-year-old birthday parties to his grandparents' fiftieth anniversary dinners and everything in between.

"Thanks for that," I told him, and he hugged me close to him.

"We should really be thinking about how to celebrate your new job, G. It sounds like a great opportunity for you. Think of all the families you'll be able to help. And while we're on the topic of families, have you thought any more about talking with Michael now that the case is pretty much put to bed?"

"Yeah, I've been thinking about telling him about my new job, you know? Like somehow he'll be proud of me. Is that weird?"

Nick was studying me closely and seemed about to say something, and then he stopped.

"No, what? Tell me," I said, and he shrugged.

"I think you should rip off the Band-Aid, G." I must have looked confused because he hurried to explain himself. "You're very important to me, babe, and I hate to see you hurt. I think the longer you wait to find out if this guy is your birth father, the harder it's going to be on you in case he isn't. And if he is, then why not get to know him and his kid? Life's short. Don't wait."

I stared at him, feeling like his suggestion was a good one. I was graduating in two weeks, I had an amazing job offer, and I was falling in love with a guy who really seemed to get me. It was time to find out, one way or the other, and move on.

"You're right. I'll call him tomorrow. Let's clean up down here and go to bed, okay?"

And that's exactly what we did.

Chapter 27

The next morning, Nick left to talk with his parents to share the news he would not be heading to Italy after all. I called Michael to see when he might be free but got sent to voicemail. I left a brief message that I was hoping to see him again soon and asked him to call me. By midmorning, I was propped up in bed, reviewing my notes and eating cold sesame noodles straight from the container. I got a text from Michael.

Hi Lennon. Out of town for a few days. Will be back in office Tuesday morning. Let me know what works for you. Michael

Even though nothing was resolved, I felt better knowing I was going to get an answer and soon. After I realized I had re-read the same page several times, I moved everything out of the way, snuggled under the comforter, and fell asleep in a bed smelling faintly of Nick—crisp and outdoorsy. I woke a couple hours later, and there was a text from Nick.

Mom is thrilled, Dad is proud. Celebration tonight at the big house. Can you join?

I was relieved for Nick and couldn't imagine his folks being anything other than over the moon. But did I want to meet them tonight, and if I did, what on earth would I wear?

Sure thing. What time?

How's 6? Need me to pick you up?

I'll come to you. See you then.

Sounds good. L.

L? L for later or *L* for love?

Whatever the *L* meant, I had roughly five hours to get ready and make the twenty-minute drive to Nick's house. My first thought was another nap, but I knew I was too excited to sleep. I checked my banking app and saw my latest paycheck from the library had been deposited. Since I didn't have a housing payment due, what with my pending move, I decided to treat myself. I grabbed my backpack and headed out on foot.

My first stop was a hair salon I had walked past dozens of times. I'd planned on getting a cut prior to graduation anyway, so why not now? They got me in a chair almost immediately, and a half hour later, I was back on the street, my short hair freshly washed, trimmed, and styled. My next stop was a nail salon and, once again, luck was on my side. I chose a neutral shade of taupe, but when the young woman who clipped and filed my stubby nails wrinkled her nose at my choice, I pointed to a cardinal-red polish. Go big, right?

After a much-needed stop for an iced coffee and a chocolate chip muffin, I headed to the consignment store I shopped at with Randi. I couldn't bring myself to pay retail. Thrifting was who I was, and I scored once more, finding a flowered sundress for tonight, a black sheath for graduation, and a perfect-fitting pair of jeans for anytime.

I made it back home in time to clean up, have a quick catch up with Randi by phone, touch up my hair, and apply a dusting of blush. I slicked on some lip gloss, and I was as ready as I would ever be. Stop overthinking things, I told my reflection in the mirror. I rarely wore mascara but had coated my lashes today, and I noted a few black specks had made it onto my cheeks. I dabbed at the area with a damp cotton ball and inspected the results. Not too bad, I decided.

I tossed clean underwear, shorts, and a T-shirt in my backpack, grabbed my keys, and headed toward the back exit, where my car was parked. I took a quick look around just in case I had another visitor, but the coast was clear. I hopped in the car and sent a text to Nick.

I'm on my way. See you in 20

Seconds later, my phone buzzed with an incoming call. I was still in the parking lot, so I accepted the call. "Hey, you. I said I was on my way," I called out, expecting a chuckle from Nick in return. Instead, I heard the sounds of a woman sobbing. It was Charlene! I grabbed the phone and took it off speaker.

"Mom? What's wrong?" I said, my heart pounding. Charlene never cried.

"Baby girl, I . . . I fucked up, hon. I'm sorry."

"Mom, where are you? What happened?"

"I was minding my own business, I swear I was. Next thing I know, they're forcing me into the back of a cop car. They said I was carrying drugs, but I swear, they weren't mine. I think they planted them on me. Cops do that, you know? It's not right. I'm telling you. There should be a law."

I was racking my brain, trying to think of a way to post bail for her. Maybe my starting bonus from the law firm? Or I could borrow from Randi? Then I remembered. "You're on probation. They aren't gonna let you out on bail, Mom. You're going back inside." There was silence on the other end, and I thought she might have hung up on me. It sure wouldn't be the first time. Tell her something she doesn't want to hear and . . .

"I'm not gonna make it, girl," she said, sounding broken, lost.

"What are you talking about?" I screeched into the phone. Had she taken something? "Mom, have them pump your stomach. You can't—"

"What the hell are you yammering on about?" she asked. "I'm not gonna make it to your graduation. That's why I'm calling. Did you think I was trying to off myself? That's the craziest . . ."

I had heard enough of her nonsense. My new boyfriend and his family were expecting me to celebrate my new job and his publishing contract. I did not have the time or the emotional bandwidth for whatever ridiculousness she was trying to dump on me.

"I can't talk right now. I have somewhere I need to be. I'll ask Randi to check in . . . Yes Mom, Randi Quinn, and she'll get a copy of the arrest report. Meanwhile, be good, don't say anything to anybody, and calm down. I've got to go," I said sharply. I ended the call and drove out of the lot and onto the street. She'd done it again. A lifelong fuckup; that was Charlene.

Chapter 28

I called Randi as I drove to Nick's house. She'd barely had the chance to say hello when I told her about Charlene getting arrested. She promised to check the police report and intervene if needed, but she confirmed what I already knew. An arrest could void Charlene's parole, and she would be heading back to prison.

"Sorry, hon," she added.

"It was only a matter of time," I said, not even bothering to hide the bitterness I felt. "I'm not mad. Just disappointed. And mad."

"Where are you going?" Randi asked, and I realized I had only told her half of my news.

"I'm meeting Nick and his folks for dinner," I said. "It's a special celebration."

"Your new job?" she asked.

"Even better. Nick's book is getting published this spring, and he doesn't have to move to Italy."

"He finished his book? That's great. But why would he move to Italy?"

Everything was happening so fast! I quickly filled her in on the promise Nick had made to his folks, how close he had come to moving, and as much as I knew about his book.

"Sounds like he dodged a bullet," she said, and I agreed. We both had.

"Ran, sorry to cut this short, but I just got to Nick's and he's . . . coming out and getting in the car with me." I watched as he hopped in and buckled up. "Nick, this is Randi on speaker. Ran, say hi to Nick." The two exchanged hurried hellos before Randi confirmed she would get the police report and wished us a good night.

Nick turned to me. "Police report? What's up, G?"

I explained how Charlene had gotten arrested and violated her parole. "I don't know the details, and Char was being evasive, but Randi's gonna check to see if she can find out anything."

"Sorry, babe, that sucks." Nick leaned in for a quick kiss. "Figured you could drive us. We're running a bit behind, so I'll direct you." I backed out of his driveway and drove along the private road leading to the big house. "I would understand if this isn't a good night—" he began, but I stopped him.

"If I broke down every time Mom got busted for something, I would never leave the house," I assured him. "I'm excited to meet your folks."

"Turn in here," Nick said, and I gasped as the family home came into view. The winding gravel driveway was lined with tall trees on both sides, their tops creating a natural arch. The grounds were lush and green and seemed to go on forever. As we drew nearer to the house, the manicured gardens, exploding with colorful flowers and artfully trimmed hedges, captured my vision, and I found myself driving more slowly, not wanting to miss a thing. The large two-story home loomed in front of us, and the next thing I knew, I was pulling onto a paved area to its left. The classic lines of the structure were blurred somewhat by the ivy adorning its stone façade, and the overall effect was warm and welcoming with the large front windows catching the last of the setting sun's rays. It was breathtaking.

I shut off the car and turned to look at Nick. "What a dump. I can't believe you had to grow up here."

He grinned in response. "Explains a lot, though, doesn't it?"

"I mean, I knew you were to the manor born and all, but wowza."

"The only wowza I see is you. Let's do this." He took my arm, and we climbed the steps to a front door that opened as we approached.

A pretty woman of about fifty came out, arms outstretched. She was dressed in a jade-green tunic worn over skinny jeans. Her feet were bare, and I noticed she was about my height as she drew me into a hug.

"My mom is a hugger," said Nick. "I probably should have warned you." He turned his attention to her. "Mom, we've talked about this. Boundaries, remember? You're scaring Lennon."

His mother released her grip on me and gave me an appraising look. "She doesn't look scared to me," she told her son.

"I'm not scared," I assured her.

She held out a hand in greeting. "I'm Bridget Flaherty Russo. And you're Lennon Gallagher. I am fairly certain I raised my boy better than that, but if we waited for him to introduce us, we'd still be waiting."

"Nice to meet you, Mrs. Russo," I said, and she held up a hand in protest.

"Please call me Bridget," she said as she took my arm in hers and led me into the house.

"Right behind you, Bridget," Nick said as he followed us into the large foyer.

"That's Mom to you, Nicky-boy," she shot back at him. I glanced toward him and noted his cheeks were flushed, but he was grinning ear to ear.

I mouthed "Nicky-boy" over my shoulder, and both mother and son laughed.

"C'mon, you lot," said Bridget. "Dinner's ready." For a small woman, she moved quickly and effortlessly across the marble-tiled floor, and I followed closely behind her, gazing at the soaring ceiling, the elegant paneled walls, and the sconces ablaze with a warm glowing light. A polished hardwood staircase seemed to reach to the heavens, and I could easily imagine a young Nick sliding down the banister. Despite the pressures of a family business Nick didn't want or need, it must have been a happy household to grow up in.

We entered a large dining room with a table easily seating sixteen and continued on through a swinging door leading to a cozy room with a table set for four. We stayed behind while Bridget continued through another door I imagined led to the kitchen.

"Breakfast nook and family suppers," Nick said. I felt instantly comfortable in the smaller space. He pointed to a door in the corner of the room. "Powder room."

I nodded before heading in that direction. I used the facilities and washed up. When I returned, Nick was seated at the round table, talking animatedly to a man who could only be his father. Not that they resembled each other in the least. Where Nick had lighter hair and a slight build like his mother, Mario Russo was dark-skinned, barrel-chested, and balding. He stood when he saw me heading his way and extended his hand. His brown eyes gleamed with pleasure as he took me in.

"Welcome, Miss Lennon. We're so glad you could join us this evening," he said in heavily accented English. "You're as pretty as Nicky said you were."

I smiled and felt my hand disappear in his. Warm and rough. A dad hand, for sure. "Thank you, Mr. Russo. I'm so happy to be here. Your home is lovely."

Bridget came in brandishing a huge tray, which she placed on the nearby sideboard. "Sit, sit," she ordered. "Nicky, pour your girl some water, would you? Unless you prefer something stronger?" Bridget asked. I noted the absence of wineglasses on the table. I had never seen Nick touch a drop of alcohol, and it made me wonder if all of the Russo clan abstained.

"Water's good for me. Thank you, Bridget." I sat next to Nick and watched as platters of food were placed on the table to be served family-style. Breathing in the tantalizing aromas of garlic, basil, and oregano, I helped myself to the dish closest to me: chicken parmigiana! I passed the platter to Nick and watched as Bridget scooped a healthy portion of ziti onto my plate.

"Allow me," she said before taking a tiny serving for herself. "Save room for salad," she added. "And dessert. Nicky tells me you have a sweet tooth."

"I do," I said, reaching over to squeeze Nick's hand. We dug in, and everything tasted as delicious as it smelled. Conversation was kept to a minimum while we ate, but I managed to respond to Mr. Russo's questions. Yes, I had been raised in New London, I had earned my degree in Psychology from UCONN, and I would be graduating from their law school in a matter of weeks.

"Let the poor girl enjoy her dinner, Mario," Bridget admonished, and Nick asked a question about one of the restaurants. "No business talk during dinner, Nicky," she scolded, and Mr. Russo mumbled something like "No personal talk, no work talk, what's left? The Yankees?"

We went back to eating, and I could only manage a few bites of salad. I was relieved when Bridget announced we would have dessert in the family room "after a bit." I offered to help clear the table, but Bridget insisted there was no need. Nick told his folks we were going to take Danny for a quick walk, and we found him sleeping on the sunporch, his fur aglow in the fading sunlight. He woke, seeming delighted for the interruption, and spun in circles around me while Nick fastened his leash. We left the house hand in hand and took off at a slow pace, allowing Danny to stop, sniff, and pee at each of the first half-dozen trees we passed.

"Your folks are great," I said, "but you already knew that."

"Yeah, they are. I hope you didn't mind my dad too much. He gets kind of intense sometimes, and then when he and my mom started arguing . . ."

I stared at him in amazement. "Babe, if you think that was an argument . . ." I shook my head and shared a couple choice memories with him, like the time on Thanksgiving when Mom's two brothers got into an argument over the last slice of pie and got into a fistfight on the front lawn, and the time my grandma called the police on my cousin

Joey, who was threatening his father with a carving knife, also on Thanksgiving. "Those are arguments," I concluded.

Nonplussed, Nick asked, "What kind of pie? Cuz if it was pumpkin, I understand. It's only around for a short while, so you have to get it while you can." I squeezed his hand tighter, and we wandered back to the house. "I will always share the last piece with you, G," he whispered in my ear.

"Good to know, and I will never threaten you with a carving knife," I assured him.

•   •   •   •   •

When we got back to the house, we made our way to the family room to find two massive balloon bouquets and more fresh flowers than I had ever seen. I stopped to check out the arrangement with the orange and pink balloons and the banner proclaiming "CONGRATULATIONS, LENNON" in a bold font.

"I can't believe your mom," I said to Nick, who was looking at a similar display of his own in shades of blue and green.

"This is how we do it," Bridget announced as she and Mario joined us. "Tell her, Nicky."

"This is how *Mom* does it," Nick confirmed, earning a grin from his dad.

"Thank you so much, Mrs., um, Bridget," I said, and she responded with a big hug.

"It's not every day we have so much to celebrate," she said. "I am so proud of the two of you."

Mario had been busy uncorking a bottle of something bubbly and pouring four glasses. He handed them to us and proposed a toast. "Raise your glasses," he commanded. "Restaurants were always my dream. All I ever wanted was to see couples in love enjoying quiet dinners and families celebrating their biggest milestones with us. I am grateful to have lived long enough to have accomplished all I ever hoped for," he began. Bridget cut her eyes at him and he continued.

"But you, my Nicky, you had a different dream, and we are so proud to see your hard work, dedication, and passion has paid off. To Nicky," he said, and we all took a sip of our sparkling grape juice.

Nick raised his glass as well. "Thank you, Mom and Dad, for all your support and for recognizing what a terrible manager/chef I would be. And congratulations to Lennon, who will be graduating in just a couple weeks at the top of her class and starting a brilliant legal career at the most well-respected law firm in the state. To Lennon," he said, and we took another sip.

I was beaming, and Nick looked pleased as well as two white-jacketed waiters entered the room, one balancing a large sheet cake and the other carrying a tray loaded with bowls of ice cream and a selection of toppings. I gasped as I realized the swirls of color on the cake were images of our faces, Nick's and mine.

"My hair is made of chocolate fondant," I said, staring in amazement at the two of us. "Yours is buttercream."

"I am going to eat your face, G," Nick murmured in my ear before sticking his finger in my mouth—my cake-mouth, that is—then licking it clean. "Yum," he said, his face smeared with frosting. "You're delicious."

"Nicky," his mother called out. "What are you doing to your beautiful cake?"

"C'mon, Mom," he said, scooping a hunk of my cake-cheek. "You've got to taste my girlfriend's face." The ice cream melted as we busied ourselves sampling different sections of Lennon-and-Nick cake. Even Mario joined in. It was the most delicious cake I had ever eaten. And the most fun.

Chapter 29

Late the next morning, I drove back to my dorm, leaving just enough time to change clothes for my shift at the law library. I had been picking up extra shifts all semester and had almost forgotten I had agreed to cover this one. Most exams were over, which meant the afternoon would be quiet. We'd had an early night last night, returning to Nick's shortly after enjoying our cake. Sticky with frosting, we had showered together (to save time, naturally, and water too) before dashing up to the sleeping loft for the hot, steamy sex we had both been imagining all evening. Afterward, I fell asleep in Nick's arms, feeling safe and well-loved. I could definitely get used to this.

On my way out of the dorm, I grabbed a stack of mail from my overflowing cubicle next to the lobby. I sifted through it quickly, mostly junk mail and flyers from restaurants in the neighborhood. One envelope had a return address from the registrar's office, so I tossed everything else in the trash and read the letter as I walked to the library. *Crap.* It was a request for the names of my invited guests for the graduation ceremony, and the deadline was . . . yesterday. I decided to swing by the office since it was on my way.

As I neared the entrance to the administration office, the big double doors opened and a heavy-set man with a flushed face and a shiny, ill-fitting dark suit stormed out. Barreling right past me, he paid no attention as he was far too absorbed in giving a thorough dressing-down to a younger, heavier version of himself. A maxi-me, if you will! Roger flushed an even deeper shade of crimson when he saw my amused face.

"Hey, Rog," I said with a saucy grin. "How's tricks?" He didn't respond to me, either because he did not have a snappy response at the ready or, more likely, his silence was due to the barrage of criticism and blame being levied at him by his father. I didn't catch all of them but my favorite was, "You were a stupid boy, and you've grown into a stupid man," followed by an angry diatribe on the amount of money "this fuckup of yours is going to cost your old man." I watched as the two men lumbered down the steps and into a waiting silver SUV complete with a driver.

I considered a parting shot like, "See you at graduation . . . Oh, wait, I won't," but by the time I decided, the Stevens men were gone. I was still chuckling to myself as I waited in the short line at the Registrar's to provide the names of my guests: Randi, Eric, and Nick. Minutes later, I slipped behind the reference desk at the library with seconds to spare to start my shift.

The first hour flew by. Randi called to fill me in on my mother's situation, which had an eerily familiar sound: drunk and disorderly, resisting arrest, and possession of a baggie of weed. Apparently, it was far less than the one and a half ounces currently legal in the state, but it was a parole violation, and Char had been arrested. After spending the night in a holding cell in New London, she had been arraigned, then transported back to the women's prison in Niantic earlier today. Randi offered to go with me to visit her, but I had already decided I was going to hold off.

"I have too much going on right now," I explained to Nick when I called him to fill him in. "It's her usual pattern, and I am not going to reward her bad behavior. I swear she just does it for attention."

"She's also an addict and an alcoholic," he reminded me.

"Oh, don't I know it. I've been meaning to ask you something. No wine, sparkling juice . . . Neither of your parents drink?"

Nick was silent for a moment before he responded. "After we lost Lily, Mom started having a problem. An occasional glass of wine before dinner morphed into a Bloody Mary or two before lunch and it went downhill from there."

"Did she get help?"

"Yeah, she went to rehab and has been doing well. Still goes to meetings. She just celebrated ten years of sobriety," he said with more than a touch of pride.

"That's fantastic. Good for her." I loved to hear success stories like that. "Do you think they liked me?"

"Yeah, they really did. Mom texted me earlier. I'll read it to you. "'Nicky, we like this girl. She is a keeper. Don't muck this up. Love, Mom.'"

I beamed happily. "I'm so glad."

"I've got a call scheduled with my publisher at six. When I'm done, I'll give you a call. Sound good?"

I told him that was perfect. I checked the time: 2:45 p.m. My shift ended at five. It was going to be a long afternoon. I had forgotten to bring my laptop with me, so I couldn't proof my final paper as I'd planned or double-check my to-do list. I stumbled out of the library at 5:01. I had busied myself shelving periodicals, returning leather-bound tomes to their rightful place, and wiping down keyboards on the shared computers, all of which had consumed only a small portion of the 135 minutes I'd had to fill. I can't be certain, but I'm fairly sure I napped with my head down on the desk for a bit as well. I made my way down the sidewalk, debating the merits of coffee, a nap, or foraging an early dinner. I started up the steps to my brownstone and jumped when I heard a familiar voice call my name.

"Hey, Lennon."

I turned to see who had spoken. What the fuck?

·　　·　　·　　·　　·

Several minutes later, I was sitting across from the last person I had expected to see today. I poured two cups of coffee and watched with detached amusement as she doctored hers up with creamer and several sugar packets. She blew on it, took a tentative sip, and frowned.

"Got any ice?" Erin asked, and I pushed back my chair, crossed the room to the refrigerator, and collected a handful of tiny cubes. I returned to my seat and, at her nod, dumped enough ice in her cup to cause her drink to rise and spill over onto the table. She started to get up, probably in search of a paper towel, but I held up a hand to stop her.

"Leave it," I said. "Now do you want to tell me what the fuck you're doing here?"

Erin held up her hands in mock surrender. "I just wanted to see you and make sure you were all right after your ordeal the other night. And oh, speaking of Roger, you should know his father is working on a deal to get him reinstated. He'll have to repeat the course as an independent study this summer, and he'll be able to sit for the bar late fall."

I shook my head, disgusted by what I was hearing. Barely a slap on the wrist. Charlene and the rest of the Gallagher clan always said rules didn't apply to the rich and powerful. The fact that none of them followed any rules, despite being neither rich nor powerful, was beside the point. I hadn't wanted to become jaded, but here was more evidence heaped on to support that claim.

"Oh, Lennon. Everyone cheats," Erin said. "It's kind of fucked up, don't you think, how once we're lawyers, we're expected to find every possible way to manipulate the system for our clients but get penalized for trying to do the exact same thing for ourselves? We should be embracing methods like these and not be bothered by flawed facts and tortured logic."

"Agree to disagree. But before you go, can you at least tell me why? Why would you help Roger? I don't understand."

She frowned as she considered my question. "Roger had something on me, okay? I did something really stupid, and if it came out, I would have gotten arrested, and a conviction would have kept me from practicing law. He covered for me, and I owed him big-time. You were collateral damage. I'm really sorry."

"If that's your way of apologizing, you suck at it."

"Yeah, well, never fear. Alex is the one who's going down for this," Erin said. "After all, the whole thing was his idea. They're looking at criminal charges, from what we hear. The guy's fucked," she added without a hint of shame. Does no one ever take any personal responsibility? I wondered.

"What about Glen and Justin?" I asked.

Erin shrugged. "They're out, I guess. I mean they could appeal, but Justin's grades were not cutting it, so I doubt they'd give him a do-over, you know? And Glen?" She shrugged again. "No clue, but I think some money exchanged hands, so he'll be set for a while. Time for him to lay low. It's the way the world works, Lennon. You should know that by now."

I wanted to leave her here in the lounge, just walk away and never lay eyes on her again. Before Randi, I'd had only a couple relationships I'd consider friendships, and neither of them had lasted all that long. To most of my middle school and high school classmates, I was just the weird, skinny loser one night away from being homeless or getting sent to juvie. Erin had made me feel those "feels" all over again, and I hated to admit it, but it hurt just as much today as it had ten years earlier. Maybe more.

I swallowed the last of my coffee. "As great as it's been catching up, I have to head out. I need to get some boxes and think about packing."

Erin looked surprised. "I thought you would stay for the summer, study for the bar. Weren't you looking to get hired at the firm you were interning at?" I wasn't about to share my good news about my job offer with her. She didn't deserve another minute of my time.

"I really do need to get going, Erin," I said again and got up from the table, grabbing our mugs and heading for the sink. She trailed behind me and watched as I rinsed them.

"Do you need any help?" she asked. I grabbed a towel and wiped away imaginary drops of water from the countertop.

"No, all set, thanks."

She smiled then. "No, I meant with packing. Can I help you with that?" For a split second, I almost caved. Helping to pack? That was something you could only count on a true friend for. But I had no plans to pack tonight. I had just made it up as an excuse to get her to leave.

"No," I said firmly. "I'm good." Her smile wavered and then vanished completely. I followed her toward the door, not feeling hospitable in the least. I merely wanted to make sure she actually left this time.

With one hand on the doorknob, she turned to face me. "Not that you'd miss me, but I'm gonna skip the ceremony. It's not my scene, and I can think of nothing worse than spending a day inside a stuffy auditorium. But you're gonna do great, Lennon," she said. "And for what it's worth, I would have enjoyed being your friend. That was real, I swear." She leaned down and kissed me full on the lips and pulled back before I could push her away. "It was real," she repeated with a ghost of a smile, right before she pulled the door open and stepped outside.

As I watched her walk away, I felt the pull of conflicting emotions. Fear I'd never see her again and anger she'd had the nerve to set me up, say those things, and then kiss me. Who did she think she was? I traced my lips with an index finger and felt a chill run through me. My grandma would say someone was walking over my grave. I think she'd have been right.

Chapter 30

I spent most of the weekend with Nick, but I buckled down on Sunday night for the final push. By Tuesday, I was caught up with most of my assignments, and the thought of spending more time working made me feel antsy. I needed to get up and do something, but what? Randi was in court today, and I didn't feel like driving to Niantic to see my jailbird mother. Nick was meeting with his writing critique group this afternoon, and I felt restless, unsettled. It was a gorgeous day, so I set out on foot with no real destination in mind. And as I walked, I realized exactly where I wanted to go.

Twenty minutes later, I found myself in front of a small brick office building. I pulled the business card from my pocket and studied it carefully, comparing the address with the number on the building: 1984 Walnut Street. The place where Michael Kelliher, M.S.W., ran his practice. I started having second thoughts on what had sounded like a good idea a short while ago. I couldn't just drop in, could I? Surely, he was with a patient right now. But as I recalled how much his business had fallen off since Data Solutions leaked his patients' confidential records, I realized he might be free. But if he was, why would he be sitting alone in his office? I was about to turn and hurry away when I heard my name being called. I looked up. Michael was walking toward me, carrying a large cup of coffee and a small bakery bag in one hand

and a set of keys in the other. Busted. No chance to get away without some sort of explanation.

"Hi, Michael," I said. "Oh, is this your office?" Realizing I was holding his business card out in front of me, I slid it back into my pocket. He seemed surprised but actually happy to see me.

"Yes, this is it," he said with a grin. "I'm glad you came," he added.

I was about to protest but chose to just return his smile. "I know I should have called," I said, "and if you're busy, I can come back another time."

"This is a great time. I'd been doing paperwork all morning and needed a break. I have someone coming at noon, but that's more than an hour from now. C'mon, let's go up to my office and have a chat. Sound good?" I nodded and followed him into the small but tastefully decorated lobby and up a flight of stairs. "I'm right down here," he said as we turned left and stopped in front of a door on the right, marked with #23 in brass, along with his name and the all-important initials. He unlocked the door and waved me in to his waiting room. Two plush love seats faced each other, flanking a gorgeous Oriental rug. I imagined the side tables were straight out of Pottery Barn along with a magazine rack, well organized with the latest editions of several weekly publications. The artwork was an interesting mix of abstract shapes and gentle colors. The vibe was soothing and comfortable, perfect to help waiting patients to feel more relaxed.

"Nice place," I said with a smile, and we continued through a door leading to a large space broken up into a well-appointed office, where I assumed he saw his patients, a restroom, and an organized kitchen with gleaming appliances and a round table with three chairs. There was another closed door at the end of the short hallway, and I glanced at it quickly. Closet, maybe? He caught me looking and winked.

"Electroshock therapy," he said, and I laughed. He really was a nice guy, and I could imagine he made his patients feel safe and comfortable. He gestured to the table. "We can sit here, if you like. I've got water in the fridge and a few cans of seltzer." He stuck his head in the apartment-sized refrigerator and called out the choices. "A couple Snapples, cranberry seltzer, water, and a can of Dr. Pepper." He looked out at me. "My son loves the stuff, and his mom won't let him have it at home. So when he comes to the office with me, well . . ." He shrugged with a "What can you do?" look, and my heart warmed to him.

"I'm good right now," I told him. I really wanted coffee, but I didn't see a Keurig or a coffeemaker on the counter. He snapped his fingers and told me to have a seat, walking over to the cabinet and pulling out two coffee mugs.

"You're a coffee drinker if I recall, and this twenty-ounce cup is way more than I need." He poured coffee from his large takeout cup into the two mugs. It was hot and steaming, and it smelled like heaven. "Perfect," he said and joined me at the table. He reached into the small bag and produced a neatly wrapped breakfast sandwich already cut in two. He held out half to me. "Happy to share," he said, and I shook my head. It too smelled delicious, but I was starting to feel nervous and didn't think I could swallow any solid food. I took a large sip of hot coffee instead.

"It's bad enough I show up unannounced and drink half your coffee," I said. "And besides, I already ate," I lied. "You enjoy."

"I'm glad you're here," he said and took a bite, chewing contentedly.

"No meat?" I asked, studying the half in front of me. I couldn't imagine not ordering one with bacon or sausage or both. He shook his head, wiping his mouth with a napkin.

"No meat," he agreed. "Gave it up many years ago. I do eat shrimp and fish, though, so I guess that makes me a . . . pescetarian," we said simultaneously. "I had a lot of bad habits back then and really needed to clean up my act." And how's that working for you? I wanted to ask.

"Oh yeah? Bad habits, huh? Like jaywalking or having too many items in the ten-or-less checkout lane?"

His face turned serious and he shook his head. "I wish that was it. No, I had a bit of a problem with alcohol and other forms of reckless behavior." He shrugged. "Got through it, but it was a lot of work."

I nodded, understanding him completely. "My mom was—well, is—a drinker, but her bigger issue was drugs. And other forms of reckless behavior," I added. Like sleeping with bartenders and passing bad checks and . . .

"I remember you told me when we talked that day. I'm sorry, that's a lot for a child to cope with. How about you?" he asked, and I looked at him wide-eyed.

"Me? You mean drinking or drugs?" I shook my head vigorously. "No way. My mother's friends used to give me sips of beer when I was little, and one of them tried to do that thing where you blow smoke into someone's mouth to get them high, but that's it. Not for me, not after I saw what it did to Charlene." His eyes went wide at the sound of her name. I waited to see what he would say next.

"Your mother's name is Charlene," he said slowly, as if he already knew it was, and I nodded.

"Yeah, Charlene Gallagher," I confirmed. "Um, did you know her?" I reached over, grabbed the second half of his sandwich, and crammed a portion of it into my mouth. Anything to get myself to shut the hell up and stop asking questions I suddenly wasn't sure I wanted answered.

He was nodding and seemed deep in thought. "Your mom, she's about my age, maybe fifty, early fifties, small, dark hair, like—"

"Like me, yeah. She used to go to the Wharf all the time, I guess." What would he say to that?

"I remember Charlene. She was . . . something." He appeared to be recalling something about her as he said it. "You said she was inside for a while?"

I considered sharing that she was back in prison, but I didn't want to go down that twisted path right now. "She says she was clean when she was pregnant with me, but who really knows? Her sister—I don't know if you remember my aunt Kelly—told me when I was real little, she was pretty good about acting responsible and all that, drinking only on weekends, smoking weed, but none of the harder stuff," I reported by rote, never knowing which of the two sisters was less reliable in their recollections of the past than the other.

"What happened?" Michael asked, and I rolled my eyes.

"Do you mean what was the inciting incident? What drove her off the deep end and into shooting junk between her toes?" I regretted my words immediately when he winced, taken aback by my outburst. Whether or not we were related, he didn't deserve to listen to my harsh words. It's just I was so sick of the bullshit, the lies, the questions by well-meaning but clueless individuals. I softened my tone as I continued.

"Well, if you ask Charlene, it was me. I was such a demon, such a bad kid, didn't listen, couldn't sit still. I was a terror, and according to my mother, she started using again to lessen the pain of giving birth to such a nightmare." There, you happy? I wondered. Is that what you wanted to hear?

He leaned across the table and held my hand between his. Such warmth and strength in those hands.

"You should never have to hear that," he said sadly. "I probably don't have to tell you that's the disease talking, not really her."

I nodded. "I was a psych major, so yeah, it makes sense, and it's probably true. But when you're five and mommy goes to prison because you're a bad girl, it's a different story."

"I'm so sorry you went through all that. Did you stay with family or . . . ?" His voice trailed off before he could add, "Or were you put in the system?"

"That was the beginning of my nomad existence," I said. "I got shuffled between staying with my grandma in Old Lyme, my aunt in New London, and various and sundry foster homes along the coastline. Whenever Charlene got out cuz of overcrowding or whatever, she would move in with my grandma and I'd stay there on weekends or if I was between foster homes." I closed my eyes briefly, made dizzy by the images of lugging my backpack everywhere I went. The one still carrying most of everything I owned.

"I'm amazed at how you've been able to turn things around, Lennon. What made you want to go to law school?" he asked.

"Two things," I told him. "I saw firsthand how broken the system is, not just the kids who slip through the cracks in the foster system, but those who age out and are unprepared to go out into the world. I want to practice family law, help the kids, create families, bring people together. Yeah," I added. "All that. And world peace." I wiped my eyes on my crumpled napkin, and Michael was nice enough to look away as I did.

"What's the other thing?" he asked, and I stared blankly at him for a moment before breaking into a grin.

"The second *thing* is my favorite person in the world. Her name is Miranda Quinn, and she's responsible for me being where I am today," I said.

"How'd you meet Miranda?" Michael asked, and I flashed back to the snarky smart-ass I had been just six years earlier. A jumbo-sized chip on my shoulder and a crap attitude to boot. Frustrated with my life and desperate to get out of the vicious cycle of poverty, crime, and isolation impacting so many of the girls in the group homes I lived in. Randi represented me in court on a shoplifting charge, my first and only offense. She and my mom were great friends back in the day, and Charlene was convinced Randi owed it to her to represent her daughter, and it was hands down the only thing of value my mother ever did for me.

"She went to school with my mom," I said simply before I began detailing all the ways Randi helped and supported me. I told Michael about Eric and Hobie and my second home down in Old Lyme. He seemed quite interested, and I chattered away until I spied a framed photo on the corner of his desk.

"Is that your family?" I asked, and he picked it up and showed me.

"I told you about my son, John, and that's my wife, Lyn," he said, pointing to a dark-haired woman with a lovely smile. "She's a second-grade teacher," he added. I recognized the two of them from my recon mission. My eyes continued to study the shot of a family sitting around a large fire pit, and there was the young blond he had been with at the café. She was holding hands with a good-looking dark-haired man about her age. "Oh, and that's my niece, Barbara. She and her husband just announced they're expecting their first child this Christmas. She's so excited. And that's Doug," he said, pointing to a large fluffy sheepdog. I barely glanced at the large canine with his tongue hanging out. It was his niece, not his girlfriend! The relief I felt was almost palpable. My maybe-dad was not a dirtbag with a sidepiece! "We got him when he was a pup, about this big," he said, his hands less than a foot apart. I smiled at the image, and we both jumped when a bell went off.

"That's my twelve o'clock," he said, and I hopped up to leave. He gathered up the remains from the table and tossed them in the trash.

"Thanks for spending time with me this morning," I said.

"I enjoyed talking to you, Lennon. Please let me know next time you're free. I would love to talk some more. If you want to, that is," he added, and I nodded.

"Sounds good, Michael. See you soon." He walked me back to the waiting area, where a young man a few years older than me was texting on his phone. He stood when he saw us and followed Michael back to his office. I saw Ariana Grande's face on the cover of one of the magazines, and for a second I thought of borrowing it and wasting an hour catching up on all the latest Hollywood gossip, but I decided to study instead. *Not today, Ariana. Not today.*

I walked slowly back to my dorm room. I would have asked Michael straight out if his appointment hadn't shown up right then. I had told Nick I would be glad to finally get an answer to this question that had been bugging me for months, and I really would. It was time.

Chapter 31

Randi invited us for brunch, so on Sunday morning, Nick and I drove from Hartford down to Old Lyme, my favorite place in the world. I was excited about Nick getting to meet my "family," the friends who had chosen me over and again for the past six years. I may have been a bit too eager to remind him who everybody was, but I was almost finished.

"And finally, Randi's stepbrother is Jake. He's married to Meg. They are the parents of Clementine, who is ten, which I find very difficult to believe. I used to babysit her, and now I think she's probably taller than I am. Not that I'm tall, but still. She's so grown up. And she's got a baby brother, Teddy, although he's no longer a baby. He's what? Six or maybe seven? I babysat him too, although not as much as Clem because—" I stopped my one-woman spiel, realizing I was rambling. "Sorry," I told Nick. "I'm just really excited."

"I am too," he said, taking my hand up to his lips and gently kissing my fingertips. "But I'm a guy, so I'm not supposed to show it. Except when . . . you know, sexy time."

"Sexy time, huh? Is that what the kids are calling it these days?"

"Sure, why not? I mean, it's definitely sexy, you've got to admit that, and I am always willing to put in the time, so . . . sexy time."

"I can work with that. Oh, and I hope you're hungry. There's always loads of food. We'll be expected to take some home, I mean to your home or, um, my room. Not to *our* home because there is no *our* home. Sorry, I guess I'm just a little nervous."

"You're nervous? Babe, I'm about to meet a dozen people who know all about me: my devilish good looks, my promising career as a best-selling, chart-topping author, the proud owner of a tiny house and co-parent to a golden retriever that likes to spoon me. And what do I know about these people? A little girl named after a fruit and a former cop who's your pseudo grandfather who goes by the name Pop. What am I supposed to call him anyway? Mr. Pop? Sir Pop? If anyone is allowed to be nervous, it's me. And we're here," he said, pulling into the driveway behind Pop's ancient Jeep Wagoneer.

I squeezed his hand, so happy he was with me. He leaned over and kissed me on the lips, a toe-curling one that made me want to convince him to drive to one of the dozens of beachfront motels lining the coast, get us a room, and . . . I let out a sigh. Sexy time would have to wait until later today. It was time to meet the family.

•　•　•　•　•

Several hours later, we were back in Nick's car heading home. It had been a wonderful day, and I could tell everyone liked Nick. Even Pop, who tended to be a bit gruff at times, approved.

"Was it too much to ask Pop if he wanted to take my car for a spin?" Nick asked, reading my mind, as was becoming increasingly frequent.

"No, I mean he was certainly interested when he learned it was a hybrid, so it probably was the right thing to do, I guess."

Nick's face broke into a grin. "Yeah, did you see the look on his face when he came back? He was positively beaming! I'm not sure if it was how quiet it runs or when I told him how infrequently I stop for gas."

"Knowing Pop, it was probably the latter. Look up 'frugal' in the dictionary, and I guarantee you'll see his picture. So didn't you just love everyone?" I asked. "Those are *my* people, you know. My favorites. Present company included, of course."

"I was glad to finally meet Randi and Eric. What a great couple," said Nick. "And you can tell how crazy they are about you." I smiled, recalling the hug from Randi as we'd cleared the dishes following an amazing brunch with all of my favorite food. "He's special," she'd whispered, "and a good sport." I assumed she was referring to Nick's enthusiasm as he'd played multiple card games with seven-year-old Teddy and his patience as Clementine described, in excruciating detail, the storyline of *Wicked*, her favorite film.

"They really liked you," I told him.

"They were all great and just as you described. Sally is a sweetheart. She invited me to speak at her book club after *CT* comes out. Guaranteed me a dozen full price sales. How cool is that?"

"It's awesome. Can I be your 'new and improved' agent? I can negotiate speaking engagements at all the best places." I started to tick them off on my fingers. "Billy's Pack and Go is the discount liquor store in town. I'm sure they would love to host you for a reading and book signing. Millie's Fluff & Fold is a no-brainer and maybe the carwash that used to be an Arby's down on Weymouth Street. What do you think?"

"You're hired. Of course, until I get my first royalty check, I'll have to pay you in kisses. Do you have a problem with that?"

"No problem at all. When can I start?"

"How about when we get home? Your dorm room, my tiny house . . wherever you're with me is home to me, G."

"Sounds good to me," I said with a smile.

Chapter 32

On the day of my graduation from law school, I woke curled against my sleeping boyfriend. I figured Danny Boy must have given up attempting to wedge his furry self between us at some point when I saw the top of his golden head peeking up from the foot of the bed. I stretched slowly, cherishing the feeling all was right in the world. Well, maybe not all, but in Gallagher world, it was pretty damn close.

First off, I was really graduating! Last night's check of the school portal indicated I was ranked fourth in the class overall. I'd earned top marks in every one of my courses this semester, which no doubt contributed to my rise in rank, but the expulsion of Roger Stevens made an impact as well.

Although I never truly appreciated the pomp and circumstance of big ceremonies, I knew this was a big deal for friends and family, and I vowed to pull up my big-girl pants and be a good sport. Randi, Eric, and Nick would be cheering for me in the stands, which was pretty cool. I couldn't help but question the timing of my mom's return to jail. For all her bravado and swagger, Charlene Finola Gallagher was a scared and very insecure woman. As proud of me as she claimed to be, I think the idea of adulting and playing the role of supportive mother, especially in the company of Miranda Quinn, the woman she blamed for ruining her life, was too much of a stretch for her. Was I disappointed? Sure, but I was also more than a bit relieved. I had accepted long ago that my mother possessed the unique ability to suck all the joy out of a situation. *But not today, Char.*

Nick and Randi had somehow arranged a party for me following today's 1:00 p.m. ceremony. They'd pulled the whole thing together this past week. I had given up on the idea because a) it seemed challenging to pull off, and b) I don't like parties or being the center of attention. But for today at least, I would smile and allow myself be hugged and congratulated. Nick had reserved a private room in Russo's North, their Hartford location, the one where he and I had met just six weeks ago. He and Randi had collaborated on the menu, deciding on food stations spread around the space, including a pasta bar, an artisanal pizza grill, made to order sushi, and several others that sounded good when I'd heard them rattled off just the other day. An ice cream sundae bar and a special cake from a Russo bakery would cap off the event. The guest list was kept small at my insistence and included Pop and Sally, Randi's siblings and their families, Nick's parents, and my aunt Kelly, who had, to date, not responded to the invitation.

I'd already alerted Nick of my desire to return after the party to the tiny house for sleep, sex, and repeat, although not necessarily in that order. After a couple days, we were heading to Cape Cod, to a secluded-sounding cottage he'd rented for us right on the water. I was looking forward to a week of fun with Nick and Danny, walking on the beach, splashing in the surf, building bonfires, and eating my body weight in lobsters, shrimp, and fried clams. It all sounded amazing to me. Nick would need to spend some time reviewing his publisher's recommended edits, and I planned to bring the books and notes I'd compiled to study for the bar exam in just two months. There was truly to be no prolonged rest for this girl, but that was fine.

I had already vacated my dorm room and would continue to split my time between Randi and Eric's place and Nick's tiny house until after taking the bar in August. Both homes were comfortable and welcoming and offered the kind of solitude I craved for my study schedule as well as my own inner peace. After that, I honestly didn't know where I would live. Beginning September 1st, I would be working for Myers, Stone & Johnson in their nascent family law department. Although I never really saw myself as a corporate type, operating out of a fancy high-rise office building with someone to prepare my briefs and someone else to bring me coffee, I'd taken the job for a few reasons. I felt an odd sense of loyalty to them, inspired by the way they handled the class action lawsuit. I knew I could learn a lot from them, especially being in on the ground floor of a newly formed department. The signing bonus, full medical benefits beginning on day one, and a starting salary in the low six figures were the stuff of my dreams. All far better reasons than a travel mug and a candy bar, for sure.

I started to roll over, figuring an extra half hour of sleep could not hurt, when I heard my phone buzzing. Nick stirred beside me but didn't wake up. I grabbed my phone. The call was coming from the York Correctional Institute. Charlene! I clicked on the call and said hello. I heard the standard recorded message about an inmate calling collect.

"Yes, I accept the call. Mom?" There was no mistaking her voice, hoarse and gravelly from years of smoking and hard living.

"Well, good morning to you too, girlfriend. You sound surprised. Didn't you know I wouldn't miss this? Saying congratulations and all?" I smiled at the very idea she wouldn't miss any of the milestones in my life. The opposite was the more likely scenario, but this wasn't the day to be keeping score.

"I can always count on you, Charlene," I told her without a trace of guile or cheek. "How are you? They treating you all right inside?" I asked as I pulled on a T-shirt and made my way down the ladder toward the coffeepot.

"Naturally," she replied. "Most of my old crew is here, and a few of the guards seemed kinda happy to see me."

"You'll be running the place in no time," I told her, only half kidding. If it weren't for the drugs and alcohol that pickled her brain, she could have been a contender, albeit in some criminal enterprise, but still.

"I guess your lawyer friends will all be there today," she said. Translation: *that bitch Randi Quinn.* I could hear the envy in her voice.

"Next time I come visit, I'll bring pictures, okay? That way you can see for yourself." There was a pause, then a long sigh, followed by a loud, hacking cough. I waited for it to subside.

"It'll be good to have a lawyer in the family, am I right?" she finally said. "We can call you for help. You said family law, yeah?"

"Not that kind of family law, Mom," I said with a shudder as I imagined a long line of Gallaghers asking for me to represent them for DUIs, bad checks, public intoxication, and so much more.

"I'm just yanking your chain, girl. When I get out of here, we'll . . ." Her voice broke, and for a few painful seconds, I could hear her trying to hold back her tears. I pictured my tiny, worn-out mother in her orange jumpsuit, clinging to a wall phone in the middle of a gray cinderblock hallway in a women's prison, and my heart broke for her and all the years she'd wasted behind bars. I realized I was crying too when I felt Danny's tongue, rough against my cheek. I gave him a hug, burying my damp face into his furry neck, and breathed in his grassy, doggy scent. My poor mom.

"Sorry, hon," she said. "I fucked up again." I started to tell her I loved her, that it would be okay, and that I'd see her soon, but what she said next left me too stunned to speak.

"I shoulda told you years ago, or at least recently, girl, but it doesn't change nothing anyways." She paused, and my mind darted around all the possibilities. Was she . . . ? "The man, the man who gave me you, sweetheart. I am almost positive, but don't quote me, 'K? Your father, he was a bartender at this bar your aunt Kelly and I used to hang out at. He was smart, taking college classes or something. That must be where you got that big brain of yours, I guess. I dunno. It was a long time ago, ya know?" She let out a long breath, and I realized I was holding mine. I'd waited my whole life for this, and now I waited for more of her words I could hang on to. Maybe even build a better life off of, taking the place of a life I'd spent paralyzed by the fear of never feeling connected.

"Mom?" I said softly.

"So, you want to know about him, yeah? Well, like I said, he was smart, going to school, wicked handsome. Kind of a player, but you know me. Always falling for the bad boys. And speaking of boys, how's that Black fella of yours? I was telling some of the gals in here about him. How my daughter's seeing a—"

I cut her off, desperate to ask the question that had plagued me for years. "Did he know about me, Mom? Did he know you were pregnant with me?"

She snorted in response.

"Are you kidding me? Yeah, he knew all right. We were only together a few times. It was different back then, you know? I wasn't looking for anything serious, at least until I got knocked up."

"What happened?" I asked.

"So, I go to see him at the bar. He was chatting up a few college girls who were slumming. Probably drinking for free. I told him I needed to talk, and he tried to blow me off. I started to get a little loud, I guess. He asked the other bartender to watch his section and took me out back. He was pissed, didn't want nothing to do with me. I told him I was pregnant and it was his, and he started laughing. Do you believe that? Your fucking father laughed at me, told me I should get rid of it, get rid of you. Nice, huh?"

Now I was crying in earnest, picturing the man I had come to know as probably my father behaving like this. What a bastard. Well, I had finally gotten answers after all this time. Not what I had hoped to hear, though. Not even close.

"So, I went to leave, but I was . . ."

Charlene was continuing on with her story, suddenly eager to share all of the dreadful details after years of stony silence. But I'd heard enough.

"Mom, it's okay. You've told me who he was, and now I know. Michael Kelliher was a jerk to you. He didn't want me." Or you, I almost added. Charlene started to laugh.

"Mike Kelliher? Big Mike, the bartender? Girl what in the hell are you yammering on about? I never slept with him. He was a good guy. Your dad was Eddie. Eddie Sullivan. Little guy, dark hair, cute as fuck, but a real bastard. Like I said, I always went for the bad boys."

·   ·   ·   ·   ·

An hour later, I was fully caffeinated and ready to seize the day. Shortly after dropping her bombshell about my paternity, one of the guards made Charlene hang up the phone, possibly aware her five-minute call had lasted several times that long. "I'm proud of—" was the last thing I'd heard.

Nick had joined me during the last few minutes of my call and knew enough to pull me into his arms and let me cry against his warm chest. Relief I finally knew the truth, anguish Michael wasn't my bio-dad, and bone-deep grief after a few short weeks of hope. I was no closer to knowing who I was. I showered while Nick made more coffee and tended to Danny's needs, then he had a suggestion for me. It was a good one, so I acted on it. I called Michael Kelliher. He answered on the first ring.

"Lennon? Are you okay?"

"Yes, thank you. I need to talk to you, Michael. Is this a good time?"

"Of course. What's going on?"

I told him about what Charlene shared about Eddie Sullivan and how he'd reacted when he found out about me. There was silence on the other end of the call.

"It's true, isn't it?" I asked.

"I remember that night," he said. "Your mom was so upset, and Eddie, well, he was a piece of work. The guy hit on every girl who walked into the bar. I felt bad for your mom. I heard enough of their conversation to know about you and how Eddie reacted. I'm sorry, Lennon. You both deserved better than that."

I was still confused. "But the Beatles' songs, and I'm Lennon, and your son is John. And you're twitchy like me, and our hands are the same and everything . . ."

"I'm not your father, Lennon. I was beginning to wonder if you thought I was. Eddie was a guy I knew from school. He was in one of my classes at the community college. He was looking for a part-time job, so I got him hired at the Wharf, where I worked."

"But that doesn't explain—"

"I drove your mom home that night. There was a Beatles CD in my car, and we listened to a few songs. I told her I loved the Beatles and how John Lennon was my favorite. She said he was her favorite too, but honestly? I don't think she was really a fan. Eddie quit the bar soon after and moved up to Springfield in Massachusetts. Your mom came into the bar every once in a while. She wasn't drinking, mind you. She would order a ginger ale, and we would talk. I think she was hoping to catch a glimpse of Eddie if he ever came by, but he didn't. If it was slow, we would talk some. If she stayed till close, I drove her home. She was sure excited about having you. She told me about all her plans for the two of you; she seemed certain you were a girl. 'That's my girl,' she would say, pointing to her baby bump. She was proud of you, Lennon. And she was clean, I swear. She really tried," he said.

"What happened to him?" I asked, not entirely certain I even wanted to know.

"Ed? He wrapped his car around a telephone pole a few years later. He died on impact, from what I heard. I'm so sorry to have to tell you that."

But I was dry-eyed, resolute in my plans for the day. I had heard so much this morning, and as far as I was concerned, the story was complete, at least the beginning and the middle. The end was up to me. I had a sudden thought.

"Michael, I know it's last minute and everything, but are you and your family free this afternoon? I would love to have you join us and meet my family."

"We will be there," he said, and I texted him the details.

Chapter 33

Today's graduation ceremony was undoubtedly much the same as those that had come before it: interminably long, mind-numbingly boring, and crowded. So very crowded. From my seat up front, I could barely hear the speakers, which, based upon the monotone droning I did hear, wasn't the worst thing. I can only imagine how difficult it was for those way back in the cheap seats. I turned a couple times, hoping to catch sight of Randi, Eric, and Nick, but it was just a grayish blur of faces, no one more distinguishable than the next.

Finally, after seven or eight brutally long hours (Nick would later confirm it was actually forty-seven minutes) they began to call the names of the graduates. We had been asked to pick up cards with our names printed on them earlier in the day, and I gripped mine in my sweaty palm. My left hand was busy waving the paper program in front of my face, trying desperately to cool down. The black polyester gown I wore over my street clothes really packed in the heat. Oh, did I mention it was unseasonably warm today? Like ninety-nine degrees (eighty-three degrees, according to Nick). My mortarboard hat slipped over my abnormally small, peanut-sized head, and the clips I'd used did nothing to keep it on straight. I looked like an idiot, although according to Nick, I looked gorgeous.

I studied the list of graduates in my program, noting the absence of Roger Stevens, Glen Harriman, and Justin Thibault from the roster. I saw my name nearly a third of the way down the list. There was a triple asterisk next to it. I looked at the legend on the back page. Three asterisks equated to summa cum laude. With highest distinction, I realized with a flash of pride. Then I checked, and there was Erin's name with a triple asterisk as well. I craned my neck but saw no sight of her. Guess she had stuck with her plan to skip the pomp and circumstance after all.

One of the teaching assistants approached our row and asked us to stand and follow her. Just as we had rehearsed earlier in the day, we filed out and up the steps to the makeshift stage. One by one, we would approach the podium and hand our card to the speaker, who would read it aloud for all to hear and drop it into a basket by her feet. As our name was being read, we were to be gliding gracefully across the stage to the far podium, where the dean and his staff were handing out diplomas. To cheers and thunderous applause, we were instantly transformed into law school graduates. Of course, the paper meant nothing unless we passed the law boards in a couple months, but I digress.

The student before me was next. He approached the podium, waited as his name was called, and marched across the stage to applause and catcalls, then over to Dean Atkins, who shook his hand and handed him a vinyl binder containing his degree and a validated parking pass in order to vacate the premises free of charge in an hour. Seemed easy enough.

The reader was motioning me forward, and I began my approach. My sweaty hands had done a marvelous job gripping my handwritten card for the past hour, so I guess what happened next was inevitable. The woman pulled it out of my hand and bent to read it. She squinted and frowned before deciding on a course of action.

"Lena Gallagher," she called out, and I glided past her and presented myself to Dean Atkins. He studied me closely, a hint of a smile starting to appear on his weathered face. He shook my hand, gave it an extra pump for good luck, and said, "Congratulations, Lennon Gallagher."

I smiled back at him.

"Thank you, sir," I said and accepted the binder gratefully. As long as they spelled my name correctly on my diploma, I could overlook the faux pas. I walked down the steps, crossed back behind the stage, and reclaimed my seat. I opened the folder and took a quick peek.

Lennon Gallagher

Summa cum laude

I half dozed through the rest of the ceremony and came to only when everyone around me stood and prepared to file out of the auditorium. There was a small cluster of grads attempting to fling their mortar boards in the air, but I was hot and sweaty and had no time for frivolity. All I wanted was five minutes in the ladies' room with running water and a stack of paper towels—a whore's bath, according to my grandma—and the opportunity to slip into my new black dress. As I joined the growing line to return my regalia, I got a text. Nick!

You did it! See you out front. Time to party G!

Yes, it was!

Chapter 34

The banquet room at Russo's North was decorated in a brilliant array of rainbow colors for my party. Balloon arrangements galore, fresh flowers everywhere, and an overflowing gift table. I'd never really had a birthday party or anything growing up, although Randi had planned a few celebrations for me over the past few years. What had I done to deserve all this? Besides graduating law school, that is.

"Do I have to open those in front of everyone?" I asked Randi as we stood together gazing at the festive table, literally groaning with thick envelopes, small wrapped gifts, and more floral arrangements decorated with small balloons. One of them featured a teddy bear holding a sign proclaiming, "I'm bear-y, bear-y proud of you!" I checked the card. It was from Seth!

"You're the girl of the hour," Randi replied. "You can do whatever you want. Just please send thank-you notes, okay?" With a wave, she made her way toward her husband.

Nick caught the end of what she'd said and pulled me in for a hug. "You can do whatever you want to me," he whispered with that searing look that always left me breathless.

"Your parents are in the room, you perv, and I guess mine are too, in a way." I glanced over to where Randi and Eric stood talking with

Michael and his wife, Marilyn. Everyone looked so happy and comfortable. Everyone, that is, with the exception of a tall, lanky blond teenager whose hair nearly covered his eyes, wearing a freshly pressed blue button-down and what looked like a Jerry Garcia-designed tie. His cobalt-blue sneakers made a strong statement and accentuated the size of his feet. He stood in a corner, silently stuffing cheeseburger sliders into his mouth at a rather alarming clip. I recognized him from my early morning surveillance and Michael's family photo. My would-be brother, John. "I gotta go talk to this kid," I told Nick and crossed the room to where he stood.

"Hey, John, right?" I said, and he looked at me with a combination of surprise (What, someone knows me here?) and dread (Oh no, someone knows me here!).

"Yeah, I'm John. Um, pleased to meet you," he said, extending his hand to shake mine. I waved it away.

"I'm Lennon," I told him. "I'm glad you could come to my party. No worries, the rager will start as soon as the old folks depart." He looked around the room at the assorted guests.

"Good to know. So the food's pretty decent, but I hope you're gonna do something about the music," he said.

I pretended to give the matter some thought. "Yeah, I'm picking up what you're throwing down, bro. You think the Carpenters are a bit too edgy for this crowd? I mean, 'Close to You' is a classic and all, but 'Rainy Days and Mondays' gets even me in a funk."

"I think you might want to consider something from this century, you know? It's risky, but I think you'll be pleased with the results." John was starting to grin, clearly enjoying our chat.

"Are you telling me my collection of 8-track tapes is worthless, dude? You're killing me right now."

"Hey, there's nothing wrong with easy listening," John said. "Certain demographics really seem to dig it." He was smiling now, and

I could see the resemblance to his father. This kid was destined to break some hearts and soon. He just needed a big sister to help him learn how to channel all that charm.

"Stick with me, kid. No, seriously stick with me. Let's go check out the grilled pizzas, yeah? Since you obliterated the sliders, I mean." He followed me to the far corner of the room where a dozen individual-sized pizzas were browning on a large open grill.

"What'll it be?" asked the uniformed chef. "I've got every possible topping you can dream of."

"Pepperoni," we called out nearly simultaneously and turned to each other with wide grins.

"I knew I liked you," I said, and John's smile grew even wider.

"Yeah, I guess my dad knew your mom or something. I think we're like, almost related. Maybe we could, I dunno, hang out sometime. I could school you on making better music choices."

My heart soared. I was thrilled. "Cool, cool," I said, and we grabbed our pepperoni pizzas and rejoined the party.

The next couple hours were a blur of all the hugs and congratulatory greetings I had imagined. Even better, actually. Nick's folks, Mario and Bridget, were so welcoming and acted like it was a quite a common occurrence to host a swanky party for a young woman they'd met only once. Randi's toast was a tearjerker, followed by Eric's, which had everyone laughing. I said, "Thank you for being here," and, "Thank you for all your support," punctuated by tearful smiles and a misplaced fist bump or two. What can I say? I clearly got caught up in the moment.

My aunt Kelly was a no-show, as I knew she would be, but it didn't feel like anyone was actually missing. The people I loved most were here, and that was all I needed. When he wasn't by my side, bringing me soft drinks and food, Nick was mingling, chatting up Pop and Sally and just being supportive. I smiled as he approached, carrying a plate of grilled shrimp.

"You've got to try these with the garlic aioli, G. Seriously, you'll love it." His boyish enthusiasm was so great I didn't have the heart to tell him I'd already eaten half a dozen. I took a shrimp from the plate and dunked it in the creamy sauce. I popped it in my mouth and chewed quickly.

"Mmmm, so good," I said. "Thanks, babe."

He grinned at me and put the plate down. "If I had to guess, I would say you are actually having a good time for yourself, you lone wolf, you. What's up with that?"

"I know, right?" And I really was. "Who am I?" I asked. He answered me with a quick kiss and a hug. "You're the belle of the ball, G. I'm so proud of you. Everyone here is."

He left me to mingle. I looked around the room and saw not only the people who had stood up for me and supported me these past six years, but I saw friends who were my family. I caught Randi's eye, and she held up her Diet Coke. "Cheers," I saw her say, and I cheered her back with mine. She was talking with her dad, and I realized I had spent very little time with my "grandparents" Pop and Sally. I started to make my way toward them when suddenly the music changed from piped-in elevator music to something more melodic and recognizable. "In My Life" by the Beatles. Oh, I knew that one. I looked around and saw Michael and John adjusting the speakers of a portable sound system. Michael gave me a thumbs-up, and John just nodded at me with a knowing grin.

If I knew how to dance, I would have started to do just that. Instead, I swayed back and forth, humming along with John Lennon. "There are places I'll remember . . . in my life, I've loved them all."

I smiled as I watched Randi and Eric start to slow dance together, followed by Jake and Meg. Nick was walking toward me, a question in his eyes. I nodded and met him halfway. I slipped into his arms, and we joined the growing number of dancers.

"I don't know how to dance," I told him.

"Don't worry," he said. "I've got you."

And so, we danced. The next song was another Beatles ballad, "Across the Universe," and we continued to make our way around the floor.

"I love you, G," Nick whispered in my ear.

"Love you more," I said, and we danced some more.

Four Months Later

The assembled crowd appeared to hang on Michael Kelliher's every word. You could hear a pin drop in the grand ballroom of the Hartford Marriott that evening.

"I only wish Sonny could be here today and know just how much he meant to his fans, his colleagues at WHRT-TV, the athletes he loved and respected, and mostly his family: his wife, Elinor, his mother, Maria, and his children, Emma and Sean. Although Sonny was unable to live in the aftermath his gambling problem created when it was exposed, his memory will live on, and with these funds, thanks to your generosity, hundreds of at-risk youth will be able to receive the care they need and the help they deserve, so no parent will have to suffer the loss of a child to untreated depression or anxiety."

I listened with pride as Michael concluded his remarks. As chairperson of the recently formed Sonny's Place, he had served as the emcee for tonight's event, a special ceremony honoring the life and legacy of Santino "Sonny" Leone, the Hartford-based sportscaster who had died by suicide one year earlier. Beginning with the half-million-dollar settlement from the Data Solutions class action lawsuit, the fund had grown to 1.9 million as donations poured in, along with proceeds from everything from one-hundred-dollar plate dinners to school bake sales and neighborhood lemonade stands. A huge social media campaign was in the works to educate the public about the variety of peer-to-peer programs, classroom initiatives, awareness events, and online support groups being planned. Renovations had already begun on a now defunct iconic department store that would house offices, meeting spaces, a clinic, and short-term housing as well.

"And I would be remiss if I did not recognize one last time the generosity of the Russo Family for organizing a number of the fundraisers, in addition to sponsoring our event this evening. Please watch your mail for more ways to get involved. Thank you and good night." Thunderous applause followed before everyone stood and started to collect their belongings.

"Trust fund kid," I said with a smirk.

"So, sue me. Wait, now you actually can sue me," he said, and I beamed at him proudly. The results of the most recent law boards had come in last night. I had passed. "Did you want to go up and talk to Michael?" Nick asked, but I shook my head.

"No, the poor guy looks exhausted, and besides, there is already a line of donors and attendees who want a couple minutes of his time."

Nick glanced at the podium, nodding his understanding. "He was pretty stoked when you told him you passed the bar, I imagine."

I grinned, thinking about the text he'd sent. "Sure was. He wrote back in all caps that we would have to celebrate. Um, you wouldn't know anything about a party being planned, would you?"

Nick's attention was suddenly absorbed by the intricate pattern of the carpeting that covered four thousand square feet of floor space.

"Oh, come on, are you kidding me? I said no parties," I reminded him.

Nick grinned and shook his head. "I believe your exact words were, 'You and Randi are not allowed to throw me a party.'"

"That sounds right, so—"

"Apparently, neither Pop nor Sally got the memo, so if you can't act surprised, at least don't tell them I told you," Nick said.

I stopped myself from doing one of my classic eye-rolls, grateful there was much to celebrate and amazing friends to join in the fun. As was usually the case with me, my mind automatically reverted to more practical matters as we made our way to the lobby. Like housing.

"Now I have no more excuses for finding my own place," I said. "I stayed with you while I was studying for the bar, then for the first several weeks after starting the new job, then while I waited to get the results. But now, what's stopping me from moving out?" I spoke as if I was fine either way, but honestly? Living with Nick in the tiny house, with occasional visits to house-sit for Randi and Eric, was like living a dream. He hadn't asked me lately if I was thinking about moving, and I wondered if he was still interested in having me stay with him.

Suddenly, in the middle of a marble-tiled lobby positively teeming with people, Nick dropped to one knee and held out a small red box. I panicked, my hands flying up to cover my mouth, drowning out my cry of, "Oh, fuck me."

"I believe you lawyers call that an 'excited utterance,'" Nick said, "and I find it both admissible and an exception to the hearsay rule." He opened the box, and I saw it contained a single key on a silver keychain festooned with a letter *G* in glossy leather. He stood and smiled down at me.

I felt tears start to form. "If you are asking me to live with you, I accept."

"Actually, I was just hoping you could drop by and water my plants, but if you want to live together, I guess—"

I silenced him with a kiss as the other guests streamed past us toward the exits.

"Right now, I'd like to make a motion we get out of here. These heels are killing me."

"Motion granted. And maybe later we can work on more excited utterances, if it pleases the court," Nick suggested.

"I'll take that under advisement," I assured him. "Now please tell me about this surprise party, would you?"

"On the advice of counsel, aka Randi, I plead the fifth," Nick responded with a wink.

I knew any objections I raised would be overruled. There was clearly a party in my future whether I liked it or not, so I would be gracious, I would smile, and I would eat cake!

"Sounds great," I said. And you know what? It really did!

The End

A Great Big Thank You to:

My beta readers who provided valuable feedback as *CLASS ACTION* evolved from a rough draft to a finished novel. I couldn't have done it without **Cam Torrens**, **Karen E. Osborne**, **A.J. McCarthy**, **Christy Cooper Burnett** and **S.M. Stevens**.

My early readers who read and reviewed advance copies of *CLASS ACTION*: **Karen Brees, Janis Robinson Daly, Scott Eveloff, Gary Gerlacher, Lucille Guarino, Linda Rosen, and Diane Nagatomo.**

My friends who willingly shared their legal knowledge and experience: Attorney **Louise Corcoran**, Attorney **Amanda Sabato** and law student **Eliza Farris.**

My editor extraordinaire, **Jennifer 'Jenny Q' Quinlan**, who never makes me cry and always makes me dig deeper in order to deliver a better story.

My family and friends for their enthusiastic and unwavering support.

My readers for reading, sharing, reviewing and promoting my work.

My fellow Black Rose authors, the best and most supportive writing community I could ever imagine; you inspire me every single day.

The staff of Black Rose Writing, especially **Reagan Rothe**, for making my literary dreams come true.

About the Author

Gail Ward Olmsted was a marketing executive and a college professor before she began writing fiction on a full-time basis. A trip to Sedona, AZ, inspired her first novel *Jeep Tour*. Three more novels followed before *Landscape of a Marriage*, a biographical fiction featuring landscape architect Frederick Law Olmsted, a distant cousin of her husband's, and his wife Mary.

Olmsted enjoys writing about quirky, wonderful women in search of a second chance at a happy ever after. When not writing, she loves being on the water, especially in a kayak. She is well known for her blonde brownies, and coffee is her love language. Visit her website at gwolmstedauthor.carrd.co.

Other Titles by Gail Ward Olmsted

The Miranda Quinn Legal Twist Series

Note from Gail Ward Olmsted

Word-of-mouth is crucial for any author to succeed. If you enjoyed *Class Action*, please leave a review online—anywhere you are able. Even if it's just a sentence or two. It would make all the difference and would be very much appreciated.

Thanks!

Gail O

We hope you enjoyed reading this title from:

www.blackrosewriting.com

Subscribe to our mailing list – *The Rosevine* – and receive **FREE** books, daily deals, and stay current with news about upcoming
releases and our hottest authors.
Scan the QR code below to sign up.

Already a subscriber? Please accept a sincere thank you for being a fan of
Black Rose Writing authors.

View other Black Rose Writing titles at
www.blackrosewriting.com/books and use promo code
PRINT to receive a **20% discount** when purchasing.

www.ingramcontent.com/pod-product-compliance
Lightning Source LLC
Chambersburg PA
CBHW060546190726
48283CB00003B/897